P9-BZI-983

The Barncastle family transforms its sprawling Victorian bed-and-breakfast into a fantasy world. Guests can rent the entire inn at Christmas for a vacation set in whatever historical period they choose. Parents Ted and Diane are skeptical that anyone will pay the exorbitant price their daughter Jayne recommends—but they're wrong. Plenty of people long for Christmas in another time.

Love Comes to the Castle by Susan Page Davis
Jayne Barncastle has big ideas for her family's bed-and-breakfast, but is the idea so big it will break them? With the rich Dillard family paying for a deluxe medieval Christmas, Jayne must come through for her folks. But how will the Dillards feel about her attraction to their widowed son-in-law, Luke?

Christmas Duets by Lynette Sowell
Sean McSweeney is the last person Marcella Goudreau wants to see during her family's Christmas vacation at Barncastle Inn, because she holds him partly responsible for her grandparents' split. Sean finds that being part of a family again brings up feelings of abandonment he'd long thought buried. While they re-create a World War II–era Christmas, complete with music from *White Christmas*, will Sean and Marcella learn to sing a duet of the heart?

Where Your Heart Is by Janelle Mowery
Stephanie Minter never expected to see Matthew Raynor again, after the way she broke his heart. But when she finds him working at the Barncastle bed-and-breakfast, Stephanie believes God has given her a second chance. As she helps Matthew re-create the pirates' life for her wards, can she prove she has changed, or will he always think of her as the thief who stole his happiness?

First Christmas by Darlene Franklin
Waverly Coe, a young unmarried mother, works as a veterinarian's assistant to Alec Ross. In addition to his practice, he serves as animal specialist for the Barncastle Inn. As they involve guests in celebrating the First Christmas, can they see past their circumstances to celebrate their first Christmas together?

CHRISTMAS AT BARNCASTLE INN

FOUR-IN-ONE COLLECTION

SUSAN PAGE DAVIS
DARLENE FRANKLIN
JANELLE MOWERY
LYNETTE SOWELL

BARBOUR
PUBLISHING

ISBN 978-1-61626-438-3

Cover design: Kirk DouPonce, DogEared Design

Published by Barbour Publishing, Inc., P.O. Box 719, Uhrichsville, OH 44683, www.barbourbooks.com

Our mission is to publish and distribute inspirational products offering exceptional value and biblical encouragement to the masses.

ECPA Member of the
Evangelical Christian
Publishers Association

LOVE COMES TO THE CASTLE

Susan Page Davis

Dedication

To all those who wish they could travel through time, and to my sisters, with whom I've traveled more than fifty years. Next Sister Week at the Barncastle!

Love is patient, love is kind.
1 CORINTHIANS 13:4 NIV

Chapter 1

The maples in the front yard showed a few red leaves as Jayne Barncastle hopped out of her silver compact. The dear old house welcomed her as always when she ventured home from Boston—not often enough these days. She gazed up at the stone walls and the east turret, where her room lay, and smiled.

Her parents had given her the tower room on the third story when they moved in fifteen years ago, and she'd reigned supreme in it ever since, with her private view of the lake and the meadow. How many dreams she'd hatched up there!

She glanced at the sign beside the driveway. BARNCASTLE INN. The name suited the stone and wooden house, a miniature Gothic castle with a hint of rambling barn. The only way the Barncastles could afford the taxes on the oddity was to share it with travelers. Her folks had run the sprawling house as a bed-and-breakfast since Jayne was nine. They'd gotten by on the erratic income—the inn was fully booked in summer and welcomed "leaf peepers" in October and occasional hardy guests at other seasons. But Jayne was sure they could do better with a little clever marketing.

The front door burst open and her mother scurried across the porch and down the steps, her arms wide and her too-early silver curls bobbing.

"Jayne! It's so good to have you home."

"Hello, Mom." They stood for a moment, engulfed in their embrace and memories. Mom smelled faintly of ginger and furniture polish, and Jayne wondered why she'd ever yearned for wider horizons.

"How did your interviews go?" Mom asked.

"Very well, thanks." Jayne grinned as her father ambled around the corner of the house with a hammer in his hand.

Jayne hugged him and patted his back. "You look good, Dad. How's business?"

"Not bad. We've got a couple coming in Friday afternoon for the weekend, and a party of four staying four days next week."

Jayne nodded, thinking plenty but saying nothing. Those numbers barely gave them the income they needed to maintain the house. Her parents wanted to retire next year, but on what? Their income from the busy season had to stretch over the bleak winter months.

Her father grabbed the handle on her wheeled suitcase, and Jayne pulled out her laptop case and closed the trunk. She walked beside her mother inside and to the kitchen, where the enticing aroma of baking biscuits made Jayne's mouth water.

"How long can you stay?" her mother asked.

"I should probably leave Sunday." Jayne sat on one of the stools beside the butcher-block worktable.

"So soon?"

"Yeah, I'll need to start work."

Her father came in from the hall. "I left your suitcase by the stairs, Jaynie. I'll take it up after we eat."

"That's fine, Dad. And I can lug it myself."

"Up two flights?"

She laughed. "I was your star bellhop before I went away to school, remember?"

The family usually ate in the kitchen, amid the polished wood cabinets, granite countertops, and gleaming cookware. This room was the heart of Barncastle Inn, not the dining room, where the guests ate.

They sat down together. Her father closed his eyes, and Jayne automatically bowed her head.

"Lord, we thank You for this food, and for bringing our daughter home safe. May we please You in all we say and do. Amen."

"Amen," Jayne murmured as she opened her eyes.

Mom dipped a generous portion of beef stew—one of her specialties—from the slow cooker and handed Jayne the ironstone bowl.

"Thank you. This smells delicious."

"So, Jaynie."

"Yes?" She looked expectantly at her father.

"What's the news?"

She smiled. "I have an offer."

"Oh," Mom said. "That's wonderful."

"You don't look very pleased."

Her mother glanced toward Dad. "Of course we're happy for you, but. . .to be honest, we had other dreams."

"Like what?"

"We missed you this summer." Her mom picked up another bowl, dipped it full of stew, and handed it to Dad.

"We hoped you'd help us run the inn this year," her father said.

"You mean. . .stay here in Vermont and help you? Now?"

He shrugged. "It was just a thought."

"Well, I did have an idea of how you might increase your business. If you're interested, I'll tell you about it later."

"Might be good," Dad said. "But you've got a job in the city, eh? I'm sure you're anxious to get started."

"Well, yes." Jayne looked uncertainly from him to her mother. Neither seemed overjoyed at her success. She'd opted for summer school to finish up her master's degree, rather than coming home to help at the inn as usual. Now she was ready to move into an independent life. They'd encouraged her every step of the way, so why the long faces?

"Actually, I told them I'd give them my answer Monday. I wanted a chance to think it over and to talk to you about the offer."

Her parents perked up at that.

"Does something about it make you hesitate?" Mom asked.

"Well, it's a very responsible position. I'd be in charge of the marketing department at a young company. It would be a great challenge, but kind of scary." Jayne sipped her water. "In some ways, I'd almost rather work for a more established firm—one that had some experienced people working with me and showing me the ropes. I get the feeling I'd be pretty much on my own at Bowker-Hatley."

"So all the blame would fall on you if something went wrong," her father said.

"Well, yes."

He nodded. "What about your other interviews?"

"There's an opening with less pay at the Ringfield Toy

company. The cost of living is so high in the city, I'd barely clear my living expenses the first year. But I'd be up for a substantial raise after that. I'm on their short list, and they say they'll call me, but this other offer. . ."

Her parents looked at each other in silence.

"Tell me about this idea you had." Jayne didn't say so, but she'd considered the thought herself more than once. But questions always arose. Did she really want to bury herself in small-town Vermont? Now that she had her MBA in marketing, would she get the same satisfaction from running a small inn, no matter how beautiful? And could the inn continue to support her and her parents? She knew how hard the work was. If she wanted to run Barncastle Inn, she'd have to hire help, especially if Mom and Dad retired.

Her parents watched her thoughtfully.

"We kind of thought you might like first dibs on the place," her dad said.

"You mean. . .buy it from you?" Jayne laughed. "With what?"

"We'd set up terms. If you stayed, we'd work with you through next summer and then turn it over to you. We figured that by now you know enough about marketing to attract more customers. If you filled four rooms every night, you could make a nice living here. The thing is, we're getting older, and we couldn't keep up with that kind of traffic."

"And we'd like to retire while we're still young enough to enjoy some travel," Mom added.

Jayne pressed her lips together. This was the moment. "About that marketing thing, Dad. I do think I could help you pull in more business. Would you be willing to hire help if you needed it?"

"Sure, if the revenue is there."

She nodded. "I've done some preliminary research. Just a sec—I'll be right back." She hurried to the hall and opened her laptop case. Inside with her computer was a folder she'd prepared. She carried it to the kitchen and slid into her chair, pushing her soup plate aside.

"What's this?" her father asked, squinting down at the cream-colored paper she placed in his hand. At the top was a small photo of the inn, with the words CHRISTMAS ANY TIME in large letters beneath it.

Her mother accepted one of the papers and began to read. "Go back in time for the Christmas of your dreams at Barncastle Inn." She glanced at Jayne, puzzled, then read on. "Have Christmas in the Victorian era, the Roaring Twenties, or colonial days. Relive your favorite childhood holidays. Hosts Ted and Diane Barncastle will transform their charming country inn into the holiday time and place you long for."

"What on earth is this all about?" Dad laid his paper on the table and stared at her.

"I don't see how we could do something like this," Mom said. "What exactly are you proposing?"

Jayne smiled at them. "Everyone has a picture in their mind of the ideal Christmas. Let's say your customer was born in the 1930s. He's old now, but he remembers those simpler days. He wants his grandchildren to have a Christmas like he did. We decorate the inn 1930s style. We make garlands for the tree by stringing popcorn and cranberries. We bring in greenery for the swags and birch logs for the fireplace—nothing modern, everything simple and nostalgic. We set up activities from the period—a sledding party and an evening of caroling. The gifts would be typical of the era—a pair of skates, a classic book, a model of Lucky Lindy's plane."

"And people will pay for this?" Her father's face projected skepticism, but Jayne waved away his doubt.

"Not only will they pay—they'll pay *extra*."

"You're kidding," her mother said. "People today want modern comfort and convenience. We lost a lot of bookings last year because we couldn't give Internet service in every room."

"That's right," Dad said. "So now we pay for expensive cable service so the guests can get their e-mail while they're here. Who's going to want to go back to the days of kerosene lanterns and outhouses?"

Jayne laughed. "I don't think you need to take out the plumbing! And they can still bring their computers. But say someone wants to be at Charlemagne's coronation on Christmas Day in 800 AD. They could rent the whole place for a week. We'd play up the castle aspects of the architecture, and Mom, you could serve wassail and leg of lamb and other dishes from the Middle Ages. The staff would wear medieval costumes. We'd hire a minstrel to come in and sing during dinner, and we could even organize a pageant, reenacting the coronation."

Her mother nodded slowly, but her eyes looked a little glazed.

"Jaynie, you keep saying 'we,'" her dad pointed out. "I'm not sure your mom and I would be up to doing all this. I mean, we've hit sixty. We're looking at retiring after the summer season next year, and there's only one Christmas season between now and then. Who exactly would do all of this decorating and event planning?"

Jayne pulled in a deep breath. "Well. . ." Her stomach fluttered. "I. . .uh. . .I could do the ads for you. Gratis."

Dad shook his head. "I just don't think we could do it, kiddo."

"Me either," Mom said. "Not without someone young and energetic heading up all this activity. I'm sorry, sweetie. It sounds like great fun, but it also sounds like a lot of work."

Dad gave her a rueful smile. "Too much work for our last year in business. Now if I were twenty-four, like you. . ."

"So what will you do with the inn if I don't want to have a part in it?" Jayne asked in a small voice. She couldn't imagine not having the castle to come home to.

"Sell it, I guess." Her father reached for his coffee cup. "Hate to do it, but we've spent enough time maintaining this place. Somebody else needs to take over."

"Yes," Mom said. "While we spend next winter somewhere warm."

"Well. . ." The dismay that ambushed Jayne shocked her. "If you did decide to sell it, this plan should increase the value of the business for you." Jayne pondered the problem while she cut a warm, flaky biscuit in half and smeared it with butter. Her throat felt tight as she swallowed.

Mom launched into an update of the neighbors and church family. Jayne and her father said little until Mom asked if they wanted seconds.

"There's pie." Dad had a faint glitter in his eyes.

Mom always made pie for her first night home. Jayne stood and gathered her silverware. "Let me help you clear the dishes, Mom."

As she carried their plates to the counter, her mother loaded the dishwasher. Jayne refilled her father's coffee cup, and Mom took a pie from the warm oven.

"You can get the vanilla ice cream, Jaynie."

"All right."

What would it be like to stay here this fall and help her folks run the inn? She'd revamp all their ads for the foliage season tourists and put the place in the holiday mood by the first of November. It would be so much fun.

She was standing in front of the open freezer surveying the stash of food when her father said, "I guess we were hoping you'd look at the inn with fresh eyes and think about keeping the business."

She couldn't disappoint them, and she wasn't ready to say good-bye to her castle home. Jayne chose a carton of ice cream and closed the door. "Tell you what: Let me place an ad for you in this weekend's *Boston Herald*. If no one books by the time I have to leave, we'll know it was a bad idea. And if someone does book. . .well, I'd have to consider my options, wouldn't I?"

Her parents exchanged a look of suppressed excitement.

"I'm game," her father said. "How about it, Diane? Shall we let the biz whiz try out her new degree on us?"

"Are you sure the guests will pay for all the extra stuff?"

"Oh they'll pay," Jayne said. "I'll advertise a weeklong package with the entire inn at their disposal—say, twelve guests—and the nostalgic Christmas celebration of their dreams for twelve thousand dollars."

"Twelve—" Her mother's jaw dropped and she turned to her husband. "Ted, she's gone crazy."

Her dad gulped. "Jaynie, that's three months' income."

"Not anymore."

They stared at each other.

"No one will pay that much." Her mother shook her head and picked up the pie server.

"They pay it all the time," Jayne said. "Cruises, European tours. We're talking deluxe accommodations, thanks to you two—" She looked around at the spotless inn and the gleaming antique furnishings. "I know exactly where to advertise, and my ad copy is irresistible."

Her mother still looked skeptical.

Why am I doing this? Jayne asked herself. Did she want to fling aside the Boston job she'd worked so hard for? And what if the idea bombed and she let her parents down? The lump in her throat told her how strongly the castle and her family pulled on her. Maybe she *had* lost her mind.

"Look, you charge a hundred and fifty dollars a night for a room for two now. Some places charge two or three hundred, and they're not as nice as this—and you'll be serving all meals, not just breakfast, and providing entertainment. Seven nights, twelve guests. That's less than a hundred and fifty per person per day."

"Meals included." Her mother's brow furrowed.

"What if they only have ten people?" Dad asked.

"The twelve grand is for the entire inn during Christmas week, no matter how many people, up to twelve."

"And if anyone books it by Sunday, you'll commit?" her father asked.

Jayne nodded. "I'll commit, Dad. For four months—through the Christmas season. We can evaluate things afterward. And I guarantee you, we'll pull out all the stops for a Christmas week that will go down in history."

He looked over at Mom. "What do you say, Diane?"

"What if they book and then back out at the last minute?"

Jayne lifted one shoulder. "We make sure the deposit we keep covers what we've spent to that point."

Dad grinned and stood, extending his hand to her. "Deal."

Her mom drew in a slow, deep breath and then stuck out her hand. "All right. Deal."

Chapter 2

L uke Gilbert's phone rang, and he laid his pen on his drafting table to answer it. He grimaced as he spotted the name on the caller ID.

"Hello, Rosalyn."

"Good evening, Luke." His mother-in-law's voice held her usual self-confidence and slight edge of superiority. "How are you and Andy?"

"We're fine. Andy's in bed, I'm afraid. He has school tomorrow."

"Ah, that's a shame. I'll have to call earlier next time. But it's you I really wanted to speak with."

"Oh?" That surprised Luke. Rosalyn almost never spoke to him anymore. She must be about to launch a tirade about how infrequently he brought her grandson to Hartford to visit her.

"Yes. I have a favor to ask you. There's an inn up there in Vermont. I'd like you to check it out for me."

Luke considered that for a moment. Was she planning to visit Andy, since he hadn't taken his son to Nana's for a few months? "Is it something you could investigate online?"

"No, it's not. You see, I'm contemplating making an investment."

Luke blinked. "Investing in Vermont real estate?"

Rosalyn laughed. "No, an investment in the family. I'm

looking for a venue for a family reunion. It's a pricey inn, but it looks respectable—quite charming, actually. But I don't want to plan a week for eleven people without someone in the family checking it out beforehand."

"Eleven people?" Here it comes, Luke thought. He picked up his pen and doodled on the envelope beside the elevated drawing he'd been working on.

"Yes. It's been so long since the entire family got together, I thought Austin and I could rent a place. You and North and Liza can all bring your families. We can relax and renew our family ties, and have Christmas together."

"Christmas?" Luke stopped doodling.

"Don't you think that's a good idea? Andy can spend the holidays with his grandparents. And his cousins, aunts, and uncles of course."

"Well, I. . ."

"Of course Austin and I will pay for your weekend expenses. You can take Andy and see if he likes the place. You know—if he's comfortable there. If the two of you like it, I'll book it for Christmas week."

"That's thoughtful of you." Luke couldn't imagine spending an entire week with his in-laws, though. He'd go nuts cooped up with the Dillards.

"Thank you. I wouldn't want Andy to be upset by a strange place and ruin the holidays for everyone else. It's about eighty miles from your place. What do you say, Luke?"

He frowned at her implication, but there was some truth to it. His six-year-old son had a hard time adjusting to anything new. Rosalyn was right, too, that Andy should know his family better.

"All right. I suppose we could go this weekend."

Rosalyn's voice thawed about twenty degrees. "Thank you so much. I'll book a room for you right now and e-mail you the details. It's called the Barncastle."

❄

Jayne and her mother made up the bed in the Library Suite together. The room hardly needed dusting, and the bathroom was pristine, but Jayne wiped it down anyway.

"Too bad we didn't have more guests this week," Mom said as they gathered the cleaning supplies, "but we've had more time to spend with you this way."

"Well, you've got five bookings for early October," Jayne said.

"Yes, and there will be more. October is usually a busy time."

As they headed down the stairs, Jayne let out a sigh. "I was sure you'd hear something on those Christmas ads by now. They've been running two days in the *Boston Herald* and the *Hartford Courant*."

"Oh sweetie, it's all right. I take it as a sign from God. I'm just sorry you spent so much on the display ads. But there's still two more days."

"I should have put it in the *New York Times*, too." Who was she kidding? She'd guessed wrong and overpriced the package. Maybe she should call Bowker-Hatley this afternoon and tell them she'd be on board in a week, ready to work.

The telephone rang, and she veered toward the small office off the kitchen. "I'll get it."

"Thanks." Mom continued on toward the utility room

with the caddy of supplies.

"Barncastle Inn, may I help you?" Jayne asked.

"Yes. My name is Rosalyn Dillard, and I'd like to inquire about the Christmas package you're offering. Is the space still available for the week before the holiday?"

Jayne's pulse raced. "Yes, it is."

"And what days would the event run?"

"Since Christmas falls on Sunday, we're making the entire inn available from Monday the nineteenth until Monday morning, the twenty-sixth. Is there a particular theme or time period you're interested in?"

"Yes. My grandson loves dragons. I'd like to give our family an authentic medieval Christmas. Can you do that?"

Jayne grinned. "We certainly can. Our staff will give your family the best of medieval adventure and pageantry, without the discomforts of the Middle Ages."

"Oh yes, good point."

"How many people in your party?" Jayne reached for a notepad and pen.

"I'm considering eleven, but I wondered if two family members could come this weekend to view the facility. Do you have a room open for tomorrow and Saturday?"

"We certainly do."

Mrs. Dillard readily gave her credit card number and a Hartford address. "Do you provide full meal service?"

Jayne did some quick calculations. "Breakfast is included in our regular fee, but our guests can also eat lunch and dinner at the Barncastle, if we know in advance. Would you like to include the meals for this weekend?"

"Could you have Friday's dinner ready for them? I think

I'll let my son-in-law decide on the rest when they arrive, if that's all right. Put any expenses they incur on the bill, won't you?"

"I'd be happy to."

"Good. You can expect them late tomorrow afternoon. And if they like what they see, I'll reserve for the Christmas package."

Jayne hung up a minute later and exhaled deeply, closing her eyes. "Thank You, Lord." She snatched up the notepad and ran to the kitchen. "Mom! You're not going to believe this!"

❄

Luke stepped out of his SUV and looked over the inn. Impressive example of Victorian architecture with some Gothic touches. The beautiful stone walls would take care of themselves, but the wood trim and cedar-shingled roofs must take a lot of maintenance. The front lawn and flower beds had been lovingly tended. Plenty of space for Andy to run and play, and a lake glistened in the last rays of sun less than a quarter mile behind the inn.

He rounded the Explorer and opened the passenger door. Andy already had his seat belt unfastened.

"All set, buddy?" Luke held out his arm so Andy could hold on to it while he slid down from the high seat. "What do you think?"

Andy stared up at the stone tower nearest them. "Is it a real castle?"

Luke smiled. "What would make it a real castle?"

"A dungeon, maybe?"

"Hmm. Well, there's no moat, so I'm guessing not." Luke

opened the SUV's tailgate and took out Andy's backpack. He held it while Andy slipped his thin arms through the straps.

Andy turned to face him, his blue eyes anxious. "Will there be a lot of people?"

Luke glanced around the small parking lot. "I only see three other cars."

Andy nodded. The little guy was too sober, Luke thought as he pulled out his own duffel bag. Too fearful. He intended to do everything possible to make this weekend a positive experience for his son. Would the castle inn be too scary for him? No way would he bring Andy back here when the house was full of Dillards if the child was frightened, and Luke hated to think what Rosalyn would say if he refused to take part in her plans for Christmas.

He smiled down at Andy and held out his hand.

❄

"Jayne! A vehicle just pulled up!" Her mother stood in the office doorway holding up her flour-coated hands. "Can you check them in?"

"Of course. Relax, Mom."

"But if they don't like—"

Jayne laid a hand on her shoulder. "They're going to love it here. Now go finish preparing their candlelight dinner. I'll make sure they have everything they could possibly want in their romantic suite."

She walked to the front desk shooting up staccato prayers. *It's up to You, Lord. Please let them like it. Don't let Mom and Dad be disappointed. You know what's best.*

The front door opened as she reached the check-in desk.

Jayne faced the newcomers with her brightest smile.

"Welcome to Barncastle Inn."

"Hi." The man smiled and looked down at his companion.

Instead of the twenty-something couple she had expected, a boy of six gazed up at his father, shivering with excitement. Jayne couldn't tell if he was glad to be inside the fairy-tale inn, or if he wanted to turn and bolt.

She extended her hand. "I'm Jayne Barncastle."

"I'm Luke Gilbert, and this is my son, Andy. We have a reservation."

"Yes, you do." Jayne bent forward and smiled at the boy. He stared at her with round blue eyes. His blond hair lay tousled over his forehead, sun-bleached a shade lighter than his father's. "Hello, Andy. I'm glad you and your dad came to stay with us. Do you like this house?"

"It's cool," he whispered.

"I think so, too." Jayne straightened. "Let me check you in, Mr. Gilbert, and then I'll take you and Andy up to your room. We put you in the Squire's Room. It's a beautiful room, with a balcony and a gorgeous view of the lake. But I have to confess, I thought a married couple was coming. This room has a king-sized bed. If you'd rather, I can switch you to a room with two doubles. Or we could bring in a cot for Andy."

Luke shook his head. "Andy won't mind sleeping on the other side of a great big bed with me, will you, buddy?"

Andy shook his head.

Jayne quickly completed the check-in. She'd have to clue Mom in as soon as possible to nix the candles and romance at dinner. The couple staying in the Library Suite was going out to eat, so Luke and Andy Gilbert would be the only ones in the dining room. They'd probably rather not have dim lights, romantic music, and candles on the table. And Andy might not go for the crab bisque and prime rib Mom had taken so much trouble to prepare.

"Do you have other luggage?" she asked as she closed the computer check-in program.

"No, this is it," Luke said.

Andy held on to the straps of his backpack, as though afraid she would try to take it from him.

"Right this way, then." She led them to the stairs.

"Do you have any armor?" Andy's plaintive voice wrapped itself around her heart. She'd told her father at least a thousand times over the years that the house cried out for a suit of armor.

"We don't." She turned to face him on the landing where the stairs turned. "But I've always thought this corner would be the perfect place for a suit of chain mail."

He nodded, his eyes huge.

Luke smiled at her over Andy's head. "Next he'll be wanting a steed."

Jayne caught her breath. "That's not a bad idea." Plans whirled through her mind as she continued up the stairs. If this little boy wanted knights and armor, the Barncastle Inn was up to the task.

❄

The inn was perfect. Luke sat on the wide, cushioned window seat in their room and held Andy on his lap, looking out over the landscaped backyard, the Barncastle family's garden, and a path leading to the shining lake. The setting sun shot golden rays over the placid water.

Andy leaned back against his chest and sighed.

"Do you like it here?" Luke asked.

"Uh-huh. Do you think they'll let us go up in the towers?"

"Maybe." He kissed the top of Andy's head. "Miss Barncastle said that we can walk down to the shore after dinner if we want to."

Andy yawned. "It's a funny name."

"Barncastle? Yes." Luke smiled. Andy was tuckered out. He'd probably put off their walk to the lake until morning. The boy had fretted all afternoon. On their ride, Andy had clutched his favorite plastic horse and stroked the four-inch figure constantly. Now he held it loosely, with the plastic knight perched on the horse's back facing the window, so he could see the lake, too.

Luke checked his watch. "It's nearly time for dinner. We'd better wash up." He set Andy down gently and walked with him to the bathroom. The tub sat on claw feet, with a shower head above it and purple-and-gold curtains that complemented the lavender paint on the walls. Every detail, from the brass faucets to the Edwardian-era framed prints, bespoke quality.

As they entered the dining room, a woman with silver-gray hair came forward, wearing a bright smile.

"Hello. I'm Diane Barncastle, Jayne's mother."

Diane's sweet face put Luke at ease. She took him and Andy to a table set with thick ironstone plates on top of wooden trays.

"In medieval times, people ate their dinners off wooden

trenchers or a thick slice of bread. But I wasn't sure you'd want to do that, so we gave you plates."

Andy stared at her. "They used bread for plates?"

Diane nodded. "Yes, and they let the gravy soak into it. After the other food was gone, they ate their dishes."

Andy laughed and looked at his father. "Can we do that sometime?"

"Well. . ." Luke looked up at Diane.

"I tell you what," she said. "I can fix your breakfast that way in the morning. I'll give you a big slice of crusty, homemade bread with your egg and sausage on top, and you can eat the whole thing."

"Yeah!"

Diane chuckled. "It will save me washing your plate."

Luke said, "You don't have to—"

"No trouble. And don't worry about the table—I'll make sure it's clean."

Luke nodded. "All right then, we'll eat breakfast castle-style."

Diane handed them each a sheet of card stock. "Here's the menu we've prepared this evening. If you gentlemen don't care for something on it, we can substitute." She winked at Luke.

He quickly perused the sheet. "First is a crab bisque, Andy. That's soup. You'll like that."

Andy's mouth drooped. "I've never had it."

"Give it a try. If you don't like it, I'll help you finish it—I love crab." Luke smiled up at Diane and gave her back the menu. "It looks wonderful, Mrs. Barncastle. Just make Andy's portions child-sized, if you please."

"All right. And please call me Diane. What would you like to drink, Andy?"

"Milk?" He arched his eyebrows as though uncertain she would have it.

"Of course."

Relief washed over Andy's face and he relaxed.

"I'll start with water, please," Luke said, "and then some coffee."

As Diane headed for the kitchen, Luke looked around the dining room. "This is pretty nice, isn't it?"

"I like the pictures." Andy was staring over the sideboard, at a large scene showing horses pulling a sled piled with logs.

"So do I," Luke said.

"I didn't know if castles had cows."

Luke smothered a grin. "For the milk?"

"Yes."

The kitchen door opened, and this time Jayne emerged, carrying a tray with two glasses. Luke realized he'd wondered if they would see her again. Andy spotted her, and a shy smile crept over his lips. Something inside Luke unknotted.

"Hello again, Andy." She set his glass of milk on the table.

Andy picked it up and took an experimental sip as she set Luke's ice water down. He lowered the glass and smiled at Jayne with his milk mustache.

"Where do you keep the cow?"

Jayne laughed. "We have a peasant down the road that we buy our milk from, sir. How do you like your bedchamber?"

"It's great. We can see the lake."

"It's wonderful." Luke was amazed that his son was talking so freely with Jayne.

"I have much the same view from my room." She leaned closer to Andy. "I've always slept in the east tower."

His eyes widened.

Jayne grinned. "No one's renting the west tower room right now. If you want, I'll take you up there in the morning. And there's a deck on top of the house, too. From up there, you get a really good view of the town and the lake. With the leaves changing colors now, it's especially pretty."

"Sounds like fun," Luke said.

"I've also come up with a few local attractions that might interest you." Jayne fished a small notepad from her apron pocket. "It's too cold to swim now, but we have a rowboat, and I'm sure we have a life jacket your size, Andy. We also have fishing gear. Folks have been known to take some nice trout from that lake. And one of our near neighbors is a veterinarian. His family has quite a variety of animals on their farm, including a pig. Have you ever patted a pig?"

Andy shot an uncertain glance at Luke. "Have I, Daddy?"

"I don't think so."

Jayne grinned. "They have a few other animals you may never have seen, too, but I'll let it be a surprise."

"Can we go?" Andy's imploring look was irresistible.

"It sounds like a great outing," Luke said.

"I'll give Dr. Ross a call." Jayne headed for the kitchen.

"I like her," Andy said.

Luke looked down into his eyes, vivid with excitement now. Andy didn't usually take to new people so readily. But

Jayne Barncastle had shown more than courtesy. She'd gone to extra lengths to make them comfortable and search for activities Andy would enjoy. He reached over and touched the boy's shoulder.

"Yeah. So do I."

Chapter 3

Jayne met Luke at the door when he and Andy came back from their walk along the lakeshore.

"Did you enjoy your stroll?"

"It was great," Luke said. "So peaceful."

"Yes. When I come home, it always strikes me that way." To Jayne's consternation, she choked up a bit. Maybe she'd stayed in Boston too long this time. "Would you like to have some ice cream near the fireplace?"

Andy yawned, and his eyelids drooped.

"How about it, buddy?" Luke asked. "Or are you still too full from supper?"

"Ice cream," Andy whispered.

Luke nodded at Jayne. "Will you join us?"

She felt her face flush. "I don't usually. But I did call Dr. Ross, so we might want to settle the details on that. Besides, Mom has some pistachio ice cream in the freezer, and I'm always a pushover for that."

Luke chuckled. "Sounds good. I'll have some, too."

"We also have chocolate peanut butter, and black cherry. Oh and vanilla."

"Chocolate," Andy said.

"There you go." Luke's smile sent a dart to Jayne's heart. "One pistachio and one chocolate peanut butter."

"Great. I'll bring it to the parlor."

Luke guided Andy to the large, cheerful room. Jayne waited long enough to hear Andy's exclamation when he saw the flames crackling in the big fieldstone fireplace. She reminded herself not to read too much into Luke's friendliness, and hurried to the kitchen. Her mother was covering a large mixing bowl with a clean dish towel.

"Breakfast cinnamon buns?" Jayne asked.

"Yes. What are you up to?"

"Ice cream for three. Luke Gilbert invited me to join him and Andy. I figured I might as well give them the details about visiting the Rosses' farm tomorrow."

Mom smiled. "That little boy is a doll."

"Isn't he? He seems quite timid, though." Jayne set three bowls on a tray.

Her mother helped get it ready, and Jayne carried the tray into the hall. As she entered the parlor, she tried to see it through the eyes of a new guest—especially those of a serious six-year-old. The fireplace dominated the decor. The glowing woodwork and soft green walls gave a peaceful backdrop for the comfortable antique furniture and reproduction artwork. Jayne had to admit her mother had great taste.

Luke sat in one of the overstuffed armchairs with Andy on his lap. The little boy faced the fireplace and leaned back against his father's shoulder, his gaze riveted to the dancing flames.

Luke glanced up at Jayne. "Ice cream's here, buddy. Do you want to sit over there?" He nodded toward the sofa.

Andy shook his head and burrowed his head into Luke's chest.

32

"Okay. I just thought it would make eating easier." He smiled up at Jayne. "I guess we're staying put, if that's okay."

"Absolutely." Jayne set the tray down on the coffee table and took Andy's bowl over. He reached for it, not meeting her gaze. He'd probably be even more anxious if he left his father's arms. Why did he cling to Luke so closely? The unexplained absence of his mother might have something to do with that. "Here you go, Andy. Chocolate peanut butter, just the way the knights liked it back in the Dark Ages."

Andy flashed an uncertain look at her. "No, they didn't."

"Oh? Maybe you're right." Jayne smiled and handed Luke his dish, hoping she hadn't made things worse for the little boy.

"Thank you, Miss Barncastle," Luke said.

"Oh please. Jayne."

"Very well, then we're Luke and Andy."

She frowned playfully down at Andy. "Are you sure it isn't Sir Andrew?"

Andy said nothing but smiled as he chopped off a chunk of the ice cream with his spoon.

Jayne poked up the embers of the fire, hung up the poker, and tossed two split maple logs onto the blaze. Andy watched enthralled as the flames licked around them. She wondered if he'd ever been close to an open fire before.

"So, about the farm." She picked up her bowl and sat down on the sofa. "Dr. Ross said any time after ten o'clock tomorrow. He's not working tomorrow unless there's an emergency, so he and his folks will be there to show you their menagerie."

Andy wriggled and nudged his father. Luke bent down

to hear his whisper.

"She said a 'menagerie.' That's a collection of animals."

Andy looked solemnly at Jayne.

"Dr. Ross told me they have a pony that you might be able to ride."

Andy's mouth opened wide. "Daddy?"

"That sounds like fun, doesn't it?" Luke said.

"Right now Alec's got something quite unusual. One of his clients left a ferret with him during his vacation. You can see that, too."

Andy swiveled his neck and peered up at Luke.

"It's a furry animal," Luke said. "Like a rat, only bigger." He smiled at Jayne. "I've never seen one myself."

"You know, I haven't either. Should be interesting."

Andy tugged his father's sleeve, and Luke bent down again to listen. A smile wreathed his face. "Not a fairy. A ferret. Different things."

Andy shook his head and concentrated on his ice cream.

"After lunch, if you think Andy would like it, there's an apple orchard on the other side of town. You can pick your own apples. It's fun, and they give you cider afterward. You can see them squeezing the apples."

"That sounds neat, don't you think, Andy?"

His mouth full of ice cream, Andy just nodded.

"Will you be able to go with us, Jayne?" Luke asked.

Jayne felt her cheeks color. She'd hoped he would ask, but hadn't counted on it. "I'd enjoy it, if you're sure I won't be in the way."

"I think we'd both like it if you went." After a minute or two of companionable silence while they ate, Luke said,

"You mentioned 'coming home' to this house. Does that mean you're usually elsewhere? If that's not too personal. . ."

Jayne shrugged. "It's not. I usually come home to help my folks run the inn in summer, but this year I was so close to clinching my master's degree, we all felt I'd be silly to put it off. So I stayed in Boston and studied all summer. I'm glad it's done and I've got the credential, but. . ." She hesitated. "I'm facing a big decision about employment. I have an offer in the city, but coming home this week reminded me of what I'll give up if I take it. And then there's Mom and Dad. . ."

Luke arched his eyebrows invitingly, but said nothing.

Jayne scraped the bottom of her dish. "They'd like me to stay. I'm just not sure that's what I should do—or what I *want* to do."

"It's a big decision."

"Yeah." She hesitated then said softly, "I'm praying about it."

"Good move."

They looked at each other, not speaking, but Jayne felt there was no need. In Luke's blue eyes, so much like Andy's, she saw sadness and fatigue, but also understanding.

Andy's spoon clinked as it fell from his hand into his bowl. Luke arched his neck to peer down at his son.

"He's asleep," Jayne whispered, leaning forward to take the dishes from Andy's lap.

"At least he finished his ice cream first. I'll carry him up to bed."

Jayne took Luke's bowl and put it on the tray. He rose carefully, shifting Andy in his arms.

"Thank you, Jayne."

"Let us know if you need anything. You can call down on the phone in your room if you want, so you don't have to leave him alone."

"Thanks. If Andy didn't feel secure here, he'd still be wound up. I think he finds this place relaxing, which is a wonderful thing for him."

"I'm glad."

Jayne walked with him out into the hallway and watched Luke carry the inert little boy up the stairs. Where they turned at the landing, Luke looked down at her and smiled. Jayne raised her hand in a friendly wave. She turned back to the parlor to collect their dishes.

Was she giving up more than she'd considered to begin her career in Boston? Luke and Andy seemed to be alone now, but they had the Dillard family—his in-laws. He must be on friendly terms with them. Did that mean there'd been no divorce? Luke and Andy belonged to a good-sized extended family. Eleven people for Christmas week, provided Luke and Andy liked the inn. So far, so good.

A sudden thought pricked her. When had she stopped taking extra pains just to get the Christmas booking and begun doing it for Andy? When she'd seen how shy and fearful he was, and then his excitement about the animals, and even the fireplace and the ice cream, her heart had tumbled. He was such a sweet little thing. In the last five hours, her goal had shifted to making Andy feel at home at the Barncastle—whether his grandmother booked the Christmas package or not. Andy's comfort and security were paramount.

Jayne carried the tray to the kitchen, where her parents

sat at the table eating ice cream. In a year, they would be gone, and the inn would be sold. If she stayed to run it with hired help, who would be here to make her feel at home in the castle? Keeping the house she loved in rural Vermont might end up as lonely as pursuing a frenetic career in the city—and she'd have more time to think about it. Would she ever have a family of her own to share life with her?

❄

A chilly wind swept in off the lake the next morning, and Luke insisted on driving his SUV down the road to the Ross family's farm.

Alec Ross and his father greeted them cheerfully. Alec told Luke about his veterinary office in the village, where he practiced with an older man, Dr. Coe. After they visited Alec's two dogs in the yard, he led them into the barn, to a cage holding a furry animal the size of a small cat.

"Is that the ferret?" Andy pronounced the word carefully.

Luke and Jayne exchanged an amused look. Jayne couldn't know how proud Luke felt at that moment— seeing Andy actually speak up to Dr. Ross and ask his own question, instead of whispering it to his father and getting Luke to talk for him.

"Yes, it is," Alec replied.

"Do they make good pets?" Jayne asked.

"Some do." Alec made sure the door was closed. "I'll take it out of the cage, and you can pat it if you want to, Andy. I'm not going to let you hold it, though, because I don't know this guy very well. He's been polite so far, but I wouldn't want anything to happen."

He put on leather gloves and took the animal carefully

out of the wire cage and cradled it in his arms then stooped so the ferret was at Andy's waist level. "You can pat his side and back. I wouldn't reach directly toward his face, though."

Andy reached out, paused, then continued. His finger-tips grazed the ferret's fur, and he smiled up at Luke. "It's really soft."

"Your dad and Jayne can touch him, too." Alec stood straighter, and Jayne reached to feel the soft pelt.

"You're right, Andy. He feels as soft as a kitten."

Luke, too, stroked the animal. The ferret began to stir and wriggle in Alec's arms.

"Time to go back in your cage." Alec slipped the ferret smoothly in through the door and closed it.

Andy stepped closer and stared as the ferret groomed itself, its long, pink tongue flicking over its silky fur.

"Want to see the other animals now?" Alec asked him.

Andy nodded.

"We have some sheep you can pat, and a cute little pig, and then there's the pony. My dad said something about putting his saddle on him." He smiled and held out his hand to Andy.

Luke held his breath, but Andy placed his hand in Alec's and walked with him to the door.

"I think Andy's found a new friend," Jayne murmured.

"Looks like it," Luke said. "Shall we tag along?"

❄

Jayne hadn't enjoyed a day so much for a long time. After Andy's pony ride, Luke drove to a small café in the village. They dawdled over sandwiches and milkshakes, with Luke and Andy telling silly riddles. Most were based on puns the six-year-old found hysterical.

"Where does the sheep get its haircut?" he asked Jayne, suppressing a giggle.

"I don't know. At the shearer's?"

Andy shook his head and shouted gleefully, "At the baa-baa shop!"

Jayne laughed. "Guess I never heard that one." They piled into Luke's SUV again, and she guided him to the apple orchard.

"We haven't had a hard frost yet," the owner told them, "so some of the varieties aren't ready yet. But you can pick McIntosh and Cortlands."

"Do we like those, Daddy?" Andy's worried frown crept back over his forehead.

"We sure do."

Jayne scooched down and smiled at Andy. "If you get a bag of McIntosh, my mom will make you an apple pie."

Andy licked his lips. "Let's do that, Daddy."

"Okay." Luke ruffled his hair and took a sturdy paper tote bag from the farmer. While he and Andy carefully picked the ripe apples, Jayne took pictures. Andy ignored her, and she got some great shots, using her close-up from several yards away.

After Luke paid for the apples and they drank cups of cider, they strolled back to the parking lot.

"I'll put the pictures in my computer and print them for you tonight," Jayne said. "I think I have some you'll like."

"Great." Luke glanced at Andy and lowered his voice. "Thanks for doing that. He's usually camera shy."

She shrugged. "He wanted a picture of him on Alec's

pony, and after that, he didn't seem to mind anymore."

"He likes you."

"I'm flattered."

Before they'd pulled onto the road, Andy had drifted off to sleep.

Luke threw Jayne a smile. "He's too old for taking naps, but all this fresh air and excitement tuckers him out."

"He's adorable. I'm glad he's enjoying his stay."

"Me, too." Luke hesitated. "Sometimes he has a rough time, especially around new people and places."

"I thought maybe." Jayne looked out the window as the familiar houses floated by. "Sometimes big people have trouble adjusting, too."

"Are you having a tough time just now?"

"Sort of." She pressed her lips together. She barely knew Luke, and he was a guest at the inn—not the person she should use as a sounding board for her dilemma. But his inquisitive glance and sympathetic half smile said otherwise. "It's this decision I have to make on whether to come home permanently to help my folks run their business, or take the job I've been offered in Boston."

"Quite a choice." He turned onto the road that led to the Barncastle. "Do you like working at the inn?"

"I love it."

"What's holding you back?"

She sighed. "For one thing, I have a solid job offer in hand. But my folks told me Monday they'd like to retire next year. I never thought the inn would bring in enough to support more than the immediate family, but now that I've studied marketing, I've concluded that it can be done.

Trying could be a lot of fun. I'd have to hire help of course." She tried not to connect the inn's success with his family's decision on the Christmas package—she wouldn't want Luke to get the idea that his or Mrs. Dillard's preferences would decide her future.

"Then there's the small town factor," Luke said pensively. "Can you be happy living out here after the social whirl of Boston?"

"I did wonder about that, but in the last few days, I've felt so peaceful. Other than having this question hanging over me of course."

Luke nodded. "I had to make a choice like that a couple of years ago."

Jayne waited, her heart aching from his wistful tone.

After a moment, he said softly, "My wife died."

"I'm so sorry."

"Thank you. Andy took it hard. We all did, but he— Well, the question was whether to stay at my well-paying job in Hartford, where I had friends and connections, or move to rural Vermont, where I felt Andy would be more comfortable."

"And you chose Vermont?"

"Yes, and no regrets. It's so much quieter, and Andy can progress at his own pace. He's doing better every day."

Better than what? Jayne wondered, but she didn't ask. Whatever troubles Andy had come through, his father was committed to doing what was best for the little boy.

Chapter 4

Luke covered Andy with the quilt and tiptoed out of the Squire's Room and down the stairs. He glanced into the empty parlor, then walked back toward the kitchen.

When he pushed the door open, Diane looked up from rolling out pastry on her work island. "Well hi, Luke. I hear Andy conked out on you."

Luke smiled. "Yeah, I thought I'd let him sleep for an hour or so."

Jayne sat at a small round table peeling apples, but she stood and laid down her knife. "How about some coffee? We've got a fresh pot."

"I'd love some. And if you've got another knife, I could help you with that."

"Seems like a fair trade to me." Jayne brought him his mug of steaming coffee then went to a drawer for a paring knife.

Diane laid a layer of pastry in a pie plate and trimmed it. "We're having a simple meal tonight, Luke—soup and salad, followed by apple pie, thanks to you."

"Andy was excited when Jayne told us you'd turn our apples into pie. I hope you don't mind."

"No trouble." Diane wiped her hands on her apron. "I won't need all of those apples, though. You'll still have a

42

bag to take home."

Jayne brought him the extra knife, and Luke reached for an apple. The afternoon sun pouring through the west windows shimmered on her caramel-colored hair. In her pink-plaid flannel shirt and jeans, Jayne gave an impression of wholesome friendliness. She attracted him more than any of the women he'd worked with in Hartford. He reminded himself that she would soon be one of those corporate women—no doubt wearing an expensive skirt suit and carrying a briefcase to her Boston office.

"I'm glad Andy had a good time today," Diane said.

"He loved it. Jayne found the perfect activities for us."

Jayne's lips quirked. "I don't think he was sure about touching the ferret, but once we got out to the sheep pen, he was all gung ho."

"He would have stayed at the farm all day, if we'd let him," Luke said.

They soon finished cutting the apples, and Diane stirred them up in a pottery bowl with sugar, flour, and cinnamon. Luke relaxed and sipped his cooling coffee.

"Say, Jaynie," her mother said, "could you put these in the oven? I need to run to the store for some fresh fruit and milk for breakfast. They'll take forty minutes."

"Sure. Go ahead." Jayne rose and walked to the work island.

"All right. You need to wrap the edges of the crusts with foil first."

Diane washed her hands and scooted out the back door. Luke got up and helped himself to another cup of coffee.

"The whole family's going to like this place," he said.

Jayne's eyebrows arched. "Do you think Mrs. Dillard will book it for Christmas?"

"If Andy and I have anything to say about it, she will." He couldn't help frowning as he thought of the peaceful inn full of Dillards, though. "Some of the family can be a little ...shall we say 'difficult'? But I think everyone will enjoy the Barncastle experience."

Jayne slid the two pies into the oven and straightened. "How do you mean, 'difficult'?"

"Well, you have to understand—I love my mother-in-law, but some might say she's...high maintenance."

"Ah."

He took another sip. "This is very good coffee."

"Thanks." She picked up her own cup, refilled it, and slid into her chair across from him. "I was surprised when you and Andy walked in. We had planned a romantic dinner for two."

Luke chuckled. "Sorry. Rosalyn said she'd take care of the booking, and I assumed she'd told you more. She asked me to come because she knew that the whole Christmas reunion depends on Andy and me."

"Oh?"

Luke hesitated only a moment. He wanted Jayne to know his situation, but didn't want to burden her. "I'm not sure it's fair to dump our family politics on you, but I have a feeling you'd be impartial enough to see things clearly."

"I'd certainly try," Jayne said, holding his gaze. "Don't tell me anything you don't want to."

He knew she would keep his confidence, and that felt good. It had been a long time since he'd had a friend he could talk over the really important things with. "I've distanced myself from the family since Edie died. Andy's mother, that is."

Jayne let out a soft sigh, as though she'd been waiting to hear that. "I'm sorry. You and Andy have been through a tough time."

"Yeah, we have." He lifted his coffee cup, thinking about it.

"How long has it been?" she asked.

"More than two years. I used to work for her father, Austin Dillard. He owns an architectural firm in the city—a good one."

"You're an architect?"

Luke nodded. "After the accident, I decided it would be better for Andy if I took a less stressful job. I never liked the rat race in the city, anyway—or only seeing Andy for a couple of hours in the evening."

"I can understand that. I like some things about the city, but it's wearing."

"Yeah, it is. And after Edie died, I had to have a babysitter all the time for Andy, and that didn't work out very well."

"I'm sorry."

Luke looked into the dark liquid in his mug. He could talk about Edie now without his voice catching, but his chest still tightened when he mentioned her death. And he hadn't talked to anyone in detail about Andy's trouble except his pastor and the counselor he'd found for Andy. He looked up. Jayne's gaze held sympathy, but something else.

"How are things now that you've moved to Vermont?" she asked.

"Better. See, Andy was in the car with Edie when she had her accident."

Jayne closed her eyes for a moment, her lashes casting shadows on her creamy cheeks. "That explains a lot."

"Yes. Though I don't want to use it as an excuse to coddle him. Andy wasn't seriously injured, but he was traumatized. He had nightmares afterward, and he seemed to withdraw from reality. It was a bad time for both of us."

Unshed tears shone in Jayne's eyes. He took another sip of coffee and cleared his throat.

"Since we moved up here, I've earned less, but the cost of living is lower."

"Tell me about it. My friend called me yesterday about apartment prices in Boston. Unbelievable."

"I'll bet. I've discovered that Andy and I can get by very simply in the country. I work at home now, and we have a lot more time together. I see progress every day. Andy's conquering his fears."

"His memories may be less intense now," she said.

Luke nodded. "His nightmares have gotten less frequent this summer. I really think he's going to be okay. But he needs a slow-paced, low-pressure environment."

"I think it's wonderful that you were willing to change your lifestyle for him," Jayne said.

"Thanks. I couldn't do anything else. And it seems to have paid off." He drained his mug.

"So, how often does Andy see his grandparents?" Jayne asked.

"My folks live in Florida, and they come up in the summer. I take Andy down for a couple of weeks in January.

I wish they lived closer. Austin and Rosalyn are a different story. They're a little upset with me because they don't think they see Andy often enough." He shrugged. "Andy finds their house stressful, and Rosalyn prods him to talk and do things he's not comfortable with. I don't like to put him through that too often."

Jayne's mouth squeezed into a sympathetic line. "When she called, she seemed eager to set up a Christmas experience Andy would enjoy. I think she chose the medieval theme for him."

"Really?"

"Yes." Jayne swallowed hard and met his gaze. "I may as well tell you, this is a new venture for the inn. You didn't see the ad?"

Luke shook his head.

"We're offering a week of Christmas in any time period the guests want—or any theme. Colonial, Civil War, superheroes, cowboys. You name it, we'll set it up."

"That's so innovative."

"Well, thank you." She smiled, and her cheeks went pink.

"Your idea?"

"Yes."

"I think it's terrific."

"Well I'm glad your mother-in-law thought so."

He looked into her eyes, and it hit him that if Rosalyn hadn't been taken with the concept, he and Andy wouldn't have met Jayne. He was starting to realize how much they would have missed.

"I'm glad, too. Rosalyn posed it as a favor to her—bring Andy here for the weekend at her expense to check out the facility, and so Andy could get used to the place. She figured if we had a good time, Andy would look forward to coming here again. She's a smart lady."

"Yes," Jayne mused. "We're delighted, and we hope we have the chance to meet the rest of your family. I've been making notes for medieval decorations and entertainment. Mom is going wild over ancient recipes, and Dad's planning some projects that will make the place seem more like a castle, inside and out."

"I hope he doesn't make too many changes. It's perfect as it is." They smiled at one another, in complete agreement.

Jayne snapped her fingers. "That reminds me. I have a couple of old friends who live about ten miles away. They belong to the Society for Creative Anachronism. Ever hear of it?"

A long-buried memory surfaced, of Luke's parents taking him and his brother to a Renaissance fair. "Aren't they the people who put on the jousts and things?"

"That's right. And they're very interested in authenticity and in educating the public about the Middle Ages. My friend Dori is a wonderful seamstress. She makes their costumes. Her husband, Bill, is more into the hardware. He makes his own armor and swords—all that sort of thing. Do you think Andy would like to visit them? Or would that be too much?"

"I don't know. Can we see if he wakes up ready for more adventure?"

"Sure," Jayne said.

"And speaking of the sleeping prince, I'd better go check on him." Luke reached across the table and gave her hand a squeeze. "Thanks, Jayne. I'm glad we had this time to talk."

❄

"This is how I'll shape the hilt."

Bill drew his tongs from the old forge where he'd heated the piece of steel in the coals of a charcoal fire. The round forge reminded Jayne of an old barbecue, but it had a handle on one side that allowed Bill to pump a bellows and blow air on his fire.

He took the steel quickly to his anvil and began hammering it around the horn, into a curved shape. Andy and Luke watched, fascinated, through the safety goggles Bill had loaned them. Jayne stood a couple of yards away with Dori. Bill had run out of goggles, and she'd insisted Luke and his son take them. She'd watched Bill play blacksmith before.

"How many costumes do you think you'll need?" Dori asked.

Jayne tore her gaze away from Andy's enraptured face and smiled at her friend. "Oh, half a dozen anyway. We'll have a full house for a week and we're serving all the meals, so we'll need to hire people to help cook and serve, as well as a chambermaid. Dad thinks he can handle the heavy work, but I don't know—we'll be hauling a lot of wood up from the cellar that week for the fireplaces, and there'll be lots of luggage and probably snow to shovel. I might hire a high school boy or two."

"And you want all your staff to dress in fourteenth-century clothing." Dori gave a dreamy smile. "I'll pull some drawings off the Internet from places that sell patterns and e-mail them to you with estimates of price for different fabrics."

"Sounds good. And as soon as the booking is definite, I'll let you know." While she spoke, Jayne continued to watch Luke and Andy's interplay with Bill. Luke encouraged Andy to speak to his new friend, and after just a few minutes of ducking his head and shrinking against his father's leg, Andy had overcome his timidity. He hung on every word Bill spoke as he formed the new sword hilt. When the steel had the shape he wanted, he dunked it in a bucket of water. Steam hissed into the air.

"That is so cool, Daddy," Andy almost shouted.

Next Bill showed him and Luke the shield he'd made for an upcoming tournament. "See this? It's my crest. I'm Sir Pantheon when I'm in tournaments, and the silver panther on a black background is my crest."

Dori arched her eyebrows and smiled at Jayne. "If all your guests are as enthusiastic as these two, you might make a regular thing of medieval-themed vacations."

"You never know. Do you think Bill would be interested in organizing some demonstrations—maybe a little fencing? We'll need minstrels and jugglers, too. Maybe some mummers."

"We know people who do all of those things, and they'll work hard to put on a good show for you. Of course, it's at Christmas. . ."

"Yes. I'll talk to you again as soon as I know for sure, so we can start scheduling."

Jayne and Dori walked closer to where Bill was helping Andy heft his leather-covered shield.

"It's heavy," Andy said.

"Yes, it's too big for a warrior your size." Bill straightened and nodded toward the far wall of his workshop. "Maybe your dad can get that smaller one down for you to try." He looked at Luke. "The one with the tree and the lightning bolt."

Luke walked to the wall where several shields hung amid tools and replicas of ancient weapons. He brought the small, round shield back and handed it to Bill.

"Here you go, Andy," Bill said. "Try this. It's the one our nephew uses when he comes to visit."

Andy grasped the handle on the back of the shield and held it up, completely hiding his face.

"Oops, a little lower, buddy," Luke said.

Bill chuckled. "Right—you've got to be able to see where you're going, Sir Andrew."

Andy's eyes glowed as he pretended to fend off blows with the shield.

Bill lowered his voice. "You know, Luke, you can get foam swords. Kids love 'em, and they can practice without hurting each other."

"I might look into it," Luke said. "Andy sure loves this."

After they enjoyed hot chocolate and cookies with Dori and Bill, Luke drove back to the inn.

"Are you awake?" he asked Andy as he unbuckled the boy's safety harness.

"Um-hmm." Andy stifled a yawn.

"Well then, I guess you can walk up to our room, Sir Andrew." Luke lifted him down and smiled over at Jayne. "I was afraid I'd have to lug him in again."

"It's been a full day." She walked beside them up the steps.

"Yes, and a good one. A day to remember." Luke held her gaze for a long moment as Jayne fumbled with the door handle.

"Do we have to go home tomorrow, Daddy?" Andy murmured.

Luke ruffled his hair. "Afraid so. But we can go to church here with the Barncastles, instead of going home early."

"Good."

Jayne swung the door open, and Andy marched inside, yawning.

"Thanks for everything, Jayne," Luke said.

"It was a fantastic day." These two had stolen her heart. Jayne knew she'd never forget Luke's sad eyes or the wistful gaze that lingered on her before he followed his son up the staircase.

❋

Luke carried the luggage down Sunday afternoon and stowed it in the SUV. He would miss this place, and not only for the excellent food and the cozy surroundings rich in heritage and history.

It was Jayne. He didn't want to drive away from her. He could tell she liked him, and unless he was mistaken, she adored his son. Would she think of them as often as he'd think of her? They hadn't even left yet, and he was trying to recall the exact sweep of her lush caramel-toned hair when she turned her head.

He went back inside. Jayne was helping Andy button his jacket. She straightened and threw him an enigmatic glance, then reached for something on the hall table behind her.

"Andy, I've had this for a long time. I got it when I was

about your age. I'm going to be really busy for the next couple of months, and I wondered if you'd want to keep him for me until the next time we meet." She held out a slightly bedraggled stuffed dragon about ten inches long.

Andy reached out and took the blue-and-purple dragon and pulled it in close to his stomach. "I'll take good care of him."

Jayne looked at Luke. "If you don't mind. . ."

"I don't mind." Luke's throat was tight, and he cleared it. "That looks like the kind of dragon that doesn't eat much."

Andy smiled. He'd smiled and laughed more this weekend than he had in a long time—since his mother died. Jayne's thoughtfulness had a lot to do with that.

"Miss Jayne?" Andy looked up at her with big, trusting eyes. "What's his name?"

Jayne's somber expression morphed into a broad smile. "Hendrick. He told me his papa was German."

"Hendrick." Andy snuggled the dragon up against his chin. "I like soft dragons."

"Me, too." Jayne held out her hand to Luke. "I'm so glad you came."

He grasped her hand, feeling that the gesture was horribly inadequate. "Listen, can I call you? Or e-mail? E-mail's good for busy people."

"Either. Both. I'd like that." She went to the desk and wrote something on one of the inn brochures. "Here's my cell phone number and my personal e-mail."

Luke took it and tucked it in his pocket. "Time to say good-bye, buddy."

For just an instant, Andy got the panicky look that had

pretty much disappeared over the weekend.

"Can we come back soon, Daddy?"

"We'll be here for a whole week at Christmas," Luke said.

Andy held up his arms to Jayne. She went to her knees and hugged him.

"Good-bye, Andy." She kissed his cheek.

Andy clung to her for a moment, his arms tight around her neck with one hand clutching Hendrick the dragon. Then he let go and squared his shoulders.

"Bye."

Luke took courage from his son's actions and from the sweet smile on Jayne's lips. He stooped and kissed her other cheek. "Good-bye for now. You haven't seen the last of us."

Chapter 5

"Luke's mother-in-law just called."

Jayne dropped her armload of split firewood into the woodbox beside the parlor fireplace and eyed her mother cautiously. "What did she say?" Her stomach had gone all tilt-a-whirl, and she realized she'd been waiting for this news since Luke and Andy walked out the door yesterday.

"Booking confirmed." Mom grinned. "She was delighted with Andy's report to her."

"Andy spoke to her?"

"Yes, he did. Luke, too, of course, but Andy's part was what impressed her most. She said he won't always talk to her on the phone, but this morning he couldn't wait to tell her about the castle. And all the neat places you took him and his daddy."

"Fantastic."

Mom flew toward her, arms outstretched. "Honey, you were so right about this. Mrs. Dillard said she's going to tell all her friends about this wonderful little B&B that Luke found."

Tears filled Jayne's eyes as they hugged each other and laughed. She swiped at them with the cuff of her denim shirt. "You're happy about this, right, Mom?"

"I'm very happy. And your father is ecstatic. He's already

muttering about crenellations and Yule logs. He wants to build faux ramparts around the deck on the roof—over the railing."

"Andy will love it!"

"Yes. But the thing that's got both of us dancing is you. Knowing you'll stay."

"I sure will. That's my part of the bargain." Jayne looked at her watch. "And it's time I called Bowker-Hatley."

"What will you tell them?"

She grinned. "That I've had a better offer."

Please thank your friend Dori for putting me in touch with the homeschool people. I was at the end of my rope when I saw that Andy just couldn't handle the public school program. I wanted him to have contact with other kids his age, but he came home every day in tears. This group has activities for the kids, and Andy's slowly getting comfortable with it. I was afraid it would be too much for me, with my work, but it's going well.

Andy's been asking me when we'll see you again. I kept thinking I'd get out from under the workload and we could set something up, but here it is November already! E-mails are great, don't get me wrong, but Jayne—I want to see you again.

Luke stopped and re-read what he'd written on the screen. Did he dare send it? Before he could talk himself out of it, he hit SEND.

He got up and walked into the kitchen and poured himself a cup of lukewarm coffee from that morning's pot.

"Daddy, can I have a cookie?"

"That sounds good. Why don't we both have one?"

Ten minutes later, Luke dragged himself back to the computer. Andy had settled down with a dot-to-dot book on the rug. Luke woke up the monitor. A new message from Jayne was already in his inbox. He held his breath and opened it.

I want to see you, too. Both of you. When and where?

He let his breath out in a huff. "Hey Andy, do you want to go see Miss Jayne tomorrow?"

❄

Luke's SUV pulled into the parking lot at a restaurant midway between his home and the Barncastle Inn. Jayne got out of her car and locked the door. She only had time to wave and register that Luke looked good—better than good—before Andy catapulted into her arms.

"Hello, Andy." She held him close and endured his choke hold hug. "How are you doing?"

He nuzzled close to her ear and whispered, "Good."

She laughed. "I'm good, too." She set him down and straightened.

Luke moved in looking a bit uncertain. She met him halfway for a kiss on the cheek.

"Thanks for coming," he said.

"Thanks for asking me."

When they got inside, Andy unzipped his jacket and hauled out a crumpled purple-and-blue wad and set it on the table.

"I brought Hendrick."

Jayne's eyes misted. "Aw. Thank you, Andy."

"He missed you."

"I thought of him often." She reached out and scratched the wilted dragon's neck. "Has he been good?"

Andy nodded gravely.

"He hasn't torched any peasant cottages lately," Luke said.

"Do you need him back?" Andy asked in a small voice.

"Would you like him to stay with you until you come to the castle at Christmas?"

Andy nodded.

"Oh, and Hendrick likes to sleep in my tower room. It puts him up high, where he can look out over the countryside. I thought maybe you and your dad would like to sleep in the other tower room when you come, and Hendrick could stay in there with you."

Andy turned to his father, his eyes aglow. "Can we?"

"Sure, if that's all right with the Barncastles."

Jayne loved Andy's eagerness and Luke's easy response.

"We don't usually rent that room to guests," she said, "but we've been using it lately, because we were full almost every weekend during October. People like it, even though it's a little smaller than the room where you slept before."

"Chelsea will be mad." Andy's mouth drew into a pout.

"Who's Chelsea?" Jayne asked.

"She's his cousin," Luke said. "My brother-in-law North Dillard's daughter."

"Why will she be mad?"

"She'll want the tower," Andy said.

Luke shrugged. "Should we let Chelsea and her sister have the tower room?"

Jayne could barely hear Andy's "Maybe."

She gave him a sympathetic smile. "Cousins can be bossy, can't they? But my mom and I were going to put the girls in the Lady's Bower. It's a special room on the back of the house. It's very pretty and frilly, and it has a little balcony of its own, overlooking the back courtyard."

"I'm sure they'll like that," Luke said.

"And the tower room is quite masculine," Jayne added.

Andy looked up at his father, his eyes like blue question marks.

Luke chuckled. "That means it's more for men than for ladies."

Andy frowned. "Does it have armor?"

"Not yet," Jayne said, "but I'm working on that. Oh, and I have a few other things planned." She looked over at Luke. "Is it better to have a surprise, or to have time to think about it?"

"Hmm. Good question. Why don't you tell me later, and I'll decide."

The waitress came, and they ordered their lunch. An hour later they walked leisurely along a path in the center of the town, where the colonial village common had become a municipal park. The breeze was chilly, and Jayne pulled her knit cap over her ears. Andy spotted a pair of spring-mounted hobby horses.

"Daddy, can I?"

"I guess so."

Luke released his hand, and Andy ran to the closest

horse and climbed on. He jounced up and down and rocked the horse back and forth.

Luke laughed. "That will keep him occupied for at least ten minutes. So, what kind of surprises do you have in store for the Dillard-Gilbert family?"

"How about fencing lessons?"

Luke stopped walking, and his eyes lit. "That's a great idea. I kept meaning to look into those foam swords your friend told us about, and I never got around to it."

"Well Bill and a couple of other fellows from his group are willing to come and offer lessons to the guests. If the family is interested, we can have them come more than once. They have foils and protective masks and jackets—all the gear needed for amateurs."

"Sounds like a blast, if North and his father aren't at each other's throats."

Jayne grimaced. "Ouch. Is the family that touchy?"

"At times." Luke smiled ruefully. "I'm glad I got out of the family business. Austin isn't a bad man, but he's not such a good boss. His son is a partner in the firm now, and they don't always agree. When they go at it, it's not pretty."

"Oh." Jayne swallowed hard. "Well, the foils are blunt-tipped, you know."

He chuckled. "I'm sure everyone will love it. And I think I will tell Andy in advance, so he can think about it and not be too scared to try it when the time comes. Having met Bill in September will help. He still talks about how Bill was forging that sword hilt."

Jayne snapped her fingers. "That's what else I need for decorations. Oh—sorry. I just want everything as authentic as possible."

Luke eyed her pensively. "Your family isn't breaking the bank to accommodate us, is it?"

She shook her head. "Mrs. Dillard made a large deposit, and we're having the time of our lives planning and shopping."

"Sounds like you're glad you decided to stay and help your folks this fall."

"I am. If I'd taken that job in Boston, I'd never have had this time with them. I didn't realize what a blessing it would be."

"Daddy!"

At Andy's shout, they turned to look at him, riding his springy steed and clutching Hendrick to his chest.

Luke slid his arm around Jayne and pulled her close beside him. "I think you're very brave to host our clan—and I can hardly wait."

Chapter 6

The folks in the Squire Room just checked out," Jayne told her mother as she walked into the kitchen. "Rachel's doing up the room, and Dad's putting up the final mistletoe garlands in the entry."

"Have all the guests had breakfast?" Mom bent over the counter, studying a sheet of paper.

"I don't think the folks in the Library Suite have been down yet." Jayne helped herself to coffee. "What are you cooking?"

Mom looked up. "I'm trying a new recipe for barley-honey bread."

"For next week?"

"Yes. Can you believe the Dillards are coming Monday? The time has gone so fast!"

"We've been busy." Jayne sat on a stool beside the work island. "The Carters asked if they could stay over until Tuesday, but I told them we're booked solid next week. They'll be the last ones to check out Monday morning."

"Usually we have a lull after the leaves are off, but not this year," Mom said. "I guess your advertising helped there."

"Are you sorry?"

Her mother looked at her keenly. "No. Why would you think that?"

Jayne shrugged. "You always loved to have a slower pace

in December, so you could get ready for Christmas. It's been a bit hectic this year."

"Yes, but that's good. We'll be handing a thriving business over to you—or whoever buys it from us. Have you thought about that?"

"I've thought about little else." Jayne clasped her hands around the warm coffee mug. "It's scary to think of owning my own business."

"You've proven you can do it. And we've had good help this fall." Her mom went to the refrigerator and opened the door. "Rachel and Stacie have been super with housekeeping, and we've got Tina coming in all next week to help me in the kitchen. Except Christmas Day. I'm afraid we'll be on our own that last day, and it's the most important." She came back carrying a jar of yeast.

"We'll be fine. Oh we've got two high school–age jugglers coming Monday night to perform, and they'll work with the kids Tuesday if they're interested. All we have to do is pay for their extra equipment."

Mom bit her lip as she scanned her recipe. "Sounds like fun to me, but I don't know how the older kids will like it. Do we have a backup plan if they think juggling and fencing are boring?"

"We've got sleigh rides and skating on tap, and the dogsled races in Bennington. Dad's planning the expedition to cut another Christmas tree early in the week. And if the guests like the costumes, Dori will come over and fit them for medieval outfits." Jayne frowned. Luke had hinted that his wife's family included several "difficult" personalities. What if they wouldn't get with the program?

"I don't know how much more you can do," Mom said. "Did that last box of tapestries come?"

"It should be delivered this afternoon. Dad's going to help me hang those in the hall."

"Good. The big tree in the parlor looks great."

"Mom, I think it's going to go over well. I really do."

Her mother walked around the island and put her arms around her.

"So do I, Jaynie. You've done a terrific job, and the castle looks fabulous."

"I just hope they like it."

Mom drew back, smiling. "Well, you know at least two of the guests will like it."

Jayne felt her face flush. "Andy's going to flip over the suit of mail Dad put on the landing, not to mention the surprise waiting for him in the tower room."

"I'm sure he'll love it." Her mother went back around the counter. "Something tells me his father will enjoy the week, too."

❄

The guest parking lot at Barncastle Inn was nearly empty when Luke drove in at ten o'clock Monday morning. An inch of fresh powdery snow turned the inn into a dream castle.

He helped Andy out and pointed to the roof. "Look at the new crenellations. Mr. Barncastle built that new wall since we were here last. Miss Jayne says we can go up there if it's not too slippery."

"Where's our room?" Andy's gaze roved the castle hungrily.

Luke pointed to the tower farthest from the parking lot. "I think it's up there. Miss Jayne said her room is in the east tower. That would be this closer one. So we're over there."

"Let's go." Andy headed for the steps.

"Don't you think we should take our bags?"

Sheepishly, his son came back to his side.

"Here, you take this." Luke held up Andy's backpack. The boy turned and stuck his arms through the straps.

Inside, Jayne stood behind the desk in the large entry hall, studying a clipboard. She looked up as they entered, and a huge smile broke over her face.

Andy ran to her. "Miss Jayne! Can we go up to the tower?"

She laughed and hugged him. "You sure can. I'm so glad to see you, Andy."

He hung around her neck and whispered, "I love you."

"I love you, too," she whispered back. She straightened and held out her hand to Luke. "Welcome back to the castle."

"Thanks. It looks great." He grasped her warm hand and felt a bit sophomoric as he added, "So do you."

"Thanks. Let's get you guys officially checked in." She unlocked a drawer in the desk and handed Luke a large, old-fashioned key.

He held it up. "Wow. Is this our room key?"

"Yes, it is. We've gone low-tech, in keeping with the theme."

"We noticed the changes outside. This place looks like it was built a thousand years ago and you're ready to fend off the Huns."

"You'll have to tell my dad that. We had to restrain him

65

from digging a moat."

She grabbed the small duffel bag that held Andy's extra clothes for the week, and Luke carried his own. He noted the swags of greenery and red berries along the railings and over the doorways in the hall. A cluster of pierced tin stars hung from the chandelier, and scenic tapestries hung above the stairs and on the walls below. On their way up the staircase, Jayne paused on the landing.

"Well Andy, what do you think?"

Andy stared at the suit of armor standing in the corner, where the stairway turned. "Wow. Did a real knight wear that?"

Jayne threw Luke a smile over the boy's head. "I don't think so. It's made to look like a real one, though."

"It's a pretty good reproduction," Luke said.

"Can I touch it?" Andy asked.

"Sure. Dad anchored it so it won't fall over easily."

Andy put out one finger and touched the knight's breastplate.

"Okay, you ready to go on?" Jayne asked.

Two flights of steps later, she opened the door to their room. Andy ran inside and stood in the middle of the floor. He turned around slowly, taking in the shields and tapestries on the walls.

"Thanks, Jayne," Luke said. "This is perfect."

She nodded with satisfaction. "Enjoy your stay. Would you like to eat lunch with the family? Mrs. Dillard called to say the others will arrive late this afternoon. We'd love it if you and Andy would eat in the kitchen with us."

A warm feeling spread over Luke. "That would be a great honor."

"Dad!" Andy had found a suit of plastic armor, sized for a six-year-old, lying on one of the beds. "Dad, look! Is it for me?"

Jayne backed out the doorway smiling and closed the door.

❋

Luke seemed completely at ease until the Dillards drove in. He and Jayne had taken Andy out to the side yard, where the lawn sloped gently away from the house, toward the lake. For a blessed hour, they'd slid and then trudged back up the hill with Luke pulling the toboggan. Andy had screamed with laughter, scrunched between the two of them, each time they flew down the hill. Jayne didn't want to end it, but finally she knew it was time.

"I need to go get into my costume," she said as they crested the knoll on the side lawn.

"Your costume?" Andy asked.

"Yes. I'm going to dress like a lady would in a castle in 1400 AD."

"What's that?"

She smiled. "I'll let your dad explain it while I get dressed."

When she came down to the big entry hall a half hour later, Luke and Andy were just coming in, scraping their boots on the doormat. "Austin's here," Luke said. The boyish pleasure disappeared from his face. "He just drove in, with Liza and North behind him."

Andy looked anxious, too. Jayne went to help him take off his snowsuit, but when the front door opened, he wriggled over to Luke and stood close against him, clutching his father's arm.

A middle-aged couple dressed in designer skiwear walked in. Jayne stepped forward. "Mrs. Dillard? I'm Jayne Barncastle. We spoke on the phone. Welcome to Barncastle Inn."

"Thank you. I must say the place is impressive." Her sharp eyes darted about the hall, appraising the burnished wood and festive decorations. "This is my husband." She spotted Andy, who was clinging to Luke's leg. "Hello, young man. Come give Nana a kiss."

Andy burrowed his face deeper into Luke's pant leg. Mrs. Dillard's frown encompassed both the boy and his father.

Jayne registered them quickly and took out their keys. Behind the Dillards, two couples in their midthirties entered, with three youngsters slinking in last. The boy had earbuds in place and stood with his hands shoved in his pockets, not making eye contact. The two girls alternately glared at each other and peeked around suspiciously. Perhaps Nana's idea of fun didn't appeal to them.

Jayne was grateful when her parents came down the hall.

"Good afternoon, folks. I'm Ted Barncastle, Jayne's father, and this is my wife, Diane. We hope you'll have a pleasant stay."

The two girls eyed their peasant retainer outfits and shot each other an amused glance.

"May I help with your luggage?" Dad asked.

"Yes, we have three more bags in the Camry," said North's wife, Hillary.

"Oh, and Ray," the Dillards' daughter, Liza West, said to her husband. "He can get my other suitcase and your laptop, too."

North went out with Jayne's father and Ray West. As Jayne distributed keys, Luke and Andy watched in silence. Once Jayne thought Luke would speak, but his jaw tightened and he said nothing.

Liza held up her key. "How quaint."

Jayne smiled. "We've put you and Mr. West in the Chateau Room, across from your parents. Your son will be in the Squire's Room." She handed twelve-year-old Michael West his key.

"That's where Daddy and I slept last time we came here," Andy said.

Michael's eyebrows shot up, and he stared at Andy as though shocked that his young cousin could talk. "Cool. Where are you this time?"

Andy grinned for about half a second, then reined in his glee. He turned his face against Luke's hip and mumbled something.

"What did he say?" Rosalyn asked. "Speak up, Andy."

"He said we're in the tower room," Luke replied. "The West Tower, that is."

"Can I be in the other tower?" Chelsea asked.

Jayne hesitated. "I'm sorry, the East Tower is part of the family's private quarters."

"No fair." Chelsea made a face of disgust.

"We've put you girls in the Lady's Bower," Jayne said, watching her face closely.

"Oh, joy." Emma turned to her mother. "Do Chelsea and I *have* to sleep in the same room?"

Her mother, Hillary Dillard, flushed slightly. She cleared her throat and turned a weary smile on Jayne. "I assume our party is using all the available rooms?"

"There is another room along the hall from the Earl's Suite, where we've put Mr. and Mrs. Dillard—Mr. and Mrs. Austin Dillard, that is. It's smaller, and it has only a single bed, but it's every bit as comfortable as the others. Each room is unique, and that one is called the Friar's Room."

"I'll take it," Emma said.

Jayne opened the drawer for the additional key. She'd almost decided not to decorate and prepare that room, as the Dillard family didn't seem to have need of it, but Mom had encouraged her to spruce it up and have it ready, just in case they showed up with an extra person.

"Here you go."

"Thanks." Emma took the key. "Now, who's going to carry my stuff up?"

"I will," Luke said.

North, Ray, and Jayne's father came in loaded down with luggage.

"Where to?" North asked.

Mom stepped forward with a smile. "Mr. and Mrs. Austin Dillard, Michael, and the Wests can come with me."

"And I'll show Emma, Chelsea, and Mr. and Mrs. North Dillard to their rooms." Jayne left the desk and smiled at Hillary. "You and your husband will have the Library Suite."

"You have to sleep in a library?" Chelsea's lip curled.

"Hey," Luke said sternly, "they're going to love it. I've seen it, and it's one of the nicest rooms ever. Two levels, and a ton of bookshelves with one of those neat rolling ladders."

"Great," said Austin. "If I need something to read, I'll know whose room to visit."

Luke lingered in the hall to help Ted sort out the luggage. Andy stuck near his father as Jayne led her contingent of guests up the stairs. She took North and Hillary to the Library Suite first. Even blasé Chelsea lost her apathy when she saw it.

"Oh Mom, this is so cool!" She and Emma headed for the circular staircase that led up to the library level above the large bedroom.

Jayne said to North and Hillary, "There's another door to the library balcony from the hall upstairs, in case that winding stairway doesn't suit you."

"This is perfect for us," North said. He strode to the window and looked out on the lake. "Beautiful property you have."

"Thank you. Would you like me to light the fire in the fireplace for you?"

"Not right now," Hillary said.

Jayne nodded. "Feel free to start it later, or to call downstairs for one of us to do it for you."

Chelsea had no complaints either when she saw her large, airy room with its floral garden theme and balcony, and Emma pronounced the small Friar's Room, tucked under the tower stairs, "awesome." Jayne felt drained as she made her way down to the kitchen. She'd told the guests that drinks would be served in the parlor at six o'clock, and she went to help her mother mix the punch.

"What do you think?" Mom asked as she entered the kitchen.

Jayne shrugged. "So far, so good. Let's hope the jugglers show up on time."

❄

Dinner was going quite well, Luke thought.

Andy ate quietly beside him, and the others chatted almost amiably while Jayne and two other women served. Chelsea and Emma only launched into an argument twice, and Liza sniped at North once. Luke didn't try to understand what she was mad about. Hillary asked Jayne about the women's costumes and declared them "darling." Luke wouldn't have used that word, but the outfits were eye-catching and flattered the ladies' figures. They wore dark skirts and laced bodices over flowing white shifts, topped by long aprons—practical and at the same time contributing to the atmosphere.

A woman in a flowing green gown came in and played the lute while they ate. Her medieval ballads lulled him, and he almost forgot how he and Austin had sparred verbally the last time they'd met. Maybe they could get through this week without a confrontation.

He looked down the long table. Austin sat in a large, carved chair at the head—lord of the castle. Creamy candles burned in three branched silver candlesticks between bowls of Christmas greens and cones, and the electric lights were turned low. He could almost believe they'd gone back five hundred years.

Two young men in bright patchwork jesters' costumes entered. The minstrel slipped away, and the jugglers began to perform, one on each side of the table. They were pretty good, and they bounced jokes off each other as they tossed and caught several balls.

They had everyone laughing until one of the balls hit the

mistletoe-festooned chandelier and ricocheted off one of the candlesticks, knocking it over into the gravy boat.

Flames leaped two feet in the air. Chelsea and Emma screamed. Everyone along the center third of the table leaped up. Luke grabbed the platter that had held bread and dumped the remaining rolls on the table. He flipped the platter over on top of the flash fire. Silence hung for a moment; then Ray said, "Well done, Luke."

Smoke hung thick in the air. Luke stared at the charred, greasy mess on the tablecloth.

"I'm so sorry," the juggler stammered.

"Of all the—" Rosalyn glared at Jayne.

Andy burst out in a wail that grew louder as they all stared at him. Luke scooped him up in his arms and headed for the hall. As he passed Jayne, she seemed on the verge of tears.

Chapter 7

Jayne pasted on the brightest smile she could muster. "Well! Won't that dunk your tabard in the rill? Ladies and knights, may I suggest we serve your pudding in the parlor?"

Austin chuckled. "Ah, Mistress Jayne, might I inquire about coffee?"

Jayne stared innocently at him. "Why, your lordship, I know not of what you speak. But we have a new beverage brought in not a fortnight past by a trading vessel. Would you like to try it? I'm told it's prodigiously bitter, but some like it."

Austin guffawed. "I'll try it, lass. Come on, gang. Let's adjourn so the serfs can clean up the mess."

Jayne corralled the two waitresses and hurried to the kitchen. She quickly filled in her parents, and they all bustled to dish up the dessert. After giving the waitresses instructions to stay calm and cheerful no matter what, Jayne went into the hall where the jugglers waited with long faces.

"I'm sorry, Miss Barncastle," the younger of the two said. "I'd give anything to undo it."

She squeezed his shoulder. "There now, Nathan, don't worry about it. Accidents happen."

"I guess they won't want juggling lessons now," his companion said.

"I don't know. I think I'll wait until tomorrow to suggest it." She handed Nathan an envelope.

"You don't need to pay us," he said. "Joe and I talked it over, and we don't think you should."

"Nonsense. You worked for a good fifteen minutes before it happened, and you were doing great. You made a mistake, but you acted maturely." *Although not all the guests did*, she thought.

Behind her, the stairs creaked, and she turned. Luke stood on the landing. "Is Andy all right?" she asked.

"He's upset. I was going to just put him to bed, but he wants his pudding. Would that be—"

"I'll bring a tray to your room." Jayne turned back to the young jugglers and reassured them once more. "I'll call you tomorrow, boys. Please don't stress about this."

Voices reached her from the parlor.

"Calm down, Mother," North said sharply. "This is a nice little inn, and we're here to enjoy it. Don't forget that."

"Oh, so now you're lord of the manor," she heard Liza retort.

Jayne turned toward the kitchen and pulled her apron up to catch her tears.

❄

When Andy was asleep, Luke tiptoed down from the tower carrying the tray of empty dishes. He left it on the desk in the hall and entered the parlor.

Austin rose. "Is the boy all right?"

"He's sleeping."

"I expect he was overtired," Rosalyn said with a bitter note to her voice.

Luke ignored her and stepped toward the fireplace.

"I'd like a word with you, Luke," his father-in-law said.

Luke's stomach turned. Was Austin going to lecture him about Andy's behavior? He went with him into a smaller sitting room the Barncastles called the Abbott's Chamber. It appeared to be a comfortable office. Austin sat down in the leather-covered chair behind the desk and gestured toward a second chair.

"Sit down, Luke. We haven't talked for quite some time."

"That's true, sir." He'd only spoken privately with Austin twice since Edie's death, in fact. Both times had ended in a bitter parting, and he hadn't much hope for a better outcome tonight.

"I want you to come back to the firm."

Luke took a breath to calm himself before answering. "No."

"Just like that? No?"

"No."

Austin scowled. "Surely you've had enough of hiding in the countryside. It can't be good for Andy either. The boy needs socialization—"

Luke stood. "I'm sorry, sir."

"Hear me out." Austin jumped up. "We've had enough of your heroics. Rosalyn wants her grandson back. Well, we both do. We miss you and Andy."

Luke bit his bottom lip, unsure how to respond.

"How can you deny a woman time with her grandson?" Austin asked.

"I haven't denied her anything. She's capable of coming to Vermont to visit. Even so, I'll try to bring Andy down to

Hartford more often."

"But the firm—we need you there, too."

"Austin. No."

"I'll make it worth your while."

"I doubt it." Luke turned and opened the door.

"Come back here! What do you mean by that? How dare you—"

Luke hurried toward the stairs, his heart pounding. Jayne stood in the kitchen doorway, a stricken look on her face.

❄

Tuesday was going well, Jayne thought. Rosalyn had set out for the sleigh ride with a dubious look on her face, but she'd come back laughing. She'd spotted a darling little shop in the village she wanted to explore that afternoon. She took Liza, Hillary, and the two girls with her, and the afternoon was quiet at the castle while Ray and Luke took Michael and Andy out sledding. North and his father seemed to have holed up in their rooms—with their computers, Jayne suspected.

It wasn't until nearly suppertime that Andy sneaked into the kitchen and crept to her side. Jayne was preparing salad dressing for the evening meal when he tugged on her skirt.

"Well hello there, Sir Andrew. How art thou?" Her smile faded as she noticed tear streaks on Andy's cheeks. She stooped and hugged him. "What's the matter, Andy?"

"Everybody's fighting again."

"Everybody?" Her mother was taking a sheet of hot cookies from the oven, and Jayne met her gaze over Andy's head.

"Grandpa's mad 'cause Nana bought a really old platter,

and Uncle North told Emma she had to take back the shirt she bought."

Jayne wished they had a pillory for the offenders. "I'm sorry, honey. Where's your daddy?"

"He went out to look at Uncle Ray's car for him." Andy gave a sob. "And Emma and Michael were making fun of me."

"Why?"

He shrugged and hid his face. "They said I'm a baby."

Jayne stroked his hair. "Oh, you know that's not true."

"I want to go home."

"Aw, Andy." She held him close. "If you went home now, you'd miss the fun. Tomorrow the fencing master is coming to give you a lesson in sword fighting."

He leaned back and blinked at her. "Really? I get to do it?"

"Yes."

"What if Emma and Michael beat me at swords?" He gritted his teeth.

"I'll bet they won't. But these are special swords that won't hurt people, and you'll wear padded clothes when you do it."

Mom came over with a plate of cookies. "Andy, I've got a couple of gingerbread men here for you and Miss Jayne. Would you like to sit up at the table with her and have some milk and cookies?" Andy nodded and swiped at his final tear.

Jayne led him to the table. "Thanks, Mom."

As she pushed Andy's chair in, the door opened and Luke peered in. "There you are, Andy. What are you doing in here? The ladies are trying to work." "It's okay," Jayne said.

Mom grinned at him. "Hot gingerbread men."

"Oh, I can't resist that." Luke came in and took a seat. He eyed Andy's face critically but said nothing about the drying tears. "I'm sorry Andy bothered you while I was busy."

"No problem," Jayne said. "I'm glad he felt he could come to me when he felt uncomfortable."

"Maybe you can tell me about it later," Luke said.

She nodded. "I think we're going to be fine, but it's always nice when your dad shows up. Right, Andy?"

Andy nodded and bit off his gingerbread man's arm.

❄

"Make sure the older kids take it easy on the little guy, okay?" Jayne smiled at Bill as he carried in the equipment for the class he would hold in the big entry hall.

"I brought an assistant along just for Andy." Bill held the door open and a small boy came in with his arms full of padded fencing jackets. "This is my nephew, Kenny. He's seven."

"Perfect! Andy will love this."

Michael appeared at the top of the stairs. "Oh cool! Real swords."

"Would you tell your cousins that Sir Pantheon is here to instruct you?" Jayne asked.

Within five minutes, all of the youngsters had assembled in the hall. Chelsea and Emma didn't even try to act bored. North and Luke stood by, and as soon as the foils began to clash, the other grown-ups appeared as well.

"Looks like fun," North said.

"Yeah, I wouldn't mind having a go at you with a sword," Liza told him.

Bill grinned at them from behind his screened mask. "I'm willing to show you folks a few basics later if you like. Let's give the kids an hour first, and then we'll suit you up. I've got some adult-size gear in the truck."

By lunchtime even Rosalyn had taken a turn, and everyone talked eagerly across the table about their lessons and the fun they'd had.

"Nice job," Dad told Jayne when she carried a tray of dirty dishes to the kitchen.

"For once, I think everyone's happy," she agreed. "They want to ride over to the high school this afternoon and see the ice sculptures."

"Good." Mom dished up portions of trifle. "We can catch our breath."

"Just keep praying things continue to go well," Jayne told her, "and that no one gets hurt or upset."

❄

Jayne organized games for the youngsters that evening in the hall, while the adults chatted in the parlor and listened to a quartet of singers. Luke gravitated out to check on Andy.

Emma was blindfolded and feeling about for her sister and cousins—and they were all laughing. She cornered Michael beside the check-in desk and whipped off her blindfold.

"Got you!"

"You sure did," Jayne said. "Here's your prize." She handed Emma a gaily wrapped little box.

Luke sidled over to Jayne. "You're doing a great job."

"Thanks."

"Can I be it?" Andy asked.

"It's your turn." Jayne knelt to wrap a soft cloth around his head.

"Ooh!" Chelsea was eyeing the faux bronze brooch Emma had unwrapped. "It looks like Viking jewelry."

"Hey Uncle Luke, are you playing?" Michael called.

"Sure, if I get Viking loot." He grinned at Jayne. "You and your folks deserve a reward. Somehow you've made this clan happy."

"My reward is working with Mom and Dad," she said. "Just pray that the peace lasts."

❄

"Everybody's going to Bennington to watch the dogsled races," Dad announced the next morning after breakfast.

"Everyone?" Jayne asked. "I thought Luke and Andy were staying here."

"Mrs. Dillard reminded Luke that the purpose of this week is to spend time together as a family."

Jayne winced. "I wonder how much family time Luke can take. I hope it's not his in-laws' way to hold him captive while they try to persuade him to move back to Hartford."

"I heard Rosalyn say something about that." Mom shook her head. "Well, it gives us some time to prepare for tonight's banquet."

"Are you sure we want the jugglers to come back?" Jayne asked.

"Yeah, give them another chance," Dad said. "Only they will perform in the parlor this time—and no candles."

To Jayne's relief, the next few days went smoothly. The Dillards gradually unwound and spent more time sitting in the comfortable parlor and talking to each other. Each day she offered several options for entertainment, ranging from lessons in snowshoeing and weaving to touring a gallery of local fine art. Hillary, Chelsea, and Emma wanted medieval costumes, so Dori came to fit them and sew the outfits, and all four youngsters attended the class in juggling silk scarves and beanbags.

By Thursday afternoon, Mrs. Dillard had progressed with Andy to the point where he sat beside her on the sofa and let her read him a story. Jayne felt that was a major victory, and she saw that Luke, too, had lost some of his nervousness. Austin offered to take the entire family to a ski slope for the day Friday, but to his surprise, they all turned him down. They already had requested more fencing instruction, and Luke and Ray were taking their sons to visit Bill's workshop and take a lesson in using the forge. A skating party on the lake filled the evening hours, and even Austin and Rosalyn went out on the ice together.

At last Christmas Eve arrived. The grandchildren displayed the juggling skills they'd learned, tossing colorful silk scarves into the air. Michael was quite proficient with beanbags. The youngsters then paired off to demonstrate their prowess with fencing foils, and the adults applauded so enthusiastically that Jayne glowed. The week was ending nearly as well as she'd hoped.

The Dillards planned to watch the medieval mystery play to be staged that night at the community church. Late in the afternoon, Jayne retreated to the Abbott's Chamber to do some paperwork while her mother and the two hired women worked in the kitchen.

The door between the study and the parlor was open

partway, and Austin Dillard's voice reached her plainly.

"Luke, I strongly urge you to reconsider. If you'll move back to Hartford, Rosalyn and I will pay for private schooling for the boy. A nanny, too, if you need it."

Jayne raised her head involuntarily. Luke would never consent. Would he?

"I appreciate the offer, but I don't think that would be best for Andy."

"Are you sure you're the best judge of what's good for him?" Austin asked.

Jayne clenched her teeth. She shouldn't be hearing this, but she couldn't leave the study without them seeing her and knowing she'd overheard.

"Yes, I do think so. I'm his father." Despite his words, Luke's voice seemed a bit unsteady. "You have to admit, Andy's doing better than he was a year ago."

"Yes, and he seems happy here. He really loved the sword master, didn't he? But Luke. . .we are his family. What can I say that will bring you back?"

"Nothing."

"Surely—"

"As I said before, I'll try to bring him to see you more often," Luke said. "Believe me, it's not my purpose to keep your grandson away from you. I only want to help Andy heal and grow strong. He does better here than in the city. He needs me with him, not a nanny."

All was silent for a moment, and Jayne held her breath. Could Luke hold out against this forceful man?

At last Austin spoke again. "All right, Luke. I can't fault you for that. The truth is, we miss you and the boy." Austin sighed heavily. "Would you consider working with me occasionally on special commission projects?"

"Yes, of course—if I can do it without traveling and leaving Andy behind."

Jayne released her pent-up breath, glad the conversation had taken a more cordial turn. A few moments later, footsteps retreated toward the hall. She put away the papers she'd been working on and walked into the parlor. Luke stood gazing into the fireplace, but he turned as she entered.

"Jayne."

She stopped and swallowed hard. "I'm sorry. I was—" She waved toward the study. "I didn't mean to eavesdrop."

"It's all right. It's not the first time that Austin has asked me to go back to the firm. I dreaded a confrontation with him. But he seems reconciled to my decision."

"Yes, I thought this time he behaved quite well."

Luke nodded. "The whole family has calmed down since we came here. I appreciate all you've done to cater to our many whims."

She gazed into his blue eyes. So much more that he hadn't said shone there. He took a step toward her, and she caught her breath.

Luke put his arms around her, and it seemed the most natural thing in the world. He lowered his head and kissed her.

"Daddy!" Andy ran in from the hall with Michael on his heels.

Jayne sprang back, but Luke smiled at the boys.

"Daddy, we learned to tumble. And we're going to

give you a show."

Over Andy's head, Luke caught her eye. Jayne smiled at him.

In the hall, the front door opened.

"I don't see why we have to go." Chelsea's strident voice carried clearly to the parlor.

"Yeah, Dad," Emma said. "It's just some stupid religious pageant."

Jayne's heart lurched. Too soon, the peace had shattered.

Chapter 8

The argument in the hall made Luke shudder. Jayne had planned for the medieval mystery play at the church to serve as a high point of the week. She'd told him how hard the cast had worked on the unusual presentation.

"Maybe you girls and I will stay here tonight," Liza said. "The others can go if they want."

Jayne looked as though her face would crumple.

Andy tugged on Luke's sleeve. "Daddy, we're going, aren't we?"

"Yes," he said softly.

"Now, see here," came Austin's deep voice. "I heard you drive in, and I was coming down to tell you we'll all leave right after dinner. Nana and I think this play will be quite an interesting part of the cultural experience, and *everyone* is going."

Jayne glanced at Luke and winced.

"Let him handle it," Luke whispered. "Liza will back down, and I'm sure once they get there, they'll be glad they went."

"Can I wear my medieval outfit?" Emma asked.

"I'm wearing mine," Hillary said cheerfully. "I'll help you girls dress."

A moment later, Liza came into the parlor.

"Well hello, Luke. Do you think this play will be any good?"

He glanced apologetically at Jayne. "I do. Jayne tells me that a thousand years ago these mystery plays were performed by rustics to portray spiritual truth, and they're not very polished, but they're funny and touching."

"I saw the rehearsal yesterday," Jayne said. "It's a different take on Christmas. Has an ancient feel to it."

"I suppose we may as well see it, or Dad will have cats." Liza held her hands out toward the blazing fire.

Luke wanted to smack her. Instead, he smiled. "We wouldn't want that to happen, would we?"

❅

Later that night, when the Dillards and the Barncastles had returned to the inn, Luke went unobtrusively to the kitchen, where he found Diane standing over the stove, stirring a large kettle.

"Hello, Luke. What did you think of the play?" she asked.

"I liked it. It was entertaining, but thought provoking, too."

"Yes," Diane said. "It made me realize how difficult it must have been in the Middle Ages, when there was no English Bible. They used drama to teach the truth of God's Word to people who couldn't read it."

Luke smiled. "Michael was a bit put out that it wasn't a detective story. I told him I thought 'mystery plays' were to reveal the mystery of Christ's incarnation."

"That's a good way to put it. I hope everyone is thinking about Christ's birth and the sacrifice He made for us."

Luke sat down on one of the stools by the island. "I think

some of them are. Ray told me he and Liza have talked lately about how they've let their faith slip. Maybe this will prompt them to go back to church. Of course, Liza only said that it made her appreciate technology and modern times more than ever."

Diane chuckled.

"I've done a little research of my own on medieval traditions," Luke said. "I wondered if you'd help me prepare a little surprise."

Diane turned toward him, her face eager. "Gladly. What are you up to?"

❄

Jayne came out of the parlor, where she'd set out punch and desserts. The Dillard family was diving into them and still discussing the play. She'd missed Luke, but Andy seemed content to sit between his grandparents, sipping the punch and nibbling on a cookie.

As she approached the kitchen door, it swung open, and she stepped back.

"Oh, excuse me," Luke said.

"Hi. What's up in the kitchen?"

"Just confabbing with the cook."

She eyed him suspiciously. "Did you have a craving for plum pudding?"

"No, but I'll do it justice tomorrow. See you later."

Luke walked away, and Jayne stared after him. He ambled into the parlor, so she went on into the kitchen.

"Hey, Mom. Why was Luke in here?"

Her mother smiled at her. "Jayne, that is a very nice young man."

"Well yes. I know."

Mom bustled about, still smiling, but offered no more by way of explanations.

❊

After serving a hearty breakfast on Christmas Day, the Barncastles retreated upstairs and left the Dillards with the run of the downstairs for their family celebration and gift giving.

In her parents' sitting room, Jayne presented them with her gifts—new luggage for her mom, a GPS unit for her dad's car, and her first payment on Barncastle Inn.

Her father looked down at her check with misty eyes. "Jaynie, this means so much. Not the money, I mean—but the fact that you want to stay here and own this house."

She felt her eyes tearing up. "I realized I can't walk away again, Dad. This is my home, and to have it as my job, too—well, it'll be tough when you're gone. I'll need to find some super maintenance person, but—" Her voice cracked, and she stopped talking.

"Oh, honey!" Her mom reached over and embraced her. "We love you so much. We didn't want to pressure you into this, but we didn't want you to lose the opportunity either."

Jayne wiped her eyes with the backs of her hands. "Thanks. I don't think I ever would have considered going out on my own here if you hadn't nudged me a little."

❊

That afternoon, Jayne and her parents served the Christmas feast to the Dillard family. The fruit, *salette*, and *pottage*, as Dad delighted in calling the salad and soup, were followed by a main course of roasted goose, broiled fish, and roast beef, with several vegetable dishes and the requisite thick bread trenchers.

"Diane, you've outdone yourself," Mrs. Dillard said as Mom poured tea for all those who wanted it.

Mom flushed with pleasure. "Thank you, kind lady. We shall serve custards and cake now, if milady pleases."

"I don't think I could eat another bite," Mrs. Dillard said.

"What kind of cake?" North asked, and everyone laughed.

Dad cleared his throat and stepped up near Mr. and Mrs. Dillard. "Milord, milady, it is the custom long held for the guests at the feast to expect to find trinkets in their cake."

Austin stared up at him. "Indeed?"

"Aye, sir."

Austin said in his most lordly voice, "Then let the cake be served, and we shall see what surprises it brings." He looked down the table toward Andy and the other children. "Mind you eat daintily, lads and lasses. No choking on the prizes, if you please."

The Barncastles quickly cleared the table and brought in the portions of cake and dishes of custard.

As Dad served him, Luke said, "You and your family should take a piece with us, Ted."

"Ah, we're but peasants," Dad said cheerfully. "We'll eat later in the kitchen, milord."

"No, I insist," Luke said, glancing at Diane, who was setting a small piece of cake in front of Chelsea.

"Yes, I think that's a splendid idea," Austin said. "Your family has served us so well all week, and I'd like to think we've become friends. Won't you please join us?"

Mom smiled at him and dipped a small curtsy. "Thank you, milord. We should be delighted."

Jayne arched her eyebrows at her, surprised that she'd agreed so easily, but Mom ignored her. Instead she reached for extra portions, which had somehow found their way onto her tray in advance. She held one out to Jayne.

"Oh, no thank you," Jayne said.

Mom leaned toward her and hissed, "Take it!"

Shocked, Jayne accepted the plate. Her father and Ray West pulled two extra chairs over to the foot of the table for her parents. Luke pulled Andy onto his lap and patted his son's empty chair.

"Sit here, Jayne."

Hesitantly, she slipped into the seat between Luke and Hillary.

Austin beamed on them all and raised his fork. "To our fellowship as friends."

"Here, here," North said. Everyone began to eat.

Jayne halfheartedly cut off a small bite of her cake. She didn't need the calories, but she was sure her mother's creation would be delicious.

"Daddy! Look what I found!" Andy rubbed away the crumbs from the tiny pewter dragon Mom had lovingly placed in his cake. Soon the others exclaimed over finding charms and coins in their own portions.

"Miss Jayne, what did you get?" Andy asked.

Jayne looked up at Luke, and he smiled at her. "Go ahead."

She cut into her cake again, self-conscious as he and Andy watched her. She'd helped her mother pick the charms and toys to put in the cake. Which one would turn up in her piece?

A metallic gleam showed through the crumbs, and she extracted the item with her fork.

"It looks like a ring." With her napkin, she wiped off the remnants of cake. She didn't remember any rings when they'd shopped for the trinkets.

"It's pretty." Andy wriggled with excitement on his father's lap.

"Isn't it?" Luke asked.

"But. . ." She stared down at the beautiful Celtic knot ring. She'd never seen it before, and it appeared to be sterling silver. "Someone must have lost this in the batter, Mom." She glanced anxiously down the table. Her mother only smiled.

Andy laughed. "Daddy, Daddy! She got it."

Jayne looked up at Luke. He smiled sheepishly.

"Do you know something I don't?" Jayne asked.

Luke's face was slightly flushed, and his eyes glowed. "All right, I admit it. Your mom helped me arrange it. I wanted to give you something that symbolized my feelings for you."

Jayne's heart thumped wildly.

"That's so sweet," Hillary said. "May I see it?"

"Good move, Luke," Ray said with a smile.

Jayne wiped the ring off carefully and slipped it on her finger. It fit perfectly. She held it out so that Hillary could examine it.

Luke touched her sleeve gently. "If you're agreeable, Andy and I would like to come back in two weeks and take you ice skating."

Jayne felt as though she could hardly breathe. "I'd like

that," she managed, wishing there weren't more than a dozen spectators to the scene. She looked at Andy. "Would you like to keep Hendrick for me for a couple more weeks?"

Andy nodded, grinning.

The telephone rang.

"Hark, do I hear bells?" Dad jumped up and hurried into the hall. A moment later he returned. "Sir Luke, your squire just sent word that your conveyance will be here this evening as requested."

Luke smiled at Jayne. "I hope you don't mind. I called Dr. Ross's father, and he agreed to pick us up for a sleigh ride after dinner."

"It sounds. . .wonderful." Jayne was keenly aware of her flaming cheeks, her pummeling heart, and the people watching her and Luke.

"Methinks I saw Cupid fly over," Ray said.

❄

At eight o'clock, Luke came down from tucking Andy in and met Jayne in the hall.

"All set. Your mom promised to listen for him in case he wakes up while we're gone."

As he held her coat for her, sleigh bells jingled and the soft thud of a horse's hooves on the snowy drive reached them. Mr. Ross greeted them cheerfully as they went out and climbed into the sleigh. The starlit night gave them a perfect view of the frozen lake as he guided the horse along the shore lane.

"It's so beautiful tonight," Jayne said.

Luke put his arm around her and drew her close. "*You're* beautiful. I love you, Jayne."

With a contented sigh, she rested her head on his shoulder. "I love you, too. You and Andy."

After a moment, he said softly, "Then I might hope you'd consider a future with us?"

"Oh, yes. You definitely could hope that."

Luke leaned over and kissed her, and she knew they had more than a wisp of hope. She settled back with his arms still around her and looked to the sky again. The gleaming stars were no match for the fireworks exploding inside her.

❄

They entered the inn through the back door. Ted and Diane sat at the kitchen table with mugs of hot chocolate before them. Luke's pulse picked up just on principle. He hadn't expected to see them so soon.

"Hey, Jaynie, you'll never guess what." Her father turned to face them. "One of Hillary's friends e-mailed. She wants to know if she can bring six couples here on Valentine's weekend with a Romance in Paris theme."

"Wow." Jayne looked up at Luke. "What do you think?"

He shrugged. "I think it's a step toward what you want for the inn. What do you think?"

Ted and Diane were watching them with puzzled frowns.

"I guess Hillary gave us a glowing recommendation, before she even got home," Jayne said.

"Yes," her mother replied, searching her daughter's face. "Jayne, what's going on?"

Jayne chuckled. "Not much. It's just that the topic of a Valentine's wedding had come up during the sleigh ride.

But we can work around this booking, can't we, Luke?" She looked up into his face, smiling confidently.

Luke's heart pounded. Life with Jayne would never be dull. He slid his arm around her waist. "I'm sure we can."

 Award-winning author Susan Page Davis is a mother of six who lives in Kentucky with her husband, Jim. She worked as a newspaper correspondent for more than twenty-five years in addition to homeschooling her children. She writes romances and cozy mysteries and is a member of ACFW.

CHRISTMAS DUETS

Lynette Sowell

Dedication

For my amazing and talented sisters, Cat and Amy,
with much love. . .

Above all, love each other deeply,
because love covers over a multitude of sins.
1 PETER 4:8 NIV

Chapter 1

Marcella Goudreau frowned out the window at the snow-covered mountains of Castlebury, Vermont. She shivered, in spite of the fire that glowed in the fireplace of the Lady's Bower. For the next week at Barncastle Inn, she and her sister, Amity, were planning a series of their own performances. The rafters of the inn's barn would echo the classic tunes from *White Christmas*. The Goudreau sisters never made it to Broadway. Amity married Pete Carruthers during her sophomore year of college and derailed that particular dream.

Marcella didn't regret missing Broadway and being a middle school music teacher instead. Christmas vacation equaled two weeks away from her students. The middle school choirs had rehearsed their Christmas songs so many times that Marcella started singing them in her sleep.

The thought of her students made her smile in spite of all that was at stake this Christmas. She and Amity, hitting the stage again like they hadn't in years. So it was only for a small barnful of guests—it was something. If only their grandparents, Memé and Pepé, would understand the significance of the *White Christmas* numbers. *White Christmas* wasn't just part of their Christmas traditions, it was part of their family's history.

Marcella turned from the peaceful scenery outside as her sister entered the bedroom. "Hey! You guys made it. How was traffic?"

"Not bad. We had to wait for Pete to get home from the office, so the worst was over. I thought the kids were going to pop, they were so excited to get on the road."

Marcella gave Amity a hug. "I can't believe the last time we saw each other was Thanksgiving." Her sister, petite and blond, with big brown eyes, looked barely old enough to be out of high school, let alone be a renowned soloist with the Springfield Symphony orchestra and the mother of two kids.

"I know. With all the symphony's performances, and kids' school stuff, it's been crazy." Amity pulled some wayward strands of her hair behind one ear. "This was a good idea you came up with, getting us all together here in Vermont. Pete and the kids are getting unpacked. They're in the Library Suite. It's amazing. You should see it. It's two levels. They have a spiral staircase, and stacks of books. What a special Christmas this will be, for all of us."

"Well, I hope it doesn't turn into a huge disaster." Marcella sighed and sank onto her bed.

"What could turn into a huge disaster?" Amity grunted as she wrangled her oversize suitcase. The monstrosity filled up part of the floor space of the room, but Amity managed to get it next to the bed.

"Christmas, that's what."

"We've got to do something. I *don't* want a repeat of Thanksgiving. When Memé threw the gravy boat at Pepé—"

"Don't remind me." Marcella studied the contents of Amity's suitcase. "How much clothing did you bring? We're only here for a week, you know."

"I wanted to be prepared. Plus, all the costumes are in the other bag. Downstairs." Amity pulled out the first of a series of button-down blouses. "Blah. I should have put these shirts in Peter's garment bag."

"We'll be prepared for the *White Christmas* numbers. I know that much." Marcella sank onto her own bed. She looked forward to sharing a room with her sister, something that hadn't happened since they were in high school and drove each other crazy. "But when Memé realizes that Pepé's going to be here too, there's no telling what'll happen."

"It's Christmas. You have to believe that what we're trying will remind them that over fifty years of marriage isn't worth throwing away over a disagreement."

Marcella rolled onto her back and sighed. The mattress was divinely comfortable. If she let herself, she could be dozing within a few minutes. But she couldn't get the problem between Memé and Pepé out of her mind.

She finally said, "It's not just a simple disagreement. Pepé's been brainwashed. And I know who's responsible."

"What are you talking about?"

"Sean McSweeney, that's who." Marcella rolled onto her side.

Amity took out a stack of sweaters and shook them out, one by one. "His new friend?"

"Yes. I mean, I was glad when Pepé said he was going to Northampton's Veterans facilities to use their weight room. He stopped complaining about his back. Then he met Mr. McSweeney. Or Dr. McSweeney. He works at the VA hospital but used to be in the Army. Anyway, Pepé always says Sean this, Sean that." Marcella reached for the nearest throw pillow and hugged it. "And then he joined a local power-walking team. They're doing a 10K relay in January."

"What makes you think he's been brainwashed? I think it's a good idea that he's gotten more active."

Marcella shook her head. "It's more than getting in better shape physically. Pepé has changed. He doesn't act the same. He used to love chess, and playing dueling pianos with me." Marcella raised her hands. "Every time I called the past few months, Memé says he's not home. She's withering away without him."

"Well, we'll get to the bottom of what's going on. I can't believe Memé kicked him out." Amity finished tucking the rest of her clothes into the chest of drawers on her side of the room. She shook her head. "Do you know anything at all about this Sean McSweeney?"

"Not much. He's a veteran, like Pepé. Doesn't seem to have any family, from what Pepé said. Likes working out, running, camping, movies. And the last time I asked about where the man lives, Pepé got angry. Said they were just fine and he was paying Sean room and board."

"Don't look so sad," Amity said as she lifted the now-empty suitcase off the bed. "We'll all be here, under one roof. You just need to believe it'll work out."

"I hope so."

Amity flashed a smile at Marcella. "C'mon, Mopey. Jayne Gilbert wants to show us the barn where we'll be having the shows."

"Mopey, right." Marcella threw the pillow at her sister. Amity ducked and the pillow smacked the closet door. Somehow, it was easier to act like a kid again at Christmastime. And one whole week, here at Barncastle Inn. Marcella reached for her coat.

Amity put on her own jacket. "Promise me you won't mope if things don't go the way we planned."

"I promise." Marcella linked arms with her sister as they entered the hallway. Sounds of big band music drifted up from the parlor below.

Jayne Gilbert, innkeeper extraordinaire, had promised the Goudreau family a week to transport them back in time, back to post–World War II Vermont. Marcella could almost imagine the inn was a short drive away from the fictional Pine Tree, Vermont, where old General Waverly waited for Bob Wallace, Betty Haynes, and company to arrive on the train to help him have a merry Christmas.

"I can't believe you cleared out your house downpayment piggybank to rent the inn." Amity paused on the landing. "But Pete and I talked. We're going to chip in for this week, too."

"It's worth every penny to me if it means seeing Memé and Pepé together again. I didn't want to put stress on your budget, which is why I didn't say anything about the cost at first."

"Girl, we would have ended up spending plenty if we'd taken the kids to Disney World for Christmas." The two women continued down the stairs. "This is going to be an experience the children won't ever forget."

"I know. This probably isn't nearly as exciting as Disney World."

"Hey, we're slowing down this week. No television, no Internet. It will be great for the kids, to have an old-fashioned Christmas."

"Jayne was genius to find the vintage radio shows for the

kids to listen to. It'll help keep them entertained while we practice our numbers."

"Sure you don't mind sharing a room with me?" Marcella asked.

"Not at all. It'll be like old times. Then on Christmas Eve, I'll join Pete and the kids in their room."

They reached the bottom of the stairs, and Marcella caught the whiff of supper, a New England boiled dinner. Her mouth watered. Pot roast and seasoned vegetables. Plus, the scent of baking bread. "Wow, Mrs. Barncastle must be quite the cook."

Jayne Gilbert was smiling as she entered the room, a coat draped over her arm. She looked about Marcella's age, and her red sweater accented her glossy dark hair. "Yes, my mother is a superb cook. I keep having to remind her that she and Dad are retired, that this is supposed to be *their* vacation, but I can't get her out of the kitchen or keep her from trying to 'help' our chef."

Marcella gave Amity a knowing glance. "We know what you mean. Our mom has worked in the food service department at Smith College for years."

Jayne slipped on her coat. "Let me show you ladies where the performances will be held so you can see the setup. We've already started advertising in the village, and we expect the barn to be packed this week."

"That's great. And you found a male soloist for the duets?" Marcella asked. She couldn't imagine singing "White Christmas" without a baritone to blend her own voice with.

Jayne pushed on the inn's main door and led them onto the porch. "Sure did. Jonathan Sevigny, a local music student.

He's home on winter break from the Boston Conservatory and will be all set to start rehearsals tomorrow. Remind me to show you the posters we had printed and distributed in town."

"Wonderful." Marcella and Amity followed Jayne from the main part of the inn. The Barncastle, as the locals called it, fairly took Marcella's breath away with its exterior and its towers. The paved parking lot had a driveway that sloped away from the house to an immense red barn that could have been taken straight out of an artist's rendering of the Vermont landscape.

They stopped at a pair of massive white doors at least twelve feet tall. Jayne reached for the handle of the door on the right.

"And here is where we'll have the shows." She slid the door away from its mate, and they stepped into what looked like a small auditorium, lined with about fifty folding chairs. "We insulated the building and ran a heating system inside, too. I know when you open the doors there's a draft, but it gives people the feeling of a barn. And it's quite snug when the doors are closed."

A raised stage ran the width of the opposite end of the barn, with two doors on each side of the stage.

"We do have a backstage area, and the two rooms off both sides of the stage are former horse stalls that we enclosed for changing rooms." Jayne's voice echoed off the timbers.

"Perfect," Marcella said. "I'll have room to set up my keyboard to the side of the stage. We brought accompaniment CDs for some of the numbers, but I'm planning to play

'White Christmas' and 'Blessings' live."

"What are your musical backgrounds, again?" Jayne asked.

"I'm a middle school music teacher," replied Marcella.

"And the two of us have always sung together from the time we were kids," said Amity. "I'm also a soloist for the Springfield Symphony. Cello. But I can play keyboard as well."

"Your demo CD was beautiful." Jayne led them toward the stage area. "I'm really looking forward to seeing the villagers enjoy your performances."

"Thank you. And we appreciate you working out a barter for part of our booking fee," said Marcella. She assessed the stage. Yes, there'd be plenty of room for them to have a Christmas tree set up for the grand finale.

"You're sure it won't feel like a working holiday to you?" Jayne looked concerned.

"Not at all," Amity was quick to answer. "We don't get to sing together nearly as often as we used to."

"I'm glad you'll have a chance to perform here, then. This is the first year we're opening performances to the town, too." Jayne glanced back toward the barn doors. "When will the rest of your party arrive?"

"Mom and Dad will be here after Dad gets off work. They'll be bringing our grandmother. Pepé, that's our grandfather, said he'll be here soon." Marcella pulled out her phone and grinned. "He actually texted me about thirty minutes ago. Imagine that. Pepé, texting."

❄

"The directions said after we get off Route 91, we go west

on Route 9 and continue through Castlebury," said Armand Goudreau. He kept glancing from the road to the paper in his hand.

Sean McSweeney negotiated the traffic rotary on Castlebury's town green. The center of the village had a gazebo with a sign that proclaimed PICTURES WITH SANTA every Saturday night until Christmas. A red brick church with a white steeple flanked the edge of the traffic circle and formed a ring with Castlebury's library, a coffee shop, general store, and a consignment shop. Straight out of a Norman Rockwell painting.

Crashing the Goudreaus' Christmas is a bad idea. Bad, bad idea. Sean shook his head. But Armand Goudreau wouldn't hear of leaving Sean alone at the apartment during Christmas week. Even after Sean explained he was used to having a solo Christmas, Armand growled at him about getting his suitcase packed.

"I'm long past seventy and you're young enough to be one of my grandkids," Armand had said. "You get your gear together and spend Christmas with us. My granddaughter has bought out some fancy Vermont inn for Christmas week. I can't let the family down."

So here they were, negotiating the traffic rotary and trying to get out of the congested traffic of a Vermont village.

"You think your wife will be there?"

"'Course she will. That doesn't mean anything. She kicked me out of our house, but she's not kicking me out of Christmas." Armand gripped the door handle. "Watch your speed before you hit something."

Grouchy old man. Sean smiled at Armand's gravelly tone

and ignored the crack about speeding. "Of course she can't kick you out of Christmas. Are you going to talk to her about moving home?"

"Why should I?" Armand studied the directions again. "She'll keep nagging me about my pills and when I should go to bed, and asking how come I don't want to play dominos with the Kurchinskis anymore."

Sean gave up for now. The more someone tried to talk sense to Armand, the worse the man stonewalled. He didn't think it was all that bad at the Goudreaus' house. He'd met Armand's wife, Ruby, twice. She reminded him of his own grandmother, who passed away when Sean was twelve. His own grandfather had died less than three months after Grandma.

It wasn't surprising when he found himself striking up a friendship with Armand Goudreau, who started working out at the gym for veterans in Northampton, Massachusetts. What *was* surprising was the Friday after Thanksgiving, less than four weeks ago, when Armand showed up on Sean's doorstep, suitcase in hand.

"She kicked me out," Armand had said.

They finally broke free of the Castlebury traffic, and twilight descended as they headed west.

After they snaked a few miles into the Vermont foothills, Sean easily saw the sign for Barncastle Inn. He turned into the drive and caught sight of the castle. Lights in the windows cast welcoming shadows on the darkening parking lot and patches of snow in the yard. Lights also glowed in a nearby barn. A cozy, welcoming place, with its pair of turrets and porch. Elegant, too. Sean hadn't brought a suit. He hoped he wouldn't be underdressed.

He found a parking spot next to a sensible gray sedan and turned off the engine. "Guess this is it, sir."

"Here we go, m'boy. Into the lion's den."

A glow of light appeared from the barn as one of two white doors slid open and three figures emerged. Two of them waved as Armand exited the car.

"My girls!" Armand called out. He started toward the women.

Sean left the SUV and shut the door, following the older man.

"Pepé!" One of the women with dark honey blond hair, hugged him tight. "We've missed you."

"I haven't gone anywhere." Armand growled, but Sean heard the tenderness in his voice. "Those kids at school giving you gray hair yet, Marcella?"

"No, Pepé." The honey-blond laughed, the sound like musical notes to his ears. She flicked a blue-eyed glance over Armand's shoulder. "Who's with you?"

Sean cleared his throat and approached. "Hi, I'm Sean—"

Armand waved him closer. "Girls, this is my roommate. Sean McSweeney. I invited him to join us for Christmas. You said we could have up to twelve people here for the week."

Marcella's blue eyes grew round. "*You're* Sean McSweeney?"

Sean folded his arms across his chest. No one had said his name like it was a disease before. "That's my name. And it's nice to meet you. Your grandfather talks so much about you both. I assume you're Marcella, and this must be Amity."

"Yes." Amity stepped up and extended her hand toward him. As she did so, she shot a glance at her sister. "Nice to meet you, too."

Right. If Sean were a betting man, he'd bet they thought Santa Claus would show up at Christmas, *not* their grandfather's roommate. Hopefully they'd let him explain about their arrangement. Which, it seemed, Armand probably hadn't.

"Mr. Goudreau, welcome," said the third woman, who until now had been looking on. "I'm Jayne Gilbert. Do you need help with any bags?"

"No," said Armand. "Sean and I can get them fine."

"Well come inside where it's warm, and I'll get your room keys." Jayne motioned toward the main house. "Supper is served at five-thirty most evenings. Tonight we have a traditional New England boiled dinner."

Sean popped the trunk and pulled out both men's bags. "I've got the luggage."

Armand was quick to snatch his carry-on, which had the weight of half a dozen bowling balls, as well as a shopping bag stuffed with wrapped gifts. "I'll get mine."

"Pepé, do you want help?" Marcella stood close by. Sean caught a whiff of her perfume. Her hair swished just past the collar of her tailored wool coat. A pretty woman with a voice he could keep listening to, even if all she did was read the dictionary.

"No, said I've got it."

They all headed to the house, a curious parade, with Sean taking his time at the rear of the group. He might as well have worn an invisibility cloak, but then he didn't need one. Ms. Gilbert had greeted him pleasantly enough, but Armand's granddaughters barely gave him a second glance.

Amity was shorter than Marcella and reminded him of a

finch with brown eyes. She flitted beside Ms. Gilbert, talking about Christmas songs and rehearsal schedules.

Invisible, indeed. Sean nodded to Armand, who held open the thick wooden front door of Barncastle Inn. Sean was accustomed to being invisible at Christmas. Not that it was a bad thing. He celebrated quietly, in his own way. Mom usually wasn't easy to deal with at Christmastime. Most years he ended up working through the holiday and enjoying time cheering up patients at the hospital.

What had he just gotten himself into?

Chapter 2

The moon lit the Lady's Bower with a pale bluish glow. Marcella blinked at the landscape just beyond the balcony outside. Sean McSweeney. Young. She'd pictured an old man, maybe not as old as Pepé, but certainly not a man about her age, or even closer to Amity's twenty-eight instead of Marcella's twenty-six.

Her sister's even breathing told her that Amity was out for the night. After stuffing themselves with Mrs. Barncastle's supper, they'd sung carols in front of the roaring fire in the parlor, made s'mores, and listened to vintage radio shows on a CD player that looked like an old radio cabinet.

Her niece Jade and her nephew Jeremy had been enthralled with the radio stories, too. Marcella hadn't even checked her e-mail on her phone, and by the time Amity and Peter had tucked the children into their bed, she was yawning, too.

Mom and Dad had brought Memé, who'd glared at Pepé as they sat down to supper, until Marcella maneuvered to sit between them. She'd found herself looking at Sean McSweeney and finding it hard to ignore him.

She liked the sound of his voice, a medium tone with a low richness to it. When he sang, was his voice bass, or baritone? Maybe he didn't sing. His brown eyes looked at her pepé with a fond expression as if he were his own grandfather, and then glanced at the faces around the table.

He's lonely. And nervous.

Marcella had glanced down when he caught her studying him. Truthfully, she hadn't wanted anyone else in the mix this Christmas. Sure, the inn had room for one more pair of guests to round out an even twelve in the group, but no one had booked the room yet.

Even now, she punched her pillow and sat up in bed. The remains of the earlier fire glowed in the fireplace. Marcella found her slippers and robe, draping her robe around her red flannel Christmas pajamas. Jayne had said something about snacks available on the dining room sideboard, in the event any of the guests had a hankering to munch during the night.

She felt like an intruder slinking along the inn's hallway to the main staircase. The carved wood was cool to her fingers as she held on to the railing and headed downstairs. What it must be like, to live year-round in a grand place like this.

Lord, please help us have a good Christmas. Our greatest gift would be Memé and Pepé getting back together, and realizing how much they have in each other. True love like theirs comes once in a lifetime.

If only Sean McSweeney hadn't come.

Marcella crossed the main reception room and found her way to the dining room, where the sideboard with its promised snacks waited. A solitary lamp lent a glow to the room, accented by the green pine garland lit with white lights.

A lone figure stood at the sideboard, staring at a row of trays. Sean McSweeney.

A floorboard creaked under her foot, and Sean darted a glance in her direction.

"Hey," he said.

"Hey," she managed to reply. "I'm looking for those snacks that Jayne mentioned at supper tonight." She slipped her arms into her robe's sleeves. Her pajamas were just as modest as her regular clothing, but the barrier of a robe made her feel even more covered.

Sean gestured to the sideboard, lined with trays of cookies and breads, covered with plastic. "*Mademoiselle*, zee Barncastle has a smorgasbord of delights for zee sweet tooth."

His faux French accent made a giggle tickle the back of her throat. She wasn't supposed to want this man around. "Sweet tooth?" She eyed the tray of breads. "Yummy, that looks like banana bread. My favorite. With chocolate chips, too."

"Chocolate chips in banana bread?"

"Good stuff." She took a slice of bread and placed it on a paper napkin. Maybe she ought to eat this in her room.

"There's a carafe of hot water, too, and some packages of hot chocolate mix."

A quick cup of hot chocolate couldn't hurt. "Oh, that's almost as good as a mug of warm milk."

"Can't sleep?" Sean reached for a cup as well, and their fingers brushed.

"No, I can't. There's a full moon shining in our window." Marcella wiggled her fingers and picked up the cup next to the one Sean chose. "Hard to sleep with the light streaming into the room."

Sean nodded. The rustic yet elegant atmosphere

reminded Marcella of another Christmas story on the silver screen, another young woman who couldn't sleep. But Bob Wallace had offered Betty Haynes sandwiches and buttermilk, and their encounter had ended with a kiss. Nope. Not this encounter.

"I guess my coming was a surprise to all of you."

"Not just you coming. You're a lot, um, younger than I thought you'd be. From the way Pepé talked, you sounded a lot older."

"I left my cane and walker at home, and yes, this is all my real hair." His brown eyes sparkled and a hint of a dimple appeared in one cheek.

Funny. Marcella smiled at him and noted his brown hair, cropped close on the sides and back, but a little longer on the top. Long enough to run fingers through. "Pepé said you were a veteran."

"I am. I earned my commission after college, then had three tours in the Middle East. Managed to get out of there intact, finished out my six year commission, and came home. The natural choice was to work for the VA here."

Pepé had served his country in Vietnam, then he came home to work in a machine shop in Chicopee until his retirement. "Thank you for serving our country." She watched him prepare his hot chocolate, unsure of what else to say.

"Look, about your grandparents. . ."

Marcella took her time emptying the hot chocolate mix into the cup, then filling it with water from the carafe. "They've been married for over fifty years. Fifty-four, to be exact. That's more than twice my age."

"I've seen troubles like this happen to older couples before."

"Well it's never happened to this older couple, and it's not right. Just because you're a doctor doesn't mean you can clinically dismiss—"

"I'm not a doctor. I'm a physician assistant. I'm not a home wrecker either. Your pepé has found his second wind in life, and he challenges me to not waste mine."

Marcella sipped her hot chocolate. "I understand. You're trying to encourage Pepé. I've noticed some positive changes in him. But this week we're trying to help him and Memé see that they have too many years invested in each other to toss each other away. You wouldn't have wanted to see them at Thanksgiving. It was the worst." She nibbled on the banana bread, savoring the moist goodness and tinge of chocolate.

"I'm not here to cause trouble." Sean set his cup on the sideboard. "In fact, I wouldn't have come at all if your grandfather hadn't insisted."

"He *can* be pretty insistent, that's for sure." Marcella crumpled her napkin up. She didn't see anywhere to put it, so she held the crumpled paper in her fist. "But I'm sure you had other plans for Christmas, someone else to spend time with?"

"No. Not really." Sean looked at his empty cup as he spoke. Then he looked back at Marcella. "Not every family is like yours. Not everyone has a picture-perfect Christmas to protect." He gave her a nod and walked away from her, out of the dining room.

❄

"Good morning," Jayne Gilbert called out as Sean crossed the entryway, heading for the front door. "Are you joining us for breakfast?"

"Ah." Sean froze. "I'm heading to town for a little bit. Do you need anything? I'll be glad to pick up whatever you need."

"No. But thank you. If you're back before ten, there's tobogganing on the hill. Or an ice skating excursion on the lake. Take your pick."

"Thanks for letting me know." He hoped Jayne didn't hear his stomach growling like a bear coming out of hibernation. Maybe they had some cross-country skis he could use. Now, *that* he could get into.

Within a few minutes, he was headed east into Castlebury and looking for a fast-food drive-through. Yes, Jayne had offered breakfast. He didn't care to face Marcella or her family this morning, not after their late-night conversation. If it wasn't for the fact he'd disappoint Armand, Sean would leave. The hospital always needed people to volunteer rotations over the holidays. As it was, he needed to be back in Northampton by Christmas night.

He didn't want to explain to Marcella, or anyone else, about his mother. They were all each other had. His brother lived in California and had his own family. They talked on holidays but since the kids had come, his brother didn't travel to the East Coast much.

She spent her Christmases with Jack Daniels or Captain Morgan. He loved her, but the few times he'd tried as an adult to have a semblance of a Christmas with her had been disastrous. He'd given up trying to create the image of a perfect Christmas.

Castlebury's streets were packed with vehicles of customers doing last-minute shopping. No fast food, but a café on the town square boasted breakfast all the time, to go, even. Sean found a parking space on a side street. He could get something to go, then take his time eating as he drove back to the castle.

The gray remains of crusted snow lined the curb, and Sean stepped over it and headed to the café. A poster in the window caught his eye.

WHITE CHRISTMAS AT BARNCASTLE INN.
JOIN SISTERS AMITY CARRUTHERS AND
MARCELLA GOUDREAU
FOR AN EVENING OF HIGHLIGHTS
FROM THE CLASSIC HOLIDAY FAVORITE *White Christmas*.
6 P.M. NIGHTLY THROUGH DECEMBER 24.
WITH SPECIAL GUEST, BARITONE JONATHAN SEVIGNY.

Marcella and Amity stood poised in matching blue glittery dresses, with large feathered fans. Marcella's dark blond locks had been coiffed into a hairdo that reminded him of the movie character Betty. Her blue eyes shone as she smiled at the viewer. At him.

White Christmas. Besides *A Christmas Story*, the movie was one of his holiday favorites. Over the years as a kid, he'd grown adept at changing out DVDs in the player. Mom would burn dinner and he would spend Christmas

Day watching movies. This one, he had to admit, he knew by heart, every song. The movies were what held Christmas together for him when he was a kid.

If only Marcella knew how good her family has it, Lord, she would trust You a little more to work this out. There are far, far worse things than one Christmas when Grandma and Grandpa aren't speaking.

❄

"I'm sorry," said the young man standing across from Marcella's keyboard, onstage in the barn. He looked pale, his skin moist. Worse, his voice cracked. "I've got strep throat. I shouldn't even be out right now. But I wanted to apologize in person." His Adam's apple bobbed as he swallowed.

Jayne looked worried. "We understand. Take care of yourself."

"I'll try. Merry Christmas, Mrs. Gilbert." With that, Jonathan Sevigny hung his head, pulled the wool scarf around his neck, and trudged down the barn's aisle and out into the cold. With that, Marcella and Amity's plans for the *White Christmas* performances started to crumble.

Marcella's hands remained frozen on the keys. Forget crumbling. This was an avalanche in the making. As if on their own, her fingers thawed and started playing the introduction to "Blessings."

Then she stopped. "Jayne, is there anyone else we can ask?"

"Ask what?" Amity's voice echoed in the barn as she entered through the door that Jonathan left open. She slid the door shut and motioned over her shoulder. "Was that our soloist leaving? I thought we were going to run through the

121

male-female duets this afternoon."

"Unfortunately, he had to cancel. Strep throat," Jayne said. "I'll have to ask around. Maybe the choir director at church knows someone. That is, if they haven't left town already for Christmas."

"Maybe you and I can work out the duets, and we can skip the male singer," Amity suggested.

"But you're the soprano and I'm the alto." Marcella looked at the musical score in front of her and started working out the key transposition in her head. "It won't work. We'd have to jump octaves and that would sound goofy. Plus, everyone hears Bing and Rosemary singing 'White Christmas.' It wouldn't be the same."

"Ha." Amity crossed her arms. "So you don't think I can do Rosemary and you can do Bing?"

"Listen to yourself. It sounds crazy."

"Honestly, Marcella. Some things you don't need to have 'just so.' People probably won't mind as much as you think they will." Amity climbed up to the stage, and slid her arm around Marcella's shoulders. "Little sister, you worry too much."

"I want everything to be just right. And we open tomorrow."

Jayne looked thoughtful. "I'll see what I can do. All is not lost. Have a little faith. I'll let you know what I find out." She climbed down from the stage and gave them a wave before she left the barn. She slid the door open.

"Hello, in there!" boomed Pepé's voice. "You girls need to get out from behind that piano thing and come ice skating." He ambled into the barn, his boots clumping on the floor. A pair of black ice skates were slung over one arm.

"You're going ice skating?" Marcella's voice squeaked. "I didn't know you knew how."

"Course I can. The Barncastles have a bunch of extra skates. I'm sure they have some that'll fit your feet, too."

"Is Memé going skating, too?" Amity asked.

Pepé shrugged. "Don't know. Think she's holed up in the kitchen, talking about making some froufrou finger sandwiches for the performances. Why anyone would want to make sandwiches out of fingers is beyond me."

"Did you ask her to come with us for a little while?" Marcella couldn't believe how childish the two of them were acting. Memé wouldn't sit near Pepé, not even across from him, at breakfast. She had asked Mom to run her into town for some last-minute gifts, then returned to the inn and retreated to the kitchen with Jayne's mother.

"Why would I invite her skating? She'd complain about the cold and how it was too slippery and why we couldn't just stay in by the fire." Pepé shook his head. "I'm not going to beg her either. But Jade and Jeremy and the little Gilbert boy and I are going to the pond. You ought to, also."

"We should," said Amity. "C'mon. I'll see if Peter wants to go, too. We can't rehearse the male duets without our male. It's just for a short while, anyway."

Marcella hadn't been ice skating since. . .well, she didn't know when. But what if one of them got hurt? She dismissed the thought immediately. *Worrywart.*

"Okay. For a little while. But then I'll get back here and start transposing if Jayne hasn't found a singer."

Chapter 3

I'm fine, I tell ya. Just fine." But Armand's voice shook as he sat on the wooden bench by the Barncastles' frozen pond. "I only slipped. The kids have slipped dozens of times and you don't have them propped up on a bench."

"All the same, sir, I need to check your ankle." Sean glanced toward the pond, where just minutes ago, they'd been playing hockey, of sorts, with sticks, as they knocked a puck back and forth.

The children loved it. Armand's great-grandchildren, along with Jayne and Luke Gilbert's son, Andy, giggled and laughed, their cheeks red, as Sean showed them how to pass the puck to each other.

Even Marcella showed up to skate, although she looked as if her thoughts were somewhere else, far away.

But now the little group gathered close to watch him examine Armand's ankle.

"Is Pepé going to be all right?" asked Jade, Amity's daughter.

"He's going to be just fine," said Sean. He winked at Jade, all of seven, who giggled and leaned on her mother. Sean assessed Armand's ankle. It was swelling already and would probably turn several colors of the rainbow. Hard to tell by the feel if there was a fracture, though. "We should probably get this X-rayed."

Armand was a diabetic, and he complained sometimes of numbness in his feet. It wouldn't be good if the man had a fracture he didn't know about.

"I'll stay with the kids while you three go see about that X-ray," said Amity. She gave her sister a pointed look.

Marcella's cheeks shot with pink, but she returned her sister's look with her own snappy glare. "Thanks, *sister*."

"Anytime. After all, you're my devoted sister." Amity sang the last few words.

"Ha," said Marcella. Except, she wasn't laughing.

Sean tried to keep the corners of his mouth from twitching. "I'll find out from Jayne where the nearest healthcare facility is and hopefully we'll get in and out."

"Pepé, can you walk?" Marcella stepped closer to Armand.

"I can walk, just hurts on my right leg." Armand reached for Sean's arm to pull himself up, then put one arm around Sean and Marcella, who moved to Armand's other side.

"It seems like it's a longer walk to the main house on the way back," said Marcella.

"That's the truth." Sean tightened his grip on Armand's waist, and felt Marcella's strong arm holding her grandfather as well.

"Something on your mind, Cellie?" Armand asked his granddaughter.

"Pepé, you haven't called me that since I was Jade's age."

"I can still see you when you were Jade's age. And you've got something on your mind. I could tell when I went to the barn awhile ago."

"We lost our male singer, Pepé." Marcella sighed. "We don't have our Bing now. The kid who was supposed to be

Bing got strep throat."

"Oh that's too bad," Armand replied. They helped him along the path, and the house grew closer. Sean took note of the man's breathing. He still sounded okay. Good thing. Sean didn't want Armand going into shock.

"Jayne's trying to find someone else who can step in. I'm not sure if she's found anyone. We go on tomorrow night. First performance."

They inched closer to the edge of the parking lot ahead, with its row of cars, between the main house and the barn.

"I bet Sean could do the parts."

"What?" Sean heard both himself, and Marcella, saying.

They both raised objections the rest of the way to Sean's car. Sean popped the door locks and helped Armand get settled, his leg stretched out across the backseat.

"Hold on. I'm sure Jayne has an ice pack somewhere in that big old house." Sean also wanted to reassure Jayne about Armand's condition and find out about any nearby clinics. Injuries like this weren't to be taken lightly in a man Armand's age, but on the other hand, he didn't want to overblow the situation.

Singing? He didn't want to talk about singing right now. He used to sing, a long time ago. After he finished his bachelor's degree and then his physician assistant training, answering the call of Uncle Sam, he'd left music behind.

"I'll be right back." Sean hurried to the house. If he had any sense, he'd head back across the Vermont state line, back to Massachusetts, and Northampton. Tonight.

❄

"Pepé, I appreciate your suggestion." Marcella shut the car door, and fastened her seat belt. "But we need a *singer*. Not trying to put Sean down or anything, but Amity and I don't have time to train someone. What if he can't sing?"

"Oh he can sing, all right," Pepé said. "He sings in the shower, could wake the whole apartment building at 4 a.m. when he gets up for an early rotation at the hospital."

"Singing in the shower is one thing. In front of people is another." A thought struck her. "You know what? I should go look for Memé. Maybe she can ride with you and Sean to the clinic, or hospital, or wherever you're heading. She knows all about your medications."

"And so do I," he snapped.

Marcella turned as far as the seat belt would allow her. "I'm sorry."

He leaned forward and touched her shoulder. "I know what you're trying to do. You are a sweet, sweet girl to think of her old Pepé and Memé. But stop pushing. I've been stubborn a lot longer than you have. Same goes for your memé, too."

"I want you both to be happy again, happy with each other. Together."

"I *am* happy. I haven't felt this good in years. Not counting my ankle, of course."

Marcella sighed. That wasn't what she meant. Not exactly. "I'm glad you're doing so well." Here came Sean, out to the car. She turned to face forward.

"I tell you what," Pepé said. "I'll sit with your memé at supper tonight. Maybe even have a little conversation if she won't bite my head off."

"You will?" Her heart gave a jump. "Just don't take it personally if she's grouchy. I know she misses you."

"I'll be on my best behavior. But I have one thing to ask of you."

Oh boy. "What's that?" She already knew.

"Let Sean sing with you. Please. He needs to be a part of this Christmas."

Marcella turned at the tone in Pepé's voice. "Okay, he can sing with us."

Sean opened the driver's side rear door. "Here's an ice pack, Armand. Put that on your leg and try not to move too much."

"You got it." Pepé took the ice pack and tucked it around his ankle as Sean closed the door. He joined Marcella in front and slid behind the steering wheel. "Bennington County Hospital. We can get an X-ray there."

They headed down the driveway, and Pepé piped right up. "Cellie here says you can sing with her."

"Cellie, huh?" He cast a sideways glance at her before pulling onto Route 9. "What if I say no?"

"I—I guess I would have to say that's all right. I'm learning people can't be forced into doing things." Marcella shrugged and studied the road ahead of them. They shot along the winding way, tall pines edging the two-lane road. Occasionally the trees would clear and Marcella glimpsed snow-covered mountains.

Now that she'd made the agreement with Pepé, she found herself *wanting* Sean to sing with her. His speaking voice had a nice enough tone. However, she'd watched enough American Idol auditions to know that just because someone's speaking voice sounded nice, that didn't mean they could carry a tune, or sing a duet, or understand the flow of music. The result could be downright painful.

"You gonna get my other ankle broken on the way to the hospital?" Pepé asked from the backseat. He thumped on Sean's headrest.

"No worries, Armand." Sean glanced at the rearview mirror. "And I doubt your ankle's broken."

Pepé muttered something, and Marcella stifled a laugh. Pepé growled a lot and that sometimes made people stay away from him. If Sean had taken Pepé in, that said a lot for the guy.

"So, um, Sean, will you at least consider singing with my sister and me?" She had to ask him plainly. "Amity and I could perform the duets, but I really wanted us to stay true to 'White Christmas,' especially the Bing Crosby and Rosemary Clooney duets. We're sort of in a jam now." Marcella made herself stop. She wouldn't beg or plead. She knew how hard it was to coax a reluctant singer to try a few notes, especially kids in middle school.

"C'mon, McSweeney, it's a few songs for a few nights," Pepé said.

Sean kept driving, and Marcella let her gaze wander from the road to him. She cleared her throat. "I think. . .I think it would make Christmas even more special."

"I'll. . .I'll think about it," was all he said.

❄

An hour later, Sean sat beside Marcella at the ER while Armand was back in X-ray. The intern on duty agreed with Sean, that he didn't suspect a fracture, but an X-ray was the best way to find out for sure.

He sensed Marcella squirming on the inside while she

paged through a cooking magazine. Twice she looked at him, opened her mouth, then closed it again and went back to studying a page of recipes.

Four nights of performances, a few rehearsals of songs he knew by heart. No big deal. He hadn't stood in front of anyone and sung in nearly a decade.

Marcella closed the magazine and placed it onto the coffee table in front of them. She pulled out her cell phone, touched the screen, then stuck it back into her purse.

"I never thought we'd end up here," she finally said. She pulled some strands of hair over her ear, then fiddled with the cuffs on her coat. Then she settled back into the vinyl cushioned seat and crossed her legs.

"Me, too. Actually, I'm surprised your grandfather came without giving us much grief."

"His ankle must really be hurting, then. I'm glad we came, though." Marcella uncrossed her legs, then picked up her purse from the floor. "Sorry. I have a hard time sitting still without doing something with my hands. Maybe that's why I love to play piano so much."

"That's okay. It doesn't bother me any." He studied her hands, with their long slender fingers. Manicured, but trimmed fingernails. "All right, I'll sing with you. I, uh, happen to know the songs."

"Oh, thank you." Marcella grabbed his arm and beamed. "You know the songs?"

He nodded, taking in the sight of her blue eyes sparkling. "I've watched *White Christmas* every year since I was old enough to use the remote." He'd never seen light in her eyes like that before. Until now, he'd seen a frown wrinkle between her eyes. She still clutched his arm.

"Thank you. Really. It means a lot. I know you care about Pepé. Maybe this is a silly idea, doing the songs, but—" She released his arm and brushed at her eyes. "He's old, Sean. Him slipping and falling today just shows me that we never know what's going to happen. I really, really hope that this Christmas, he'll see that his marriage to Memé is a treasure, and that she'll let him back in. Literally, and figuratively. I always looked up to them, how good they were to each other and what good care they took of each other."

Sean nodded. "I know I've only seen part of the story. But I hope you understand, Marcella, that I never once encouraged your pepé to move out. Whether your memé kicked him out, or whatever actually happened."

"Either way, it's a mess. Something I know my family never saw coming."

"Families have an almost uncanny ability to hurt each other." The words had a bitter taste as he spoke them. "That happens when you love someone and you're vulnerable."

"So, what about your family?" Marcella asked. "I realize I don't know much about you, and here, you're seeing our dirty laundry."

He tried not to snort. "Your family is a stack of starched cotton linen shirts, neatly folded, compared to mine."

"How's that, if you don't mind me asking?"

Sean shrugged. Now it was his turn to fidget, and he made himself stop. "Mom and Dad split up when I was seven. My brother Vance went with Dad to live near Boston, I stayed with Mom. Dad and Vance sort of do their own thing. They really don't have the time to get together.

Especially with Vance living in California now. And, Mom, well, she did the best she could. She lives in Easthampton."

"Oh that's close to where we live. I teach in Westfield, actually. Is she all alone at Christmas?" Marcella frowned. "Should we invite her to come up to Vermont and join us? Maybe I could talk to Jayne and see what we can work out. I know Jayne's parents are here visiting, too, but in a house that size there ought to be spare room—"

"No, no." Sean held up his hand. "My mom is fine by herself at Christmas. Really."

"But you won't see her on Christmas Day, and she's so close."

"I'm going to stop by Christmas night, on my way home from here. I'm due at 11 p.m. at the hospital." He almost felt apologetic, but Marcella didn't know his mother. Nurturing wasn't a word in her vocabulary. Not like Mrs. Goudreau, anyway.

A door opened, and out came Armand in a wheelchair, pushed by a nurse. "You were right, Sean, m'boy. I didn't break it. You should have gone to medical school."

Sean tried not to sigh with relief at the interruption. Mom here at Christmas would be an absolute disaster. He couldn't imagine what would happen.

Chapter 4

So, let's start again from the beginning," Amity said from where she sat at the keyboard. "Really listen to each other and try to blend at the chorus."

Somehow Marcella had ended up on the barn's stage next to Sean, and Amity was the one hogging the keyboard. The floorboards creaked under their feet. She'd pictured Sean standing beside the keyboard while she played the song. However, Amity insisted that Marcella and Sean would be able to blend better if they stood closer together. Blend, right.

The familiar notes of "Blessings" echoed off the barn walls. Sean more than knew the words to the song. He felt them, Marcella could tell, by the way he enunciated the words. A few tears burned her eyes. When he sang his part of the verse, Marcella watched. The man who spent so much time maintaining fortified walls around his life knew what it was like to lose sleep.

Of course, she should have known that from the first night at the inn, when she'd wandered into the dining room looking for a snack. She'd never asked about the source of his insomnia.

Now it was her turn to sing. She closed her eyes, thinking of counting sheep, and all the blessings in her life. *Thank You, Lord. Even with what's going on with Memé and Pepé, I thank*

You for everything You've given me. Us. My family. Sean.

Her eyes flew open.

The music stopped. "What's wrong?" asked Amity.

Marcella glanced at Sean, then at her sister. "I got distracted. Sorry." She rotated her neck, side to side, and swung her arms a little. "Whew, my muscles are tight." She needed to take her own advice, advice she'd give her students, and tell them to relax, think about the song, and just. . .sing.

"We've been practicing since after breakfast," Sean said. "I could use a break. Wanna go for a walk?"

"You mean me?" Marcella shifted on her feet.

"No, I mean the girl at the café in Castlebury that served me breakfast the other morning."

"Huh?"

"Silly," Amity chimed in. "He means *you.*"

"We really should practice. . . . We go on tonight. Jayne says the barn will be packed."

Amity stood up from the keyboard. "Well, *I'm* taking a break. Pete and the kids and I are going to string popcorn for the little Christmas tree in the Library Suite, and make paper ornaments."

"I guess we're going for a walk." Marcella reached in her pockets. No gloves. They were probably in her room, and she didn't want to run inside for them.

"We can meet back here after lunch," Amity said. "Jayne is sending a hairstylist to do our hair around five o'clock."

"C'mon," said Sean. "See you around one, Amity."

They ambled off together, and to Marcella, walking beside Sean seemed natural. Amazing, what two days could do to someone's impression of a person. She would love to know if he had a girlfriend. In the time they'd spent together, he'd never even hinted at such.

Usually a guy was quick to point out that he had a girlfriend, or fiancée, or someone special. Not Sean. He wasn't quick to reveal much about himself anyway. Like the way he'd avoided talking about his family. What was the deal with that? Now he was smiling at her as he slid one of the barn doors open. "After you."

"Thanks," she said as she stepped onto the parking lot. She could feel Amity's gaze boring into her. Her sister would definitely grill her tonight as they settled down in their room for the evening. Last night had been taken up by settling Pepé in and making him comfortable and Amity reading stories to Jade and Jeremy. But tonight after the show, girl talk.

"We can walk to the pond, if you'd like." He paused by the inn's steps. The sunlight glinted off his hair. "Or, if you're game, we can try sledding."

"Sledding. Really. I'm trying to loosen up, and you suggest sledding."

"Well, it's a little late to head for the slopes, and there are some perfectly good hills, and sleds right here at the inn." Sean nudged her arm.

Who was this man? "Yes, and I could end up like Pepé, with a sprained ankle, and then where would we be?"

"You say you can't sit still for long? I can't stay inside for too long. I think there's enough snow for us to do some sledding. Besides, I think sledding will loosen you up just fine."

"I need to change clothes. I can't wear this." She gestured to her slacks and loafers.

"Fine. I'll meet you back here in ten minutes."

"You got it."

They both entered the inn together. Pepé waved at them from the front parlor.

"You two doing all right? How's the music going?"

"It's going," replied Marcella. Maybe they ought to stay inside, or at least she should. If Pepé needed help. . .

"I'm looking forward to seeing what you kids have cooked up." He pulled an afghan onto his lap, his sprained ankle propped on an ottoman.

"Armand, I've brought your snack." Memé emerged from the dining room, carrying a tray. She stopped short. "Marcella."

"Hi, Memé." Marcella gave Memé a half wave. "What are you and Pepé up to?"

Memé glared at Sean. "I'm getting your pepé his morning snack. Can't go too long between meals. Mrs. Barncastle made some scones."

"I could have gotten it myself." Pepé's tone was sharp, but then he glanced at Marcella. "But thanks, Ruby. I appreciate the snack."

Memé nodded as she set the little round tray on the end table beside Pepé's chair. "I know it isn't the best with your diet, but I brought some fruit, too."

"My diet is fine. I'm off my diabetes pills, you know."

"No, I didn't know." Memé took a step back. She rubbed the sleeves of her fisherman knit sweater.

"Me either, Pepé." Marcella joined them by Pepé's chair. "That's great news."

"With Sean's encouragement and my doctor's okay,"

Pepé said, gesturing to Sean, "I got hold of my exercise and diet, too. See?" He lifted his arm, flexing his biceps.

"You did the hard work, Armand." Sean cleared his throat.

"Well, that's really nice to hear." Memé shrugged and walked away toward the dining room.

Marcella's heart sank. "Sean, I'll be right back. I need to talk to Memé."

"What did I say?" Pepé was asking as Marcella strode off after her grandmother.

She found Memé in the dining room, by the window seat. Sunlight streaming through the window panes made Memé's hair glow white and silver.

"Memé. . ."

"I don't know him anymore." Memé sighed. "I tried to do the right thing. He is still my husband, and I want to help take care of him."

"I know you do." Marcella slipped her arm around Memé's shoulders. Oh, they were thin. When did Memé get old? "I'm happy he's started taking better care of himself. I want both of you to be around to see more great-grandchildren someday."

"I want that, too. But I hurt, Cellie. If it's not my hip, then it's one of my knees. I didn't have weight to lose like your pepé." Memé wrung her hands. "The idea of going to a weight room makes me shiver."

"Did you tell him this?"

"I tried. But he didn't listen. Said I was making excuses."

"Won't you ask him back home?"

"No. I won't. I won't be criticized and put down because

I'm not some muscle workout *fiend*. Not until he says he's sorry."

Marcella sank onto the nearest chair. "Did you talk to Dad? Maybe he can explain to Pepé." What a mess. She saw both of their positions. Memé hurt; she was aging. Pepé was aging too, but he was seizing life in a way she wished Memé could. Maybe not in the weight room. If only they wouldn't be so closed-minded to the other.

Memé turned to face her, raising her hands as if in surrender. "I should have gone into town with your parents for an early lunch and to pick up one of the gifts they had personalized yesterday. But my hip hurt. I figured I would stay here. Now I see what I get rewarded with."

"It's Christmastime, Memé. I think especially now, you two can find a way to meet in the middle."

"I don't know." Then Memé's expression brightened. "But I do know I'm looking forward to my girls' Christmas show tonight. Even with that Sean singing with you."

"Oh Memé, I hope you love it. Amity is brilliant. She even wrote a script of monologues between each song. And *that Sean*, as you call him, is an answer to prayer. He's a great singer." She smiled at remembering the first time she heard him sing.

"Hmm. . ." Memé found a chair and sat. "I don't know about that one. I'd watch out for his kind, if I were you. Nice as pie, but always a little angle for them."

"You know, I thought that at first, Memé. Now I think I was wrong about him. He's a good man, who truly seems to care for people."

"Oh, dear." Memé shook her head. "You're sweet on him.

Get out now, before you're too far gone and you lose part of your heart. I have a bad feeling about him."

"I–I'm not sweet on him." She couldn't be. She'd only met him a few days ago, but they'd spent quite a bit of time together with two mornings and one afternoon of rehearsals. "I think that if you spent more time with him, you'd like him, too. Even Mom and Dad like him."

"I think you're protesting a little too much." Memé waved her pointer finger at Marcella. "You watch. Be careful. If he could get Pepé to bail out on fifty-four years of marriage, he could hurt you, too."

❄

The bottom of the hill came rushing in Sean's direction as he slid down the slope, the cold air slicing down his throat. He couldn't help the grin on his face. A squeal rang out from Marcella, on her own wooden sled.

He pulled back on the rope and dug in his heels, feeling awfully like he was ten years old again. Snow sprayed up from his feet and the sled skidded to a stop. Marcella did the same with hers, and she laughed from where she sat.

"I forgot how much fun this was." Her cheeks were red, and her breath made little white puffs in the air. "When was the last time you went sledding?"

Sean stood up from the sled, brushing snow from his jeans. "I can't remember. We lived in an apartment, third floor walkup, but there was a school down the street from our house that had a little hill. I might have been twelve, maybe?"

Together they pulled their sleds back up the hill. With every step, he realized he was starting to fall for the woman beside him. Maybe it was Christmas, the music, the feeling of being with a mostly normal family. He glanced at her. A week ago, he couldn't have imagined being with Marcella Goudreau. She'd been the faceless granddaughter of his elderly friend.

"What?" she asked when they reached the top of the hill. "I don't have broccoli in my teeth, because I can't stand broccoli."

He laughed. "No, I don't see any green leafy vegetables in your teeth. . .You're very beautiful, Marcella Goudreau." He touched her coat sleeve. She looked down at his gloved hand.

"Thanks." Her eyes sparkled as she smiled at him.

"So, uh, is there anyone special in your life?"

"My family, of course. I have some great friends at work, and at church." She blinked, swallowing hard. "But you weren't meaning special like that."

"No, I wasn't." He took a step closer in her direction. "I don't play the field, and I don't want to overstep if there's someone in your life. Like a boyfriend."

"Nope." She shook her head. "No boyfriend. I—I haven't really had the time, and then there just wasn't anyone I seemed to click with."

He released the sled's rope and pulled Marcella into his arms. She slipped her arms around his neck. Their lips met, and the cold around them seemed to melt away. The scent of her perfume, her fingers reaching his hair, made him continue the kiss.

Then he slowly released her, but not before letting himself brush her cheek with his fingertips. "I think I overstepped. Maybe it's being here, with you, with your family. It's made me see possibilities and take a few chances."

"Well, I'm glad you did." She cleared her throat. "I like you, a lot. I was preparing myself not to. Especially when Pepé made me allow you to sing with us. The more I found myself trying *not* to like you, the more I found myself wanting to."

"So what are we going to do now?" He took her hand.

She cast her glance down the bottom of the hill. "We only have one sled now. Guess we'll have to decide who takes a trip down to get the other one."

"That's not what I meant."

"Oh." Marcella's blush increased. "I guess we try to know each other better. Things we like, things we don't like, what our goals in life are, how we react in sticky situations. I know you're a believer, Pepé told me that much, so that's a great common ground to have."

"Yes, it is." Sean nodded. "But Cellie, don't turn everything into a project."

"Wow. Do you think I really try to turn everything into a project?" She crossed her arms across her chest.

He hadn't meant to sound harsh. "Sort of. Sometimes. I mean, I want to enjoy the time we have together. It feels like the rest of the world, the real world, has slipped away while we've been here at Barncastle Inn."

"It seems that way to me, too, and we've only been here a few days." She uncrossed her arms, letting go of the sled rope. "Like it or not, Christmas Day will come and go, and then we'll be back to reality. There's only so much time we have here."

She almost looked disappointed, and he laughed. "Don't sound sad. I have a feeling that after Christmas, we'll still find time to spend together. If you want to, that is. And I have a feeling that your grandparents will start doing the same, too."

"Maybe you're right. I just want things to go as I hope they will."

He didn't ask. "Sometimes, you just have to trust God and let Him do what He's doing." He reached for her sled rope. "Now, I think there's enough room on here that we can both head down the hill together."

The instant they whooshed down the hill together on the sled, Sean regretted it. He was getting way ahead of himself with Marcella. Once he'd taken the chance and kissed her, everything between them had changed. He needed to explain about his mother, how dealing with her could be. If Marcella was someone who valued an intact family, without drama or issues, then his wasn't one to be a part of.

They both dug their heels in to slow the sled down, then tumbled off in a pile of arms and legs and sled. The world spun. Marcella screamed.

Sean found himself looking up at the blue sky. He rolled over to see Marcella lying on her side, doubled up with laughter. She reached for his hand and squeezed it.

He felt his own laughter bubbling up inside.

Chapter 5

The parking lot of Barncastle Inn held two rows of cars, and moonlight glinted off well over a dozen vehicles. Jayne's husband, Luke, helped act as valet for the visitors, packing the cars and SUVs into the yard area and behind the inn.

Marcella's heart soared as she peeked out from the room behind the stage. She'd grown to like the Gilberts and wanted this new idea of theirs to take hold for their business. Tonight, only a few seats in the barn remained empty.

Jayne left one of the front seats and took the steps to the stage.

"Good evening, and welcome to the Barncastle. We're trying something new this year at the inn, and we wanted to include Castlebury in our festivities. Tonight, and for the next three evenings, we're featuring highlights from a classic Christmas favorite, *White Christmas*."

She glanced back toward the room where Marcella, Amity, and Sean waited. "We're taking you back to Vermont, just after World War II, when life was simpler. Heroes had been forgotten, and life went on. We bring you. . .the Haynes sisters." The lights went low.

"That's our cue," said Amity, adjusting the top of her glittery blue dress, reminiscent of the ones worn in the movie.

"Go get 'em." Sean's voice was low, close to Marcella's ear. "You look gorgeous."

"Thanks," she whispered. She allowed herself to give him a quick kiss before she grabbed her feathered sky-blue fan and followed Amity to the stage.

The first notes of "Sisters" came from the sound system as Marcella stepped to her mark, spun on one heel, and held up her blue fan in front of her face. The lights came up.

Backs to the crowd, Marcella and Amity turned in unison, holding their fans aloft, then gradually lowered them. *Here we go.*

"Sisters, sisters. . ." The music carried her along. Amity, and her, singing the song they'd sung nearly every Christmas since they'd first seen the movie. Growing pains and teenage drama. Saying good-bye when they went to different colleges, then home again on semester breaks with Mom and Dad. More good-byes after Amity married Peter.

Mom and Dad beamed at them from the front row, along with Memé and Pepé. Memé and Pepé, sitting side by side, with Pepé on the end, his foot still propped up on a chair with a pillow.

The song came to its end, and Marcella grinned at Amity, breathless. The crowd roared its applause. Now it was time for her lines. *Focus, Marcella.*

"Thank you for joining us. I'm Marcella Goudreau, and this is my sister, Amity Carruthers. We have always loved to sing together, and *White Christmas* is one of our favorite Christmas movies. We'd like to thank Jayne and Luke Gilbert, the good proprietors of the Barncastle, for having us.

"*White Christmas* first came to the big screen in 1954 and has become a tradition for millions of viewers over the years. The movie has special significance for our family, because right after our memé and pepé saw *White Christmas* onscreen at the Paramount in 1958, Pepé proposed to her while he was walking her home."

Some in the group made acknowledging sounds like *ohhhhh*. Marcella smiled.

"When the Haynes sisters went to Pine Tree, Vermont, they didn't know that Wallace and Davis were coming as well. Like our grandparents, love was in the air for these two couples."

The lights went low, and Marcella dashed backstage to the empty room where her thick red pajamas and bathrobe waited. She changed, then zipped back out to the darkened stage. Sean was already there, standing at the ready.

The lights came up as she strode onto the stage. "Oh, it's you." It reminded her of her first night at Barncastle Inn.

"You're up late," Sean said.

"I can't sleep." She shrugged and smiled at him. No playacting here. She found her smile easily.

"I know just the thing to help you sleep." Sean paused, with this being Amity's cue to start "Blessings."

Then the song about counting blessings instead of sheep began.

Marcella allowed herself to be lost in the sound of his voice, his gentle eyes looking her way. She remembered their kiss earlier that afternoon, when it seemed like everything paused in time around them. She felt the same way now.

Marcella echoed back the chorus to him, and then they

blended their voices together, their hands clasped as they faced each other. Amity ended the song with soft notes on the keyboard. As the applause began, Sean leaned toward her and gave her a simple kiss on the forehead.

The lights went low again, and she whispered to him, "*That* wasn't on the script."

"I know."

Her heart hammered in her chest as she turned to face the crowd when the lights came up.

She found her voice. "At Christmastime, we often get caught up in the busyness of the holiday. So many things try to claim our attention, and we forget the simplicity of what Christmas means. The blessings that God has given us far, far outweigh the grief or difficulty that life can bring. A sleepless night can go away when we take the focus from ourselves and our worries."

The barn door slid open and a woman entered, bundled in a thick wool coat and wearing a long multicolored scarf around her neck. Ash blond hair was coiffed into a short, flippy hairdo. She waved at them, then settled onto an empty chair in the back.

Marcella glanced at Sean. He stood there, his jaw tight, and hands curled. Then he uncurled them and rubbed his pant legs.

"Christmas in Pine Tree, Vermont, wasn't without problems either," Marcella continued. "General Waverly had served his country, then had gone on to sink all of his resources into his inn. With the unseasonably warm weather, the inn didn't have guests and was in danger of closing.

"Bob Wallace brought his entire New York show to Pine

Tree. That wasn't enough. When Bob realized that General Waverly wasn't just losing his inn, but was losing hope when he learned the Army wouldn't let him reenlist, Bob knew he had to help show the general how much he was still appreciated."

At the thought of the fictional General Waverly, at the thought of her very real Pepé and all he meant to his family, Marcella's throat hurt. The lights went down.

In the dimness, she asked Sean, "Are you okay?"

He shrugged. Something was wrong, but she had no way to ask him what.

The evening continued with more songs and cheers from the crowd, and laughter at the song "I Wish I Was Back in the Army."

The glow of performance ignited inside Marcella and she shoved her concern about Sean to the side, if only for a few moments.

Their grand finale began. The famous "White Christmas" song. Amity looked elegant in a crimson ball gown trimmed in white fur, and she took her seat behind the keyboard. Marcella loved the feel of her own dress. Jayne's friend Dori, a local seamstress, had been the genius behind the creations. But Sean nearly took Marcella's breath away in the vintage Army uniform that Jayne had found online.

When they sang, though, Sean would barely meet her eyes. She reached for his hand as they sang, her heart sinking.

She could barely drag the last words out, and the final notes drifted away.

The air hung thick between them and a roar filled the barn. Amity joined Marcella and Sean onstage, and they took their bow.

After the applause drifted away, Marcella addressed the crowd. "Thank you for journeying back with us to a simpler time, and we hope you've been reminded of the *real* gifts of Christmas, gifts you can't put in a box. Love, giving to others, just like God gave His best Gift to us that first Christmas many years ago. Jayne?"

Jayne moved to the stage. "Thank you all once again for coming. At the back of the barn, you're welcome to enjoy hot chocolate, apple cider, and fresh homemade doughnuts."

As people left their seats, Marcella glanced at Sean. "Hey, what's going on?"

He tugged at his tie. "Nothing yet. Or at least I hope not. I need to take care of something. I'll meet you for some hot chocolate."

"Okay." She watched him leave the stage area.

❄

"Mom?" This wasn't happening. He was going to wake up in Barncastle Inn's Earl's Suite and find this was a bad dream.

"Shawnie!" His mother had a new haircut. The last time he'd seen her, Thanksgiving weekend, she'd worn old sweatpants and a tired T-shirt proclaiming that Holyoke's Venus Gym for Women was "the best workout planet in the universe." Now she wore dark denim jeans and a fuzzy pink sweater topped by a cream colored wool coat. Gold earrings, even. The fringe of a long multicolored scarf reached her knees.

She brushed the front of his dark olive dress uniform jacket. "Look at you. In a vintage uniform. Reminds me of when you first got your commission, how handsome you were in your class A's."

"You're here. In Vermont." If anyone else heard him, they'd probably think he was the most ungrateful son. If only they knew the whole story. He gave her a hug, sending up an unspoken prayer that somehow, she'd be a mother for once instead of his "best friend."

"I know, I know—" She raised her hands as if in surrender. "I know we haven't had a real Christmas since. . .since. . ."

"Ever?"

"Right. Ever." His mother smiled at someone passing by, heading for the table with the hot chocolate. "But things have changed. Truly. I've had a wake-up call, and I decided to come up to Vermont for Christmas. I know the inn probably doesn't have room, so I found a hotel right off Route 91. It's a drive to Castlebury, but close enough."

"But your job? What about work? Don't they need extra help right now? The store's probably packed right before Christmas."

"I, um, I took a few days off." His mom shrugged. "I told Quinlan's I needed a few personal days, so they told me to go right ahead."

Something didn't feel right. She was too cheery, too bright. So polished, too. "Wow. You're here."

"When you said you were bringing your friend to Vermont to spend Christmas with his family, and that it was an old-fashioned Christmas, I admit I thought it was a crazy idea. I got thinking. We haven't had much Christmas, you and me, so I want that to change. Starting now. I know you probably don't believe me, and I've stunk at being a mom, but—" She looked at him, a pleading look on her face.

"C'mon. I want you to meet the Goudreaus." Sean

slipped his arm around her shoulders.

"I have to say, when you told me you were taking in a seventy-five-year-old man as a boarder, I thought you were nutso," she said as they approached Armand who was wolfing down a doughnut and talking to his son.

"Armand, Mr. Goudreau, I'd like you to meet my mother."

She stepped forward. "Heather McSweeney. So you're my son's new roommate." She looked at Marcella's father and beamed.

"No, I'm Frank Goudreau. My father actually is the one who rents a room from your son." Marcella's dad looked like his collar was an inch too tight.

His mom batted her eyelashes at him. Honestly—

Armand gave a roar that probably was meant to be a laugh. "Dear, I'm the sad sack that your son's taken in. Armand Goudreau." He extended his free hand in her direction, which she shook vigorously.

"Dad, I'll get you a chair. You shouldn't be up on that ankle." Frank Goudreau made a beeline past them and toward the chairs.

"I hope you don't mind. I'm going to be here for Christmas. If there's anything I can help you with, just let me know." She smiled at Armand. "My son and I haven't had a real Christmas in simply ages, not counting the three Christmases he was serving in Iraq and Kuwait."

"Well, his family is welcome here, Mrs. Goudreau." Armand ate his final bite of doughnut, then continued speaking around it. "Your son has been a godsend to me when I needed a hand."

"You *must* let me know how many people are in the group—genders, ages. I would love to pick up a few gifts for everyone," she said.

Sean had a whole pile of questions for his mother, not least of which was, where did she get money for gifts? He no longer gave her cash, but if she needed food or help with utilities, he would take care of that. Sometimes.

"Sean, you, Amity, and Marcella did a fabulous job tonight," a voice spoke at Sean's elbow. He looked to see Jayne Gilbert. "Is this your older sister?"

"No, this is—"

"I'm his mother, Heather McSweeney. I'm in town for Christmas."

"Mom, this is Jayne Gilbert. Jayne and her husband, Luke, run Barncastle Inn," explained Sean.

"What a lovely place. I imagine it's even more beautiful in the daylight." Oozed charm, something that came naturally for her.

"Thank you. We truly count ourselves blessed to be given the responsibility of running the Barncastle. You said you're in town for Christmas. Where are you staying?" Jayne asked.

Oh no, no, no. . .

"I'm not exactly *in* town. I'm at the Holiday Inn just off Route 91 in Brattleboro," his mom replied. "Although this place looks a lot more like a Holiday Inn than where I'm staying." Her laugh rang out in the barn.

"I didn't know she was coming," said Sean. He didn't want Jayne to think he was trying to smuggle his mother in for Christmas.

"Well, that simply won't do. You can't stay all the way in Brattleboro." Jayne shook her head. "We'll find a place for you here. I hope you're ready for an old-fashioned World War II–era Christmas, though, just like the Goudreaus ordered."

"Sounds lovely."

Lovely? Mom didn't use words like *lovely*.

"I'll see about getting the Tower Room ready. If you'd rather not drive all the way back to Brattleboro tonight, you can stay here. We have some extra toiletries on hand and probably a change of clothing," Jayne offered.

"I would like that, very much." His mom's gaze flicked past Jayne. "Oh, now who's this?"

"Did you get some hot chocolate yet, Sean?" asked Marcella. "Hi, Jayne."

"Wonderful job tonight. All I hear are raves from the crowd. I'll tell you about it later." Jayne smiled. "We'll have standing room only tomorrow evening, once word gets around. Mrs. McSweeney, I'll get you a key for your room within a few minutes."

"Dear, it's *Ms.* McSweeney, but you can call me Heather."

Jayne nodded. "Sure enough, then. I'll remember that." She scurried away, leaving the two women eyeballing each other.

"Oh. Mom. Uh, this is Marcella Goudreau. Armand's granddaughter," Sean explained.

"You two were *a-maz-ing*," his mother said, stressing the syllables in the last word. Sean tried to lean closer. She hadn't been drinking, had she? No telltale sign of alcohol on her breath, at least from where he stood. "Isn't it great,

Shawnie, that Jayne has an extra room for me? We'll have Christmas as a family."

"Christmas as a family," was all he could parrot back.

Chapter 6

O kay, spill," said Amity from where she sat in front of the fireplace in the Lady's Bower.

"Spill what?" Marcella joined her sister on the carpet where she sat, cross-legged. She reached toward the flames. "I wish I had a fireplace in my condo."

"You and Sean. We didn't need a heater backstage, because you two kept things warm enough, just looking at each other."

Marcella wasn't sure where to begin. And Sean's mom showing up tonight? Now that was bizarre. Jayne welcomed her right into the inn, and Heather McSweeney was now comfortably tucked into the west Tower Room. Sean acted like he wanted to explain, but for the rest of the evening his mother had hovered around like one of those birds around a water buffalo.

"I like him," was all she could say. "I like him a lot. I never imagined that a few days of music rehearsals, then Pepé spraining his ankle, and then Sean and I going sledding today. . ." She thought of the kiss they'd shared on the hill.

"Well, I'm glad. Because he seems to like you a lot, too. Just be careful, though," Amity said.

"You sound like Memé earlier this afternoon." Marcella smiled at her sister as light from the flames reflected off her face. "She doesn't trust him. I can see why, with what's happened with Pepé."

"I think things are turning around, though, for them. Did you see them tonight, Memé walking with Pepé back to the house?"

"No. I didn't see that. Heather was busy telling me all about how Sean was when he was a little boy." Marcella stared into the glowing fire. "It sounds like they had a tough time, her being a single mom and raising him, with his father having custody of Sean's older brother near Boston. I think it's nice that she's here. Even though it was odd how Sean acted when she showed up."

"Why odd?"

"Sean acted as if, well, as if he didn't want her here. And she seems very sweet. I think the next few days are going to be very interesting. Maybe this will be good for them, like it has for Memé and Pepé, and us."

"You could be right. I have to say, Cellie, it was a good idea, coming here for Christmas." Amity punctuated her sentence with a contented sigh. "The kids don't seem to mind not having 200 TV channels, no video games. They've loved making old-fashioned homemade crafts. You should see the coffee mug that Jade painted for Pete, and the change dish Jeremy made for him. Tonight, I read to them until they fell asleep."

Marcella's heart swelled with longing for her own family. "I hope to have a family like that one day."

"It's worth it, meeting the right man." Amity squeezed Marcella's shoulder. "I know you'll meet him, if you haven't already. God has a way of working things out when we least expect it."

A heat wave shot through Marcella's stomach. *Sean.* But he was right, they needed to take their time. So far she'd enjoyed getting to know him. Very much. *Lord, help us find our way.*

❄

Sean stood in the doorway of the Tower Room, where Jayne had found a space for his mother to stay. "Mom, tell me what's going on. I mean, really going on."

His mother, wearing sweatpants and matching top that Jayne had lent her, looked plenty cozy where she sat on the curved window seat. At any other time, Sean would have loved to examine the details of the room, from the carved wood trim framing the windows, and the inset stained glass capping the windows.

"I know I've stunk as a mother. It was hard, trying to be Mrs. Crocker, or Betty Crocker. Never could get that right. I did the best I could. But I felt like you were trying to trade me in for this rich family." She raised her hand and waved it, as if trying to brush away the Goudreaus' presence at the inn.

"Mom, they're not rich."

"Oh-ho, so you say. I looked up the Barncastle site online and I know how much it costs to rent this place for the week. They're rich."

"Marcella and her sister are doing this for their grandparents. Armand and his wife are going through a rough patch, and the girls figured being here would help the whole family." Sean rubbed his forehead. "I don't know why I'm explaining this to you."

"Marcella, now, is she the one you were practically eating up with your eyes earlier tonight?" His mother blinked like a cat who'd found a bowl of cream.

Her words made Sean's stomach turn. "Mom, don't make my relationship with Marcella sound that way. We've gotten to know each other since we've been here, and she's special. Really special. We're taking things slow." In his heart, though, he knew when Christmas came and went, he wanted to see her as much as possible, and not just as Armand's granddaughter.

"Easy, Romeo. I'm just teasing." She uncrossed her legs and stood, then went over to her purse on the bed and pulled out a small notepad. Something silver flashed inside her purse, but she snapped the bag shut before Sean got a good look at it. She'd better not have brought booze with her.

"Well, don't. Or no teasing like that, anyway."

"How many people do I need to buy presents for?"

"You don't have to buy anyone gifts."

"Don't argue with me. Who in the whole big, happy family is here this week? I don't want to come for Christmas without giving them anything."

Unbelievable. Not six weeks ago, his mother couldn't pay her light bill and he'd let her sit in the dark until her payday came around. Tough love. He never imagined he'd be put in a position like that. Or this. *Lord, how can I help her without enabling her?* He shouldn't have mentioned he was going to Castlebury, Vermont, for Christmas. He could only imagine how she tracked him down.

He sighed before continuing. "There's Armand and Ruby, Marcella's grandparents. Her mother and father—you met Frank earlier, and her mother, Beth. And Marcella's sister, Amity, and brother-in-law Peter, and their two kids,

Jade and Jeremy. That's it. Counting you and me, that makes eleven of us."

He'd already brought his gifts. A coffee basket for Marcella's parents, and a gift for Armand and Ruby. Plus, a family movie night basket for Amity and Peter, with a Christmas tea basket, all made by one of the nurses who worked on his floor. He didn't know what to get for Marcella yet, though. Bath products were a little too personal a gift, even now.

"I'll get everyone gift cards, that way they can get whatever they want." Mom wrote on her note pad. "And children, what fun. I love seeing children's faces when they open gifts."

He bit back the words he wanted to say. *Funny, I never remember you watching me open gifts, even when you had the money to buy them yourself.* He never realized how much his attitude toward his mother smelled worse than a garbage can in July.

"I know they'll appreciate whatever you do, Mom."

"So what's on the schedule for tomorrow?"

"Marcella, her sister, and I will be rehearsing in the morning after breakfast. I'm not sure what the rest of the family is doing. I think the Gilberts have some baking planned. Then in the afternoon, Mrs. Barncastle— that's Jayne's mom, visiting from Florida—will be teaching knitting to anyone who wants to learn. Then, there's going to be a hayride for the kids."

She frowned. "Well, keep me out of the kitchen unless they want the whole place to go up in flames. Now, that knitting stuff. I might try it."

"Knitting?" He still didn't buy his mom's reasoning for being here at the Barncastle, even with him spending Christmas here.

"Knitting." She looked up from her notepad again, and yawned. "Oh, I'm beat. All the chilly air tonight, after the drive up here, and I'm ready to crash."

"I should probably turn in, too." The events of the day tumbled through his mind, and he wanted to be alone. "G'night, Mom."

"'Night, Shawnie." She smiled, and waved.

He closed her door, thankful the hallway remained empty. Once inside the cozy Earl's Suite, he closed the door behind him. Jayne told him when they checked in the other day that she'd put him in the smallest room, but he didn't mind. After all, he was a tagalong. The more he thought about it, he should probably contribute something special to their Christmas celebration. He didn't know why he didn't think about it before now.

Plus, the matter of a gift for Marcella. Until a few days ago, she'd been a stranger to him. Now, she'd found a place in his heart. If he took Mom shopping tomorrow, maybe he'd find something in the village shops for Marcella.

Sean looked out the small square window of the suite. The dark form of the barn loomed across the parking lot.

Before he turned in, he took a few moments to pray. "Lord, I thought I'd be able to keep to myself this Christmas, even being with the Goudreau family. And here I am, right in the middle of everything. Then tonight, Mom coming. Please don't let her ruin anything."

Chapter 7

December twenty-second greeted them with a sparkling sunrise that lit up Sean's bedroom. After breakfast, Sean asked Marcella if she wanted to go for a walk. He knew they'd spend a couple of hours rehearsing and going over notes from last night. There was no place to jog, but the trails on the Barncastles' grounds were an inviting alternative.

"So, before you tell me that I'm trying to overplan everything, hear me out," said Marcella as she ambled beside him.

"Okay." He reached for her hand. "Go ahead."

"I play a game with my students every year, especially the choir kids." Her breath made white puffs in the air. "It helps break the ice. I call it Three Questions."

"Three Questions?"

Marcella nodded. "You get to ask me any three questions and I can ask you any three questions. They can be silly, or serious. But no yes or no questions. That's the only rule."

"You are incredibly cute." Sean shook his head. "Okay. I'll play. But I get to go first."

"Ha, so you like being in charge?"

"Hey, I get to ask a question first." They ambled along under the pine trees. Sean found himself breaking a sweat, walking the slight incline.

160

"Okay. Ask. I'm ready."

"Why did you become a music teacher?"

"Because I like music and teaching." Marcella kept walking and didn't continue speaking.

"And?"

"I answered your question." She grinned at him.

"I'd like to know more than the obvious."

"I love music, yes. To me, the world is full of music. Nature is. Even the Psalms talk about the trees of the field clapping their hands. Music touches our hearts. We communicate through music, to each other, we share with music. We can also worship with music. I always feel closer to God with music. I'm hoping that will happen for my students, too." She stopped for a moment. "There, is that better?"

"Yes. Much better. So, you get to ask me a question now?"

Marcella's eyes glistened. "Yup. So how come you became a physician assistant?"

"That's easy. I realized my freshman year of college in Biology 101, how fascinating the design of the human body is. I honestly didn't think I had the resources or the patience to go through more than ten years of training to become an MD, so for me, backing up a doctor by working as a physician assistant was a logical choice."

He recalled more often than he wanted to, working in a hospital in the Middle East. Helping his wounded brothers made him realize that once he left the military, he didn't want to stop. The memories plucked at him now, bittersweet. The draining heat seemed a lifetime away from the cold of Vermont.

"Good answer. I think it's amazing. And you knew just

what to do to help Pepé. I know a lot of that was basic first-aid training, but you made me feel like it was going to be all right. Even if Pepé's ankle *was* broken. Which, I'm glad it's not."

They reached the pond. "Guess we'd better turn back now."

"Two more questions for the way back."

"Yes, Miss Goudreau," Sean couldn't resist saying.

"Ha. I'm not Miss Goudreau for this week and next. I'm just Marcella." She shivered, and Sean slipped his arm around her.

"Better?"

She nodded.

"Okay. Hmm. . . What else can I ask you? And no, that's not my second question." What did he want to know about her? Everything. However, he was opening doors of his heart he thought he'd kept tightly locked for everyone's safety. "All right. What's the best thing you've ever read?"

"I read all kinds of books, when I can find the time. Lots of fiction. I always come back to the book of Psalms, though. Besides some of the psalms being originally written as songs, I find them really encouraging. Especially if I'm having a bad day."

The house grew closer. Maybe they'd reach it before Marcella had the chance to ask him another question. The question about being a PA wasn't a hard one to answer. She'd asked before about his mom, and he knew she hadn't been satisfied with the answer he gave her.

"Good answer," he said. "I like to read. Don't have a lot of time, though. But give me a good suspense or legal thriller. I like those a lot. Right now I'm going to a men's Bible study at church on Thursday mornings, so most of my reading is for that at the moment." Now they were rounding the curve behind the inn.

"My turn again. Guess it'll just be two questions instead of three. But that's enough for now." She stopped, and he did, too. "One thing I do want to know. Your mother. Why didn't you seem happy to see her? I mean, I don't mind her being here. Especially since I heard she would be alone at Christmas. That wouldn't be right. But I get the feeling you really don't want her here."

He knew she asked not because of nosiness, but because she cared. He looked across the parking lot to the barn. They were due to rehearse at ten.

He tried to choose his words carefully. "Marcella, my mother's an alcoholic. I've learned to deal with that over the last many years as best I can." What else to say? He wasn't sure how to explain broken promises, disappointment, learning to lower his expectations from a woman who he once desperately wanted to love him more than she loved herself.

"I—I'm sorry. I don't know what to say."

"I wanted to warn all of you. She figured out somehow that I was here, and Jayne said there was room, and the whole thing turned into an avalanche. I have no idea what she's going to do or say. When she's not drinking, she's the most friendly, charming person you'd like to meet. But when she's. . .like I said, you never know." Now that he'd spoken the words, it didn't seem so horrible. In fact, Marcella might be an ally, now that she knew. He only prayed nothing

163

happened to ruin the beautiful week they'd all been having.

❄

Sean's words followed Marcella around the rest of the day, and stayed on her mind during the second evening of performances. Thankfully, no incidents with Heather McSweeney. Marcella awoke the next morning to the memory of Sean's goodnight kiss from the evening before, in the shadow of the barn. She gave a happy sigh, too, realizing that tomorrow was Christmas Eve. She listened to the sound of the shower running. Amity had dragged herself out of bed first.

The sound of running water stopped, and eventually Amity emerged, clad in a robe and her hair wrapped in a towel. "You getting up?"

"Eventually." Marcella sat up and fluffed the pillows behind her so she could lean on the headboard. "I'm making an executive decision, since I'm the baby of the family. No rehearsal this morning. We need a break. I want to make cookies with you guys since I missed out yesterday. We know the songs well enough." Maybe if Sean had some time with his mother, things would turn around for them both as well.

"Good. It's Christmas, remember? And Jayne is thrilled with the performances." Amity removed the towel from her head and started rubbing her wet hair. "And I'm glad you're finally realizing it's okay to relax."

"Ha. I guess I am." Marcella could hardly wait to roll out some cookies.

When they found their way downstairs, Sean and his mother were absent from the breakfast table.

"They're having breakfast in the village, and Heather

wanted to shop," Mom explained. "I must say, her showing up here was a surprise. Did you know she was coming?"

"No, Mom," said Marcella. "Sean didn't either. They've been a little...estranged during the holidays. I'm glad they're here. Christmas is a good time to reconcile." She glanced at her grandparents, actually seated side by side this morning.

"What?" asked Pepé. "I think it is, too." But he wouldn't glance at Memé. Okay, so there was still a little bit of work to do in that department. At least there weren't any flying gravy boats.

"I saw presents with my name on them," chimed in five-year-old Jeremy.

"Where?" Dad asked.

"Under the big tree in the parlor. I only shook one."

Everyone around the table erupted with laughter. "Very good show of restraint, Jeremy." Marcella's dad chuckled. Marcella grinned, grateful that the conversation had steered away from Sean's mother.

"Okay, gang. Let's finish up breakfast," Mom announced. "We have a gingerbread house to construct, plus gingerbread men who need decorating."

"We're helping today, too, kids," Amity said. "Aunt Cellie and I are taking the morning off."

"Hooray!" Jade hugged her mother. "I *miss* you when you're not having fun with us."

Amity leaned closer to Jade. Her glance at Marcella told her that they'd made the right decision to scrap their practice plans.

Not long after the breakfast dishes were cleared away, they set to gluing the gingerbread house together with white royal icing. Marcella didn't think her efforts would win them any prizes, but she basked in her niece and nephew's laughter.

The front door of the inn opened.

"Hello, hello!" a female voice rang out. Sean's mother. The sound of rustling drifted into the dining room as well. The door closed, and footsteps grew closer.

Sean and his mother entered the dining room. Marcella wanted to give him a hug, but ever since the morning they'd asked each other questions, he'd seemed to distance himself. If he wanted a little space, that was okay. All she knew is she wanted to keep spending time with him, long after Christmas.

"Look at that gingerbread house," Heather exclaimed over the four walls, now held together with icing. "I've never seen that done before."

Marcella's heart went out to the woman. She looked lonely, just like Sean had when he first arrived. "It's not as hard as I thought it would be. Do you want to join us?"

Surprise flashed across Sean's face, followed by a furrowed brow.

"No, no," said Heather. "I'll just visit in the parlor with Mr. Goudreau."

"Uncle Sean, will you help us?" Jade piped up.

"Sweetie, he's not really your uncle. How about calling him *Mister* Sean instead?" Amity said.

"But I want an uncle." Jade frowned.

"Me, too," said Jeremy. Marcella smiled at that. Of course he'd want what his big sister did. Just like she did.

"I'll help, kids. Don't know how much good I'll be at

this." He stepped closer to Marcella. Suddenly, she really liked cookie baking. If his mother didn't want to participate, they couldn't force her.

❅

The barn's audience swelled tonight. After this evening's performance, followed by their final one on Christmas Eve, Marcella knew it would be a Christmas to remember.

They made it through all the sets of songs, until just before the finale. While Sean spoke the words this time, giving Marcella's voice a break, the barn door slid open.

"Shawnie!" Heather called out as she stepped through the door. "Sing it again. That's my boy, everyone! I am *so* proud of you." With each word, she stepped down the main aisle and closer to the stage.

Normally Heather's big personality filled the room. Tonight, it crowded everything and everyone else out. People turned to face her and murmur. Maybe this was a new part of the routine. Or Marcella hoped that's what they were thinking.

She glanced at Sean. The old adage, "the show must go on" applied here, but how would they do that without Sean stopping to quiet his mother?

As if knowing what Marcella was thinking, Amity began to play the "White Christmas" introduction.

"You two take it from here," Sean said. Lower, he added, "I'm sorry, Marcella." He stepped from the stage and headed straight for his mother.

"My son, my only son that counts, anyway." Heather's voice rose above the music. She stood by the front row, near Mom, Dad, Memé, and Pepé. "He takes care of people. He takes care of you, Mr. Goudreau."

"Mom, let's get some coffee." He reached for her elbow.

"I don't want coffee. Lemme finish." Heather yanked her arm away from Sean's reach. "In fact, he's been so good to you, Mr. Goudreau, better than your family."

"What are you talking about?" Dad asked.

"Pepé Goudreau has changed his will. He's giving everything to Shawnie here. Cutting *all* of you out. *All of you*." Heather sliced her hand through the air horizontally.

"Pepé?" Marcella asked from the stage. "Is that true?"

"Mom, we're going. *Now*." This time Sean reached for her elbow and didn't let go. "We'll talk about that later. Now isn't the best time."

Sean knew about this? If something happened to Pepé, Sean was set to receive what was left of her grandfather's nest egg? It wasn't like Pepé was Donald Trump or anything, but Pepé had invested carefully over the years. His and Memé's modest home had skyrocketed in value since they'd built it in 1960. Being family, though, was never about the money, or keeping yourself in the inheritance.

The notes for "White Christmas" still chimed out as Amity continued to play.

Sean wouldn't even look at the stage as he marched Heather out of the barn.

Sing, Marcella. She opened her mouth, and the words came out just fine. But inside, her heart started to splinter.

Chapter 8

In less than thirty minutes, they were in Mom's car, on the highway headed south, back to Massachusetts. "I'm taking you home, Mom." He'd left their room keys on the Barncastles' front desk.

"Fine, go ahead." She'd quieted from her earlier boasting and ranting. She fell silent and glared out the window at the darkness. "I'm your mother, and you're being disrespectful."

He didn't know what he was going to do. This latest humiliation had done it for him. He had *no* idea where his mother had gotten the idea about Pepé changing his will. Armand had mentioned it a few times, but Sean knew nothing specific.

Something beautiful had been put in front of him, the idea of his life with Marcella in it, and then snatched away by this latest catastrophe.

"I talked to that Pepé today," Mom finally said as they took the exit for Easthampton, heading toward his mother's apartment. "He told me he wanted to give you everything. He did. He was going to tell everyone this week."

"Whatever you talked about, it wasn't your place to tell everyone."

"But I'm so proud of you, Sean. You turned into a good man despite me and your deadbeat father."

Never argue with someone who's drunk, he reminded

himself. He bit back a retort about his father. He'd get her settled in back at her place and then what? His own vehicle was still in Vermont. Somehow, he'd go back for it. After Christmas.

❄

"Okay, Dad, what's going on?" Marcella's father asked as they all sat around the dining room table after the performance had ended and the town guests had left. "What was Heather talking about? Did you change your will?"

"Yes. Sort of."

Marcella could barely taste the spiced cider or the buttery, cakey doughnut. She couldn't believe it. Pepé, leaving everything to Sean? Had Sean been using them all, just as Memé suspected? She'd heard of scam artists, playing up to the elderly and swindling them out of their nest eggs.

If that were so, then she didn't know him after all. How could you fall in love in less than a week? But that's where she'd been headed. After the first shocking moment of realizing that Sean McSweeney *wasn't* as old as her grandfather, she'd cruised along from distrust and anger to feelings that now sliced into her heart. Love, trust, expectancy.

"I was mad at everyone." Pepé sucked down a sip of coffee. "So I went to my lawyer and changed everything."

"Of all the stupid, witless—" Memé said. "I oughta be glad I kicked you out. Should I have gotten my own lawyer, too?" She stood, ignoring the warm doughnut on the plate in front of her.

"Mother, let Dad explain. Please." Marcella's dad had a tone in his voice that reminded her of a young boy.

"I may be old, but I don't want to live old. You are all so busy with your lives, that people didn't have time for me. What if *I* wanted to go to the weekend at Cape Cod, too? Nobody asked us." Pepé glared around the table. "And Ruby. Every time I asked if you wanted to do something with me, you never wanted to. I want to try new things."

"You're cutting us out of the will because *I* didn't want to go to a gym and work out?" Memé sounded incredulous. "Unbelievable."

"Dad, you could always come with us. But all we've heard for a while is how much your back hurts if you have to walk or ride in a car for any long distance. You complain about the prices everywhere, and slow service, and how the food just isn't good enough for you." Dad sighed. "So when we went to the Cape last June, we didn't ask you because we didn't think you'd have a good time."

Thankfully, Jade and Jeremy were with Andy, the Gilberts' little boy, so they could all have their family meeting. But maybe the kids should have been here, to see the grown-ups trying to work out their issues with each other. Marcella nursed her own stinging feelings. Pepé felt left out?

"No, Ruby." Pepé addressed Memé. "I want you to meet me halfway. You *assumed* I wanted you to come to the gym. Did you know we could go to a pool and do water aerobics? It's fun and it would help your hip. Sean told me about it."

"I—I didn't know that." Memé stared down at the table.

Pepé chomped a bite from his doughnut. "Maybe we've all been wrong about a lot of things, is all I can say. I'll talk to the lawyer as soon as we get home."

Marcella knew she should be rejoicing that they were

getting all the drama between Memé and Pepé cleared up at last. This is what she wanted, by coming to Barncastle Inn for Christmas. Feelings were still sore, but finally, both Memé and Pepé were admitting hurts on both sides.

Somehow, though, she knew that someone was missing from the table. And she didn't know at the moment if she wanted him back or not.

❅

Sean slept on his mother's beat-up old couch, something he never did. He woke early on Christmas Eve day, and set to cleaning the house while she slept. Where did you draw the line between helping and enabling? How could he at least try to have a halfway normal relationship with his mother, without her spoiling everything?

He found cheese slices and bread, and prepared some grilled cheese sandwiches for them. Not much else to eat. But he noted an empty liquor shelf and a trash bag full of empty bottles.

"I got fired from Quinlan's, Sean," Mom said after she dragged herself into the kitchen and they sat down to eat their sandwiches. Her attitude had done a complete 180-degree shift from the disastrous night before.

"All those gifts you bought? Where'd you get the money?" Unbelievable.

"I cashed my last check." Her eyes were shadowed with dark circles, her normally swishy hairdo looked matted, unkempt.

"Mom, you can't live like this. Do you remember when your lights were turned off last month? I wouldn't pay the bill and made you wait until your next check came around?"

She nodded. "I was so angry at you."

"You need to get back with your support system. They can't do it for you; I can't do it either. You have to want to make the change and get the help you need. Above all, let God help you, too." Anytime he'd mentioned God in the past, Mom would either shut down or blow up. "I finally, finally meet someone special, really special, and now I don't know where we'll be. Know this, Mom. I'll be here for you. But I won't be cleaning up your messes." How tough must tough love get?

"I know, I know." She stood, went over to the kitchen window above the sink and looked at the frozen world outside. "I wish it would snow again, cover up all that gray slush outside. Snow makes things so fresh and new looking." Her sigh reminded him of Memé, far older than her forty-six years.

Love covers a multitude of sins—just like snow, covering up all the slush and winter mess outside. *God, what do I do?*

"I didn't mean to get drunk last night." She turned to face him. "I poured everything out of the bottles before I left for the Barncastle. I thought I'd make one effort to get something right."

"But you brought liquor with you."

She bowed her head. "I held one bottle back. Then yesterday, after shopping and taking a nap, I felt thirsty."

But she'd poured everything out here and cleaned house, in a manner of speaking. "Why didn't you come find me, or find someone else?"

"I didn't want to ruin anyone's Christmas. The Goudreaus seem like happy, positive people. I felt like I didn't belong there, no matter what I tried."

"Mom, your perception is wrong. They didn't even know I was coming; Armand didn't tell them. Sure, they were surprised at first. But they accepted me anyway." Right now, he missed Marcella so bad, and it hurt worse than a toothache.

His mother returned to the kitchen table and sank back onto her chair. "So I ruined Christmas."

"It's still fixable, you know." Or so he hoped. But the idea of facing them all again, after what happened last night. . .

"Well, if we go back, I'm not going empty-handed." Mom slapped the tabletop with both hands. "I'm going to make cinnamon rolls."

"Cinnamon rolls?"

"Of course. Don't you remember? I used to make them for us on Christmas morning. I'm a disaster in the kitchen, but I know how to make good cinnamon rolls. I can do that much." She darted toward her tiny pantry and started pulling out flour and sugar. "It won't take long."

A flash of memory exploded in his mind. Seven years old, and Dad had left them. No Vance, either. And no money. He padded along in footed pajamas to the kitchen, trailing the scent of warm, buttery cinnamon.

"Cinnamon rolls, Shawnie. Fresh out of the oven. And we can eat the whole pan together. Just you and me."

His mom pulled eggs from the refrigerator, and butter. "My pantry's skimpy. But I can bring them this much."

Sean's throat burned as his mother scurried around. He didn't think he had any good Christmas memories with his mother. But here it was, in the form of cinnamon rolls.

They had a long way to go, but today, Christmas Eve, was a fresh start. Like a new blanket of snow.

※

The trees cast long slanted shadows across the lawn of Barncastle Inn. Marcella looked out toward the frozen pond beyond the grove of trees. "He's not coming back."

Amity joined her at the window. "I don't know what to say except I'm sorry. I hate to say it, but maybe his mom going off like that in front of everyone was a blessing in disguise. Sometimes we need a little shock to make a change. I know that Memé and Pepé have been busy, making up for lost time with each other."

Marcella nodded. "I don't even have his cell phone number."

"Pepé probably has it."

"I don't want to bother him and Memé. And I don't know what I'd say to Sean. I want to believe him, that he didn't know about the will."

"If he was just out for the money, he wouldn't have come here," Amity said.

"I hope not. I'm so embarrassed, though, that this all happened in front of Jayne and her family, and half their town." Marcella went over to the mirror at the vanity to touch up her makeup. They needed to be down at the barn in thirty minutes, to run through their rearranged songs, without Sean. The transposition hadn't been so bad. But it wouldn't be the same without him, without his rich baritone.

※

"Jayne said she didn't know exactly what was happening. Most of the crowd thought it was part of the show, that she was a long-lost mother proud of her war hero son. I'm glad I started playing the piano, so nearly everyone missed the part about Pepé and the will." Amity finagled her way to see herself in the mirror as well. "Pete and I had lunch with Jayne and Luke today. We're planning to keep in touch after Christmas, since the kids got along so well. And you know what? They even prayed with us about Sean and his mother and our family situation."

Marcella blinked hard and found a tissue. She didn't want to cry and muss her makeup. The Barncastle Inn was more than a massive, elegant home. Love filled every corner. Maybe that's why special things happened here this Christmas.

Please, God. Let Sean come back. Even his mother. If he's going to be in my life, she probably will be, too.

"You look perfect." Amity gave her a shoulder hug. "Smile. Tonight's performance will be the best ever. And then later, we'll go into town for the midnight candlelight service at Jayne and Luke's church. The kids get to open one present when we get back here. And then, Christmas. We did it, Cellie. Memé, Pepé, Christmas."

She nodded. "Maybe we didn't have as much to do with it, though."

Only one more thing would make her Christmas complete.

❄

Unbelievable. Sean hit the brakes, and his mother's car slowed to a crawl. Just over the Vermont border, a four-car pileup had shut down northbound Route 91.

"Those poor people," Mom murmured as they passed

the scene, directed onto the shoulder of the road. "Christmas Eve, too."

The scent of cinnamon rolls filled the car, and Sean's stomach rumbled. "Lord, guide the rescue workers, touch all the families involved in that accident. Thank You for protecting us tonight."

He prayed aloud, not caring if his mother objected. She didn't.

"I'm proud of you, Sean," was all she said. "I wish I could believe like you."

"I hope you do, one day."

He took the Route 9 exit. Not long now, and they'd be back at the Barncastle. He glanced at the clock on the car. Six-thirty. Maybe he'd make it in time for the finale, the one that had been ruined last night. Just in case, he'd donned the vintage uniform he'd worn last night.

Because he and his mother weren't running away anymore. He couldn't hide, and to her credit, Mom wouldn't either. Hopefully the Goudreaus would accept them back. The thought of facing Marcella's father made his nerve falter a bit. What man wanted his daughter to be with a man who had a load of baggage?

They negotiated the traffic circle in Castlebury center, empty except for a few other vehicles on the road. Everyone was either snug in their homes or with family. So was he.

The Barncastle's lights welcomed them as they turned into the driveway. He squeezed the car into the last remaining parking space. A figure was walking across the parking lot.

Luke Gilbert met them at the car. "You're back. Welcome,

welcome. Both of you." He shook Sean's hand.

"I brought cinnamon rolls for you and your family." Mom held up the pans. "I've got more in the car. I baked all afternoon."

Luke nodded. "Well, thank you. I know we'll enjoy them."

"Did I miss the program? Is it over yet?" Sean asked.

"No. I think Marcella is doing her last speech before the finale."

Exactly where she was last night when the whole thing fell to pieces.

"Cool." Sean tugged on his tie.

"Go get 'er, Shawnie," Mom called after him as he quickened his steps.

He could hear Marcella's voice, talking about Christmas. A few flakes descended from above. Sean smiled as he tugged on the door. The barn door slid open, and a few heads turned.

Marcella froze onstage, her voice silenced. Snow fell around Sean and some flakes drifted into the barn.

Sean strode up the aisle. Marcella left the stage, the red skirt of her gown swishing the floor.

He took her in his arms. "I'm back."

"You're back."

"I'm sorry I left," he whispered in her ear as he hugged her. Applause drowned out his voice.

"We'll work it out, just like Memé and Pepé have," she whispered back as he released her.

Amity started the introduction for "White Christmas," thankfully, in Sean's key. He flashed her a grateful glance.

"We have a lot to talk about."

Marcella nodded. "We'll talk. After the song."

"Merry Christmas, Marcella." He knew she'd love the gift he'd found for her, a snow globe of a castle that looked very much like the inn, all decorated for Christmas, with a music box in the bottom that played "White Christmas."

"Merry Christmas, Sean. And I love you."

"I love you too, Cellie."

With that, he took her hands in his own, and they began their duet.

Lynette Sowell is the author of five novellas and five novels for Barbour Publishing and Heartsong Presents. She divides her time between editing medical reports and chasing down stories for her local newspaper. But she also loves to spin adventures for the characters who emerge from story ideas in her head. She hopes to spread the truth of God's love and person while taking readers on an entertaining journey. Lynette is a Massachusetts transplant who makes her home in central Texas with her husband and five cats, who have their humans well trained. She loves to read, try new recipes, take Texas road trips, and spend time with her family. You can find out more about Lynette at www.lynettesowell.com.

WHERE YOUR HEART IS

Janelle Mowery

Dedication

To my parents, who raised me to understand
and celebrate the true meaning of Christmas.

But lay up for yourselves treasures in heaven.
MATTHEW 6:20 KJV

Chapter 1

Stephanie Minter gripped her sword with both hands and prepared for the enemy's next strike. The two swords slammed together and made her hands tingle. She flipped her wrists and blocked the next hit. She spun around and swung her sword, only to be blocked.

Arms tiring, she changed her stance for better balance then dipped the point of the sword toward the ground to fend off another attack. She slashed at the enemy, thrusting several times, forcing her foe backward. With the advantage on her side, she kept swinging. Another thrust or two and she'd win.

A second adversary joined the first. The two swung at her, each taking turns, backing her one step at a time as she parried each strike. Then her heel caught on something. She lost her balance and plummeted to the ground. They were on her faster than she could blink, standing over her, the tips of their swords ready to plunge into her. She dropped her blade and held up her hands.

"You win."

The older of the two leaned closer. "So you'll come with us?"

Another voice called from a distance. "You all packed and ready, Stephanie?"

Jennifer and Brandon Tolliver glanced up at their father,

then speared her with their eyes. "You're going?"

She grinned. "Yep, my bags are already in the SUV."

The two kids shared a glance. "Why didn't you tell us instead of making us fight you?"

"I wanted to see how much you've learned about sword fighting."

"Oh, man. . ." The nine- and seven-year-old voices blended in outrage.

Two hours later as they neared the Barncastle Inn, Stephanie tried to hold on to her smile. Both children were using her arms as pillows. Sleep was a luxury she hadn't enjoyed since she accepted the invitation to join Steve and Emily Tolliver and their children for Christmas vacation. The holidays would have been the perfect time for a break from her role as nanny, but she'd come to love the children and didn't feel the need for some time off. Not to mention how much the children had begged her to come along.

The only cloud on the trip would be if Jayne Barncastle remembered her as the woman who broke her cousin's heart. At least Matt wouldn't be there. Last she heard, he still had his carpentry business in Pennsylvania. Just knowing Jayne was his cousin was painful enough. Seeing Matt would hurt too much.

Matthew Raynor. She still remembered every crease, crevice, and smile line on his face. But it was his eyes that had weakened her knees from the moment they met. If she hadn't run off to New York to make a name for herself in the photography world, they'd probably be married by now.

She did her best to push him from her mind and take in the scenery. Vermont was beautiful. And the farther they drove, the more she fell in love with the state.

"There's the sign for Barncastle Inn. Only another mile and we'll be there."

Steve sounded tired as he reached for his wife's hand. He needed a break from his corporate law business as much as Emily needed one from her interior design job while she carried their third child due in a few months. Stephanie planned to do as much as possible with the children to give the parents a rest.

They wound through trees for several minutes before the inn could be seen, and when Stephanie caught her first glimpse, she craned her neck several times trying to keep it in view. She roused Jennifer and Brandon, then pointed so they could see what looked like a castle.

Brandon crawled across her lap. "Whoa, look at that!" They squealed and pressed their noses against the window. Without a doubt, this would be a Christmas they'd never forget. And if the exterior was any indication, they were going to love this place.

As soon as Steve unlocked the doors, the kids had theirs open and all but fell outside into the snow while shoving their arms into their coat sleeves. Stephanie almost stepped on them in her haste. They stared at the inn until the front door opened and a woman wearing a bright smile descended the porch steps. She held out her hand to greet the parents.

"Welcome to Barncastle Inn. I'm Jayne Gilbert."

Steve interrupted his stretching to shake her hand. "Steve and Emily Tolliver." He placed his hands on the kids. "And this is Jennifer and Brandon, your friendly neighborhood pirates."

Jayne laughed and bent to meet them. "I'm guessing it's more like Blackbeard or Black Bart. And you—"she touched Jennifer's cheek"—could be the rough and tumble Anne Bonney or maybe the slightly sweeter Grace O'Malley."

Jennifer's eyes widened. "There was girl pirates?"

"There sure were. Several of them. Most were pretty rough. Some say downright ferocious."

"Can I be a nice pirate?"

Jayne smiled. "Absolutely. You're a pirate, and most of the time, pirates do what they want."

Brandon grinned and rubbed his chin. "I'll be Blackbeard. He sounds tough. Do ya got any whiskers I can wear?"

Jayne ruffled his hair. "I'm sure we can come up with something. And Jennifer, we have some clothing for you that most women pirates wore. I think you'll both have a lot of fun with all we have planned."

Steve opened the hatch of the SUV. "But you can't get started until we get everything carried into our rooms."

"Ugh." Both kids' shoulders slumped.

In an effort to get things moving, and if she were honest, get away from Jayne before she was recognized, Stephanie stepped forward and grabbed her bag. "The sooner we hurry, the sooner we can look around."

"That's right." Steve stopped her from leaving. "Jayne, this is our nanny I told you about, Stephanie Minter."

She couldn't tell if the look on Jayne's face was one of familiarity or a struggle to remember where she'd heard the name, but Jayne extended her hand anyway. "Nice to meet you. I hope I can count on your help with some of our skits."

"That's great, and I have a few ideas I'd like to run past

you, maybe work them into your plans."

"Good. We'll get together after everyone is settled and has a chance to look around."

A gust of wind blew up from the lake, making everyone pull their coats tighter. Jayne shoved her hands into her pockets and nodded toward the house. "If you'll follow me, I'll get you out of the cold and into your rooms."

As they headed up the walk, Stephanie took in as much of the stone exterior as she could, taking snapshots with her mind. Matt had told her about the place, but this was so much more than she ever imagined. She couldn't wait to explore.

She hustled to catch up to the group. It looked as if Jayne had gone all out decorating for Christmas, yet managed to add touches of pirate lore for the sake of the Tollivers. From the top of the stairs, Stephanie glanced over the railing and gasped at the sight of the huge Christmas tree.

"Jayne, this place is beautiful."

"Thank you, Stephanie. All the decorations you see have been collected over the years, mostly by my mother. She's always had great taste. She helped me put all this together."

Brandon ran his fingers along the handrail. "Do we get to slide down the banister? Didn't pirates do that?"

Emily covered her face with her hand. "No, Brandon, you don't. You'd ruin all the garland wrapped around the railing." She looked at Jayne. "I'm sorry."

Jayne laughed. "Not a problem. It just proves he'll like the planned activities." She flipped through a ring of keys and motioned to a door. "This is the Library Suite, now named the Jolly Roger. Steve, you and Emily will be in here.

I believe you'll find it large enough for your children to visit whenever they want as well as private when you want to be alone."

She opened the door and led them inside. Through all the *oohs* and *aahs*, envy struck Stephanie in a big way. She could lose herself in this room. She just might have to visit Barncastle Inn again on her next vacation and ask for the Library Suite, though she doubted she could afford a corner of the basement.

Jayne headed down the hallway and pointed at the doors to the next two rooms. "The Barnacle is for Brandon and The Parrot is for Jennifer." She opened each door for the children and smiled at their squeals and shouts. "I guess that means they're acceptable."

Stephanie laughed. "We may not see them for a while."

If that's what Jayne did for the Tollivers, she couldn't wait to see her room. Just across the hall from the children's room, Jayne motioned to a door with a large colorful feather attached with a placard stating, THE PLUME. Jayne opened the door.

"I hope you'll be comfortable in here."

Stephanie stepped inside and held her breath. The blend of Christmas garland and other decorations with the fluffy feathers attached to long green and red swags added vibrant color and life to the room. She could be celebrating the birth of Christ on a tropical island. The children would have to drag her out or come for a visit if they wanted to spend any time with her.

She finally turned to Jayne. "I don't know how you do it, but this room is amazing. I almost feel like I know you just by how you decorate."

"I'm glad you like it." She motioned to a small table with two chairs. "Since the children still seem enthralled with their rooms, how about we sit and go over our ideas and see how they'll mesh?"

They'd just gotten started when a boy about the same age as Jennifer and Brandon poked his head through the doorway. Jayne smiled and waved him in.

"Andy, I'd like you to meet one of our guests. This is Miss Minter. She's the nanny to Jennifer and Brandon, whom you'll meet soon."

The words were no sooner out of her mouth when the children raced into the room. They slid to a stop and gaped. Stephanie smiled at Jayne.

"Hey you two, come meet my son, Andy."

Jayne made the introductions and, typical of the young, they took to each other right away. Andy leaned against his mother. "Can I show them the barn?"

The tone of Andy's voice made Stephanie want to tag along, especially if Jayne decorated the barn even half as much as the inn.

Jayne touched her arm. "Do you mind or would you rather wait so you can join them?"

"No, let them go. I'll find them when we finish." Besides, this vacation was for the children.

The three ran out of the room. Jayne called after them, "Make sure you wear your coats."

Stephanie shook her head. "I was about to say the same thing. Funny how we have to tell them that."

"Even funnier, they would have gotten all the way to the

barn before they realized they were cold."

They laughed, then got down to work. Half an hour later, Jayne leaned back in her chair.

"You've really done your homework. Adding your ideas will make the events I've planned even better. Trying to add the real meaning of Christmas to a pirate theme hasn't been easy. This is going to be great."

"Good. I'll enjoy working with you." She glanced at the window. "Oh goodness. It's almost dark. I should go check on Jen and Brandon."

"Tell you what. Go look around the grounds and see what you want to use for your plans. I'll round up the kids and get them cleaned up for dinner. In case you ever need one, you can always find a battery-charged flashlight on the wall next to the door."

"Great. Thank you."

On the walk outside, Stephanie listened as Jayne sketched out the layout of the grounds, and watched her head to the barn. The bottom half of the building was of stone much like the inn, with the top half made of wooden planks. Half tempted to follow Jayne just to see the ship she'd mentioned during their talk, she instead wandered toward the nativity set. Handcrafted from wood, the collection was impressive in the details, from the expression on each face to the wrinkles and nails on the hands. Stephanie almost felt the need to introduce herself as she resisted the urge to touch each piece. She knelt in front of the baby Jesus and traveled back through time to the night of His birth. Warmth filled her chest at the thought of the precious gift.

She touched the manger then looked underneath. She'd

need help with her plan but it looked like it would work. As much as she wanted to stay, she needed to see more of the grounds. By the time she made it to the barn, Jayne and the kids were gone. They'd left the lights on, though. The ship Jayne and her staff had built for the skits was just as incredible as the nativity set. They'd outdone anything she could have imagined. From windows for the cannons all the way up to the masts, it was as if they'd taken a ship from one of the many movies and landed it in their barn. She couldn't wait to see the skits Jayne had planned.

A glance at her watch sent her scurrying for the inn. Before she made it to the back door of the house, lights glistening off the icy lake caught her attention. The sight kept her feet moving until she stood at the gate to some steps leading to the lake's edge. She dropped onto the nearby concrete bench and wished once again she had her camera. As beautiful as it was here, this wouldn't be the last time she'd fight that wish.

One day, Lord. You know the desires of my heart, and I know I'll one day have another nice camera.

"Stephanie! What are you doing here?"

At the familiar voice, Stephanie's heart threatened to pound from her chest as she turned to face Matt.

Chapter 2

The porch light shining behind Matt's head glowed like a halo. Or maybe it just looked that way because Stephanie still loved him. She wanted to run up the porch steps and wrap her arms around him, but no doubt he wouldn't allow any kind of embrace. By his expression, he still wore his hurt close to his heart.

He made no move to join her. "How did you know I was here?"

"I didn't." She headed toward the porch. "I'm here with the Tolliver family."

His frown deepened. "I don't understand. Are you related or something?"

She climbed the steps and stopped in front of him. After two years, all she wanted to do was touch him. He shoved his hands into his pockets. She took a breath and shook her head. "I'm their nanny." She paused and examined his face. "How've you been?"

He tilted his head. "You left to make your fortune as a famous photographer. How'd you become a nanny?" He took a step back. "Never mind. It's not my business."

He turned to leave. Stephanie reached out to him, touching his arm. He stopped.

"I'll tell you the story if you have the time and would like to hear it." When he glanced at her, she motioned to the porch swing. "There's something I've needed to say to you. I'd like to do it now if you'll let me."

He stared at the swing in silence for several moments then sat as close to the end as possible. Following his lead, she sat at the other end, giving him his space. She pulled her stocking hat down around her ears then shoved her gloved hands in her coat pocket. He wasn't wearing much of a coat.

"Are you warm enough? We could go inside."

"I'm fine." He stared straight ahead, his foot pushing the swing into a slow rock. "You highlighted your hair. It looks nice."

"Thank you." This was hard. Even harder than when she faced her family so long ago. She gazed at the lights glistening off the ice and took a breath. "I know I hurt you, Matt, and I want you to know how sorry I am. What I did was selfish and thoughtless. Stupid." Her throat swelled as tears threatened. "I was so stupid."

"What's your last name?"

"What?" She looked at him. "It's still Minter."

"So you didn't marry that guy?"

Oh wow. His pain was worse than she thought. "I didn't go to New York with Larry to marry him."

"So you were just using him."

She blew out a long breath, creating steamy little clouds. "Yeah, I guess so. And I just ended up getting used."

He finally looked at her. "How so?"

She made a face. "Our second day in the city, he sent me out to get some food, and when I returned, he was gone—along with all my photography equipment, including the antique cameras my grandpa gave me." She took another breath. "And there I was, alone in a big city with no money and no equipment to make money."

"Why didn't you just come home?"

"More stupidity. But mostly I was embarrassed. It took me almost six months before I could face my family." She shrugged. "Of course they forgave me, but I couldn't forgive myself."

"How did you survive those first six months?"

She lifted one corner of her mouth. "I wandered down the streets looking for work. I saw a help-wanted sign in the window of an ice-cream parlor. They hired me on the spot. Must have been the desperate look on my face. Or maybe it was my growling stomach."

The corners of Matt's mouth lifted. "Ice cream, huh? Did they know you could eat them out of business?"

Stephanie laughed, glad to see even a slight smile from Matt. "I kept that bit of news a secret for all of about two weeks. But thankfully by then, the family that owned the shop had taken me under their wing and overlooked that little weakness. They let me live with them until I could afford a place of my own."

"How did you come to be with the Tollivers?"

"They're friends of the family who hired me, the Vickers. When the Tollivers' other nanny got married, the Vickers told them they should hire me. I've been with them for almost a year. The kids are great."

"And your plans to get rich and famous from photography?"

She looked across the frozen lake again, remembering her wish for another camera mere minutes ago. "Gone. No longer important to me. Oh, I want to own another nice camera again because I love taking pictures. I can't count the number of times I've wished for my cameras back because of scenes just like this. This place, this house, it's all beautiful."

She could feel him staring and turned to meet his gaze. He gave a slight shake of his head.

"You're different. I can hear it in your voice."

"I'd like to think I can learn from my mistakes. And the Vickers had a lot to do with it. They were a great help." There was so much more to tell, but she wanted to know about him, what he'd been doing the last two years. "How about you? How's your carpentry business? You here visiting Jayne for Christmas instead of spending it with your parents?"

Matt put one arm along the back of the swing and propped his ankle on his knee. "I moved my business from Pennsylvania to here. Jayne called one day and told me her idea of using this inn for special Christmas packages, calling it Christmas Any Time. She said she needed someone to build sets for some visitors' wishes, like a pirate ship for instance."

Stephanie turned in the swing. "*You* built that? It's incredible. You did a great job."

He smiled. "You saw it? I think it's been my favorite set so far."

"This wasn't your first set?"

"No, Jayne had a special request a few months ago."

"What'd you have to build for that?"

He looked down at the porch flooring. "A little boy had cancer." Matt's voice was low and soft. "He loved the story

Jack and the Beanstalk, but he was too sick to take part in an actual event, so his parents asked if there was any way we could reenact something similar." He shook his head. "I about broke my neck coming down the beanstalk after Jack."

She raised her brows and tried not to laugh. "You played the giant?"

He shrugged. "I did the best I could."

"I bet it was great."

He shrugged again, then stood. "I've got a few more things I need to do before tomorrow. I want that boat in shipshape."

She laughed as she stood next to him. "That was bad."

"I know."

"You need some help?"

A dark form came around the corner of the porch. "There you are, Steph. I've been looking all over for you."

Before she could recover from her shock, the man raced up the steps, grabbed her in his arms, and spun her around, ending with a loud, smacking kiss. She struggled to get free and was released. She stared, unable to believe her eyes, then turned to Matt. His nostrils flared and his eyes flamed. With a nod, he descended the step and disappeared around the house.

❄

Matt couldn't get away from Stephanie fast enough. She hadn't changed a bit. She'd only become a better actress.

He stomped across the yard and entered the barn. Was he more angry with her or himself? How could he have softened enough to let her hurt him again? He flipped on the lights and stared at the ship. The excitement of working with the young pirates had dimmed. Might even be gone, because now he knew he'd also be working with Stephanie. If Jayne knew she was coming and didn't warn him. . .

He ran his hand across the ship's facade. He'd worked hard on getting it just right, spent hours on the Internet downloading pictures to use as guides. He'd poured himself into this task just as he'd done in all the others—since Stephanie ran away to New York, and working with wood was all he had left.

A week. Only a week. He could manage to put up with seeing her that long; then he could get back to living again. He hadn't done that in the last two years, but now it was time to start.

❉

"What are you doing here, Greg?"

"Oh now, is that the way to greet your future husband?"

Stephanie gritted her teeth and clenched her fists. "I'm *not* marrying you." *I don't even like you.* "Did Steve invite you?"

"Why else would I be here?"

"Because I wouldn't put it past you to just show up and hope they'd let you stay."

Greg put his hand over his heart. "Now you're just being mean. Why do you want to hurt me?"

Grrr. "I'm going to find Steve."

Greg grabbed her arm. "Hold on. I really was invited. I take it by your reaction my brother didn't tell you."

"Steve never said a word." *Or I wouldn't have come.*

"Probably because they knew you wouldn't come." He shrugged. "I heard about their pirate theme and thought it would be fun. I could help them walk the plank and swing from the mast."

"Or hang by the neck until dead."

Greg laughed. "Or there's that." He nudged her with his elbow. "I really rub you the wrong way, don't I?"

"You have a certain knack."

He stepped around to face her. "I just want to be with you. Like I've said a hundred times, I'm in love with you."

"And like I've said a hundred times, get over it. I don't love you, nor will I ever." She tilted her head as she peered up at him. "Why can't we just be friends?"

"Because I'll always want more."

"This is all you'll ever get."

She slipped past him and entered the inn. Why was it so hard for him to take no for an answer? She'd started off being nice, kind in her refusals. Now she had to be blunt and it still didn't help. Worse yet, what had Matt thought? He looked pretty mad. All the progress they'd made tonight was destroyed because of one thoughtless act. For the second time. Her running off in a selfish act was the first. She may never get a third chance.

Chapter 3

What do you mean, I have to work closely with Stephanie? Why can't you do it?" Matt propped his forearm on the table and leaned toward his cousin. "Did you know she was coming and didn't tell me?"

Jayne made a face. "No, I didn't know she was the nanny. And I would have warned you she was here if you'd have come inside first."

He sat back in his chair. "Yeah, well when I thought it was her, I couldn't help it. I had to know for sure. Besides, you could have called."

"I've been a little busy."

He tapped the tabletop. "What is it she needs done that requires my help?"

Jayne smiled. "She's got some great ideas, Matt. Wait till you hear them."

"I'm waiting."

"I'd rather you hear them from her."

"Why?"

The kitchen door opened. Stephanie stopped when she saw them sitting at the table. "I'm sorry. I didn't mean to interrupt anything."

Jayne stood and motioned for her to sit. "You're not interrupting. Have a seat. I'll get you a cup of coffee while you fill Matt in on your plans."

Stephanie didn't move but stared at Matt. He wanted to strangle his cousin for putting him in this position. Instead, he nodded toward an open chair. Stephanie's smile was timid as she sat.

He was feeling mean and Stephanie became his target. "Is your boyfriend joining us?"

Stephanie frowned. "My boyfr—" Her mouth formed an *Oh*. She placed her elbow on the table. "Greg isn't my boyfriend. Never has been. He's Steve Tolliver's brother."

Matt looked at Jayne, who nodded. He narrowed his eyes. Jayne needed to be a little more forthcoming with information. He returned to Stephanie. "If that's the case, don't you think Greg's a little too familiar with his brother's nanny?"

"Yes, I do. And I've told him as much, repeatedly."

By Stephanie's expression, there was more to the story, but her answers removed his edge. Not to mention she had that innocent look again. He took a breath. "Jayne tells me you need some help with plans for the kids."

"Do you have time?"

"I took the week off to be here for any help needed."

Jayne set a cup of coffee in front of Stephanie and refilled his cup. "Would you like some cream and sugar, Steph?"

"She likes it black." As soon as the words were out of his mouth, Matt wished he'd have bitten his tongue. He caught the raised eyebrows on Jayne's face and scowled.

Jayne set the carafe in the middle of the table. "I've got to finish breakfast. You two get the plans hammered out."

As Stephanie laid out her thoughts on the treasure hunt, Matt grew more impressed. She'd given everything a lot of thought. He raised his brows at how she wanted it to end.

She leaned back, her expression hopeful. "Do you think it's possible, or have I gone too far?"

Matt stared at the table trying to picture how he'd be able to make her idea possible. "So the kids will be opening their gifts Christmas Eve?"

"Only some of them. They'll get the rest Christmas morning." She made a face. "You don't think it's possible, do you?"

He ran his hand across his chin. More than ever, he wanted to make it happen. "Let's go out and take a look."

Jayne stopped stirring the scrambled eggs. "Will the family be down soon?"

"Oh I'm sorry, Jayne. Yes, Emily said to tell you once they were all dressed, they'd come down together."

"Great. While you're out there, Stephanie, be sure to tell him the rest of your ideas."

Matt waited for her to get her coat then led her outside. "What other ideas? Are they anything like this treasure hunt?"

She smiled and once again he had the feeling there was something different about her. He tried to focus on what she was saying.

"Nothing as hard as what I'm asking you to do. I've done a lot of research on real pirates instead of what everyone's been led to believe in all the movies. I'd like to pass that along to the kids."

"Like what?"

"Well, for instance, a lot of the time, a pirate's punishment was to be placed in a pillory. I was kinda hoping you'd be able to build one for me."

He raised his brows. "You're gonna put those kids in a pillory?"

"Only for a few minutes so they can see what it was like. But if it's too much, we can skip that part and give them other examples."

"You're planning to get rid of the fallacy and stick with the facts. You mean you're not going to let them walk the plank?"

She laughed. "Oh I'll let them do that. If they didn't, it would break their hearts."

"Good, because I've built a little cage filled with those balls that they can jump into."

"That sounds great. Might have to walk the plank myself."

He cast a glance at her. He'd forgotten the fun side of her. They arrived at the nativity scene. He knelt beside the manger and ran his hand over the smooth wood remembering how fun it'd been to carve the characters.

"I love this set." Stephanie lightly touched the figures of Joseph and Mary before she crouched across the manger from him. "Do you know where they got this?"

The answer caught in his throat, unsure how much he wanted to reveal. He finally shrugged. "I did it. Well, a friend helped carve the details. I'm not artistic enough to do that."

Her mouth had dropped open. "Oh Matt, it's beautiful. You do great work."

His heart thumped and he fought the feeling. "Thank you. Now, let's see about getting your idea to work."

Electricity was already available since the scene was lit

at night. He stared above them. The last part would be the most difficult but as he thought of the possibilities, he grew more excited.

"I think I might be able to make this happen. It'll take some work."

"If I can help, let me know."

Before he could answer, the kids raced out of the house, Andy with them. He'd hoped the Tolliver children would include Andy. They seemed to be getting along great. Stephanie rose and started walking away.

"I don't want them asking what we're doing. I'll try to distract them."

Matt wanted to see her interaction with them. The more he saw, the more impressed he became. Over the last two years, he'd allowed his hurt to turn her into a cruel person, but everything he'd seen and heard since last night made him question that assumption.

She'd dropped to the ground and started scuffing out a snow angel. An odd feeling grew in his chest. Unable to stop himself, he scraped up a handful of snow and shaped it into a ball. Then he made a second. With careful aim, he flung a snowball at her. It hit her chin. She screeched, sat up, and gaped at the children.

"All right, who's the wise guy?"

All three kids pointed at him. Mouth open, she stared. He grinned and hurled the second ball at her. She rolled just in time to keep it from hitting her. Then she jumped to her feet, her hands full of snow.

"Now you asked for it."

She heaved her snowball at him. It landed a foot in front

of him. He laughed.

"You have me scared."

But she had already scooped up more snow. The kids joined in, and snowballs were flying everywhere amidst squeals and laughter.

A large snowball came from the direction of the inn and caught Stephanie in the back. They all turned in time to see Greg cast another ball, hitting Stephanie in the face. As fast as the game started, it ended. Greg ran toward her while laughing. He helped her rub the snow from her face, then replaced it with a kiss.

Stephanie shoved him away but Matt had seen enough. Andy ran after him.

"Where you going, Uncle Matt?"

"I have work to do. You have fun."

He had to get his hands busy before he flattened Stephanie's suitor.

❄

Hands on hips so she wouldn't slap Greg, Stephanie gritted her teeth. She moved away from the children and kept her voice low. "Do that again and I'll talk to Steve, and either you or I will be leaving."

"Come on, Steph. It was just a friendly kiss."

"Never again, Greg. I mean it."

He put up his hands. "All right. No more kisses." He flipped up his collar and tucked his chin inside. "So what are we doing today?"

"Not we. You. You get to keep the kids entertained while I get everything finished for the skits and games."

"I can help with that."

"No, you can't. Play with the kids, and keep them away from the barn for a while."

He eyed her then smiled. "See, you do need me."

She shook her head and fought a smile. He'd be considered charming to any girl who was interested. "You're hopeless." She headed for the barn and heard Greg call out to her. She turned. "What?"

"I'm not giving up."

"You're wasting your time."

"It's my time to waste."

Then she might be spending Christmas with her parents after all. With Matt here, that notion wasn't as appealing as before.

Chapter 4

"What are you doing out here?"

At the disembodied voice in the darkness, Stephanie yelped and spun around. There stood a grinning Matt. She whacked his shoulder. Laughing, he raised his hands in defense and then pointed a finger in her face.

"You know only guilty people get that scared."

She slapped at his finger, her heart still pounding. "That's not always true—but guilty people who sneak up on women in the dark get smacked." She propped her hands on her hips. "Why do men get such a thrill out of scaring women?"

He tilted his head and looked into the sky, then shrugged. "Probably because we're hoping the woman will throw herself into our arms."

That thought sent her heart pounding again. She narrowed her eyes. "Is that true?"

He smiled. "There's probably a smidge of truth to it. So what *are* you doing out here?"

She turned back to where she'd been looking. "It's this treasure hunt. First, I can't go by paces because theirs will be so much shorter than mine, so I'll have to use landmarks or something."

"And second?"

"It can't be buried treasure. The ground is frozen solid."

He nodded. "True, but we can use hay or something. I doubt that part will matter to them. As for the landmarks, let's wander a bit and see what we find." He looked around. "Where are the kids?"

"Jayne took them and their parents into town." And Greg, thank goodness. "She said something about knowing someone who has a collection of pirate memorabilia."

"That's right. So we have a couple hours?"

"That's what I'm figuring. Maybe more because they plan to eat in town."

"Then let's get to it."

Almost two hours later, they sat in Jayne's kitchen munching on sandwiches and chips. Stephanie looked over her notes and nodded.

"This will work great. Now I just have to come up with some pirate-sounding poems leading them to these landmarks."

Matt smiled. "You mean trying to rhyme with stuff like 'arr' and 'matey'?"

Stephanie laughed. "Something like that."

"Sounds like fun. Let's see what we can come up with for the 'W' tree." His brows went up. "Tree and matey rhyme."

She laughed again, picturing the group of trees whose odd growth pattern had made them look from a distance like a giant *W*. It was a landmark at Barncastle. "Yes, they do, but we need phrases leading them there."

She took another bite of her sandwich and ran the words through her head. She looked up and caught Matt staring. "What?"

"You have—" He motioned to his lip then pointed at

hers. "There's some mayo there."

She looked for her napkin then realized she'd forgotten to grab one. Before she could stand, Matt reached and touched her lip with his finger, pausing while their eyes met before he pulled away.

"I got it."

His low voice sent a shiver through her. Or was it his touch? Didn't matter. All she knew was that she wanted him to kiss her.

The kitchen door opened and the kids ran in followed by Greg. His eyes went from Matt to her, then narrowed. Stephanie knew he'd quiz her later. She'd tell him the same thing she always had. It was none of his business. She turned her attention to the excited kids while Matt slid her paper out of their sight.

Jennifer waved something under her nose. "Look what we got, Steph. That pirate man gave us eye patches and these swords."

"And Daddy bought us these hats."

Stephanie touched the items. "These are great. Now you really look like pirates. You can wear these tonight when we start all the pirate games."

Brandon took a stance with his sword. "Yeah! And we can start talking like them too, like that man did today." He frowned then and moved next to Stephanie. "Why did he keep saying 'eye' all the time? Is it cuz he wears a patch over one?"

Stephanie laughed and pulled him into a hug. "Not that kind of eye, Brandon. It's the pirates' way of saying yes."

Matt stood and held out his hand with a pretend sword.

"Aye, me boy." He made his voice raspy like they'd all heard in the movies. "If ye'd like to fight, ye'd say 'aye.' If not, ye'd say 'nay.'"

Brandon grinned and swung his sword toward Matt. "Aye, we can fight. I'll win since you don't have a sword. Then I'll make you walk the plank." He lowered his sword and touched his neck. "Trying to use that voice makes my throat hurt."

Matt laughed and scooped him up. "We'll let you be a pirate without that voice. How's that sound?"

"Good." Brandon leaned back and touched Matt's face. "You gonna wear a patch like us?"

Matt set Brandon back on the ground. "Aye, and a beard if I can grow one fast."

As Stephanie watched and listened, her heart reaffirmed her knowledge that she was still in love with Matt. Maybe even more than before. He turned to her then and caught her staring. She looked away as her face heated.

"What time do the games start tonight?"

Thankful for Jen's question, Stephanie tapped the girl's nose. "Right after dinner. We'll all go to the barn for some fun."

"What'll we do till then?"

Stephanie needed to work on her treasure hunt. "Maybe you should get Matt a sword and show him how well you can fight."

Both kids ran from the kitchen.

Matt turned to her. "Why do I feel like I just fell into a trap, or was fed to the wolves?"

She smiled and shrugged. "Paranoia?" She stood with her

211

paper in hand. "Just make sure I get to watch."

He narrowed his eyes. "Uh-huh. Now I'm getting nervous."

"No need. They're just kids."

"With you as their nanny."

She grinned and winked. His brows flew up. She laughed and went in search of Jayne to see if she had a rhyming dictionary. Greg entered and grabbed her arm as she tried to pass.

"Can we talk?"

"Can it wait?"

He glanced at Matt. "I guess. Not long, though."

"Good."

When Jayne found out about the sword fight between Matt and the Tolliver kids, she managed to delay the battle by asking the kids to teach Andy how to fight. She wanted everyone to have a chance to watch that evening.

The kids were the first to finish their supper. They asked to be excused, then ran to their rooms to get dressed into their outfits. Stephanie gathered her notes, consulted with Jayne, then headed to the barn. She sat in one of the chairs near the pirate ship. Someone dropped next to her. She looked up. Matt wore his own pirate outfit, a wooden sword strapped to his side, a patch over one eye, and a tricorn on his head.

She fought a grin. "Oh, my kingdom for a camera."

"Stop it. What have you gotten me into?"

"A great night of fun."

"Uh-huh. And a date with a doctor."

Stephanie laughed and shook her head. "Just a night of

fun and laughter. I promise."

Greg entered and sat on her other side. "I thought we were gonna talk."

"And we will. It's been busy."

Jayne entered. With her were Luke, her husband and Andy's father, along with Andy and all the Tollivers. She had them sit in the middle. "You ready, Steph?"

"I hope so."

Jayne handed her a small camera. "We may need proof of what happens. Do you mind?"

"Not at all." She joined Jayne up front and faced the families. "We've all seen how the movies portray pirates. Some of it's the truth. Most of it's been stretched. We'd like to take a few minutes to clarify the facts and the fallacies."

Brandon frowned. "Fallacies?"

"Untruths or wrong beliefs."

Jayne held up a bar of soap and a toothbrush. "Did you know pirates rarely, if ever, bathed or brushed their teeth?"

The kids all looked at each other, then Brandon jumped from his seat. "We don't have to brush or take baths. Yippee!"

Jennifer and Andy joined him. Jayne laughed and waved them down.

"That didn't mean *you* could quit being clean. Especially you, Andy. I can't speak for the Tollivers."

"But I can." Emily wore a wide grin. "Our pirates will be clean."

"Aw!"

Stephanie bumped Jayne. "You'd better go on before we have a mutiny."

"Mutiny! Yes, of course." She pointed at each of the kids.

"Do you know what mutiny is?"

Jennifer raised her hand. "I do. That's when all the workers stop listening to the captain and try to take over."

Stephanie sent her a wink. She really had been studying.

Jayne nodded. "That's right. Now, do you know what they did to those leading a mutiny?"

"Uh, killed them?"

"Sometimes, and they weren't very nice about it. But sometimes they marooned them on a tiny island with very little food or water."

Brandon frowned. "That's not gonna be one of our games, is it?"

Stephanie laughed. "You don't want to miss breakfast?"

"Nope."

"You won't. We won't maroon you. We just wanted you to know what most pirates were really like."

"Do we get to walk the plank?"

Jayne smiled at Stephanie. They'd walked right into their plan, just a little sooner than expected. "That's another false belief. Most pirates didn't make others walk the plank. That's something Hollywood made famous."

The kids shared another look and their shoulders drooped. Andy made a face. "We wanted to walk the plank."

Stephanie stood. "Well that's good, because even though it's not really a true pirate act, we decided to let you do just that. But first, you have to have a sword fight with Captain Matt. If you win, he walks the plank. If he wins, you walk the plank."

Matt's mouth dropped open. It was all Stephanie could do not to laugh. "All right, Captain. Board your ship. And don't forget your pirate swabbies or there won't be a mutiny to enjoy."

He walked past her and leaned close to her ear. "You're about to see a mutiny all right. I can't believe I let you talk me into this." He smiled at the kids. "Arr. Come aboard, me mateys. It's a party we be having."

The three children cheered as they stood and slid on their eye patches. They trailed Matt up the stairs to the ship. Stephanie couldn't stop staring. Matt had never looked so good, though she'd never tell him that, not dressed as a pirate anyway. She snapped a couple shots.

He stood at the wheel and pulled his wooden sword. "All right, you swabbies, grab a mop and get to work."

The kids looked at each other then pulled their own swords. Jen held hers out at Matt. "We ain't doing it."

Brandon held his high. "And you ain't captain no more."

Matt jumped from the wheel to the main deck. "What's this?"

Andy joined his new friends. "This be a mutiny!"

Stephanie couldn't help but laugh. The kids tried so hard to sound tough. She took a couple of pictures then glanced at the parents. They each wore a wide smile. Greg wasn't watching the show. His eyes remained on her. She ignored him and returned to the mutiny.

Jen stepped forward, pointed the tip of her sword at Matt, and took her stance. "And we be fighting ye."

"Well, shiver me timbers."

Brandon lowered his sword. "Huh?"

Laughter rolled from those in the seats. Steve cupped his mouth. "It means he's ready for you to fight him. Take him, kids."

Jennifer swung first. Matt met her sword with his. The two parried for several moments, then Brandon stepped up. From her own experience, Stephanie knew Matt had his hands full. He had to dodge a couple of swings from the kids as he fended off their wooden blades. Gasps could be heard from the observers. Then Andy joined them and their efforts had Matt moving backward. His foot caught on a coiled rope and he went down.

Matt grinned as he dropped his sword and raised his hands. "Blimey, mates. I give."

The kids didn't stop. Jen put the tip of her sword near Matt's chin. "It's the plank for ye, mate."

The parents hooted. Brandon and Andy poked Matt in the ribs. "To the plank. Ye be walking."

Matt pushed to his feet. "Aye, me mateys. It's the plank for me." He met Stephanie's eyes and shook his finger at her. As he walked, the kids poked him with their swords. He stepped onto the plank and looked down. "Whoa, me hearties." He pointed down. "Uh, Steph. Some water, please?"

"Oh right." She ran behind the curtain and pushed the large, wheeled cage of foam balls to where Matt would land, then set the brake on each wheel. She bowed. "Your water, Captain."

The parents started clapping. "Jump, jump, jump."

Matt shook his head, held his nose, and leaped from the plank. The balls bounced out the sides as he landed. The kids peered over the side.

"We want to jump."

Matt scooted out of the way. "Come on."

One by one, the children took turns jumping into the balls, climbing out, and walking the plank all over again. Even the parents, all but Emily, took a turn walking the plank. Jayne bumped Stephanie.

"Go on. Take your turn."

She handed her the camera. "You'd better take this." Then she climbed the steps and headed toward the plank, but Matt stood in her way, two swords in his hands. He handed one to her.

"Arr, me beauty. Ye must earn the plank."

She grinned. "Is this *your* mutiny?"

"Aye, lass. 'Tis a sword fight or a flogging with the cat o' nine tails."

They'd caught everyone's attention now. The audience stood to watch and cheer. Stephanie raised a brow and reached for the offered sword.

"'Tis a fight we'll be having then, me bucko."

And the fight was on. The wooden swords clacked together over and over as they warded off each attack. Eventually, her arm growing tired, Stephanie stepped back and they circled several moments. Then she lunged and he dodged. He swung and she deflected. He came at her with a barrage of thrusts. She eluded by running to the other side of the mast. When he tried to follow, she swung at him. He sidestepped and came at her again.

Panting, she warded another attack. There was only one way for this fight to end. She climbed onto the plank and parried his attack a few more times before she pointed at her side. Matt slowed his assault as he frowned, then understanding dawned in his eyes.

With a mock leer, he lunged and slid the blade between her arm and side. She groaned and dropped her weapon. It clattered to the deck as she bent over, grabbing her side. She winked at Matt and tumbled into the cage.

Amidst much applause, the kids jumped in after Stephanie. They played several minutes before Stephanie had her breath back enough to climb out. Matt stood at the edge to help her. He gave a slight bow.

"You're pretty good. I started wondering if I would win."

She leaned close to his ear. "I let you win."

She gave him another wink and raced down the steps before he came up with some kind of revenge. She didn't get far. Greg slipped his arm through hers and led her away.

❄

Matt's ear still tingled from her whisper. He wanted to wrap her in his arms and give her a kiss. Tonight only proved beyond a doubt he still had feelings for her, even after all she'd done in the past. She was still fun and very beautiful, yet she wasn't his. That was proven by the fact that she had just left with another man. Again.

He couldn't watch. He climbed the steps to the ship's deck with the intent to bury his frustration by jumping in the foam balls with the kids.

Chapter 5

Before Greg could get her outside, Stephanie yanked her arm free. "What's so important, Greg. I was having fun."

"But not with me."

"You could have joined in. People older than you were jumping and having a good time."

He cast a glance over her shoulder. "I want to spend some time alone with you, Steph. Let me take you to dinner tomorrow. I want to prove I'm a good guy you can fall in love with."

"No."

"Why not?"

His scowl annoyed her. Everything about him annoyed her. She closed her eyes and blew out a breath. "First of all, I'm here for the kids, not for you. We have plans for the kids tomorrow evening."

"Then let's go for lunch."

"No."

He reached to touch her. "Why not?"

She pulled away. "I don't love you, Greg, and I never will. Not the way you want."

"So you do love me a little."

She groaned. "Not that way. And if you keep this up, you may lose our friendship, too."

"What is it about me that keeps you from loving me. Am I that bad?"

She motioned to a bale of hay and they took a seat. "You're not bad. One day you'll meet a girl who'll think you're perfect. I'm not that girl."

"You could be if you'd just give me a chance." He motioned toward the ship. "What's that Matt guy got that I don't?"

Where would she start? The list was long. "What makes you think Matt has anything to do with this?"

"Because you don't look at me the way you do him." He took a long look in Matt's direction. "He's not good enough for you, Steph. I mean, look at him. He's a carpenter. And wearing a goofy costume."

Stephanie did as suggested and looked at Matt. She loved the way he played with the children, that he didn't worry about what it looked like to put on a pirate costume but wore one for the sake of the kids to make sure they had fun. He was selfless two years ago, but he seemed even more so now.

"See. You're looking at him that way again. I could give you so much more."

"There's nothing wrong with being a carpenter, Greg. Christ was a carpenter."

"You're seriously going to compare Matt to Christ?"

He was wearing her out. "Don't be ridiculous. Just the occupation. He loves what he does. What's wrong with that?"

"I love what I do. And I love you. And if it takes putting on a pirate costume to show you how much, I'll do it. But you've got to promise to give me a chance to show I'm better for you than him."

She shook her head and stood. "Stop it, Greg. Keep this up and you'll ruin everyone's vacation."

He stood and grabbed her arm. "Give me your word. At least give me a shot."

She tried to pull her arm away but he held tight.

"Is something wrong?"

She turned. Matt stood only feet away. She jerked her arm again. This time Greg let her go, but the muscles in his jaw were jumping as he stared at Matt.

"This is none of your business, Raynor. We're having a private conversation."

"Steph?" Matt looked from Greg to her. "You want me to leave?"

Shoving down an urge to scream in frustration, she threw up her hand. "You two do what you want. I'm going to bed."

She stomped from the barn. If it weren't for the kids, she'd be on her way to her parents' house first thing in the morning.

❄

The afternoon sun felt good on Matt's back as he raised the top half of the pillory to check the strength of the hinge. It held tight and didn't even wiggle. Now for some kind of latch.

"Put your head in. Let's see how it works."

He smiled at Stephanie's voice and turned. "You first."

"No way. Knowing you, you'd get me in there and walk away."

"Don't tempt me."

She moved closer and whacked his arm, then fingered the pillory. "This looks great. Is there anything you can't do?"

Win your heart.

He shook away the thought. He'd been hurt enough. Why set himself up for more pain?

"It's not perfect but should work good enough to hold a few kids." He lifted the top half again. "If you want to help, stick your head in there. I need to get an idea of how high off the ground to make this thing."

"Nope. Besides, I'm a lot taller than they are."

"Oh come on. I promise I won't leave you in here. Look, it doesn't even have a latch. You can escape whenever you want."

She eyed him for several seconds then looked at the pillory. It was all he could do not to laugh at her distrust but he fought to keep a straight face.

"You've been asking every day if there's something you can do to help. Here's one way."

She wrinkled up her nose. "Oh all right." She pointed her finger at him. "But this better not be a trick."

"Would I do something like that?"

"Yep."

He laughed as he held the top open. She sent him one more look then put each arm in place before placing her neck on the middle slot. He carefully lowered the top half wishing like crazy he had some way to hold it closed.

"All right, you're what? Five-six?"

"Uh-huh."

"And I'm guessing the kids are no more than four feet tall."

"Right."

He leaned on the top board of the pillory, successfully keeping it closed. "Let's see. So to make them bend over like you and make it as uncomfortable as possible in the least amount of time. . ." He rubbed his chin, not even trying to do the math. He leaned lower, keeping his arm on top. "Does your back hurt yet?"

She turned as far as possible to see him. "It's getting there. You can let me up now."

"What's that?"

"I said, this feels awkward. Let me up."

"You want out?"

"Yes."

"But you haven't been in there very long."

"Long enough. If you doubt it, let me put you in this thing."

"Oh but Steph, I'm smart enough not to get put in that position."

She craned her neck and stuck out her tongue. "You'd also better be faster than me cuz when I get out of here, I'm gonna strangle you."

"Who says you're getting out of here?" He placed both hands on the top board then leaned low enough to look her in the eyes. Their noses were only inches apart. It was all he could do not to kiss her. "I could have used this little contraption two years ago."

Her expression turned serious. "I wish you would have. I'm really sorry, Matt."

"What other forms of pirate punishment are you planning for the kids that I can practice on you first?"

She gave him a slight smile. "Well, let's see. There's the cat 'o nine tails."

"You're not using that on the kids."

"No, but I'll be telling them about it."

"What else?"

"They were tied to the mast, tossed overboard, hanged, marooned, set adrift, clapped in irons—"

"Oh now that sounds like something—"

"Now stop that."

He laughed. "Anything else?"

"Keelhauling."

"I've heard of that. What exactly is that?"

She smiled and batted her eyes. "I'll tell you if you'll turn me loose."

She was so adorable, he wanted to keep her there forever, but her neck and back had to be getting tired. "You drive a hard bargain." He tilted his head. "And I'm feeling generous."

He lifted the board. She stood and massaged her back.

"Thank you, kind sir." She turned her head from side to side, then rubbed. "That really is an awful torture." She motioned to the pillory. "Care to try it for yourself?"

He smiled. There was only one thing he'd care to try. Maybe it was time to get everything talked out so there'd be no walls between them. But was he ready? Is that what he really wanted? All something he didn't have the answers to yet.

"I'll pass. We should move this before the kids get back from the lake and see it."

"To the barn, then?"

"You have the treasure hunt finished?"

"Nope." She raised her brows. "Point taken. I'll leave you alone."

She headed toward the house. He wanted to call her back but the words wouldn't come.

Time. Maybe that's all that was needed. Or maybe it wasn't meant to be. "Lord, help me. I don't know what to do."

"Talking to yourself, Raynor? That's a bad sign, ya know."

Greg stood several feet behind him.

"And you'd know that how?"

Greg grinned. "She deserves better, Matt. If you have any feelings left for her, you'd know that and walk away."

"And leave her for someone like you?" He shook his head. "See ya, Greg."

He pushed the pillory toward the barn, questions rolling through his mind. Just what was the relationship between Stephanie and Greg? Was there or had there ever been any relationship? And the biggest question was, could he ever trust her again?

Chapter 6

Stephanie perched on the stool next to Jayne and glanced at everyone's faces. Greg wasn't among them. She wouldn't mind except she'd thought this was one part of the skits he needed to see. . .a reminder of what Christmas was all about, as well as why they were at the inn in the first place.

She eyed the three children. "I know you love to be punished, right?"

"No way. . ." Brandon shook his head while Jennifer and Andy set Stephanie straight. He shrugged one shoulder. "I don't get into trouble."

As the parents laughed, Stephanie raised her brows. "Oh, really? So when you used the jar of peanut butter to paint the bathroom, your mom was so happy she didn't do anything?"

He made a face. "It wouldn't have happened if you'd been with us then."

"Oh, it was *my* fault." She nodded and laughed. "The logic of a seven-year-old."

Jayne smiled and patted her leg. "Get used to it." She turned to the kids. "Let's take some time listing all the pirate punishments, done to each other as well as how the law punished them."

Jennifer raised her hand. "Some were hanged."

"That's right, done mostly by the law when a pirate

was caught. What else?"

They spent a good deal of time naming the consequences of doing something wrong, from marooning and being tossed overboard, to being set adrift or keelhauling.

Andy raised his hand. "What's keelhauling?"

Stephanie pulled out a picture of a ship and pointed as she spoke. "That's when a pirate was tied to a rope that looped under the ship, then was thrown overboard on one side and hauled under water to the other side, usually resulting in the sailor's death."

The kids looked at each other and made a face. Stephanie motioned for the children to follow her onto the ship. "There were other punishments you haven't mentioned yet. How about this one?" She pointed at the handcuffs and irons lying on the deck. "Which one of you wants to try this one?"

Brandon ran to them. "I will. This doesn't look bad at all."

"Great." Stephanie put the irons on the boy then led him across the deck and locked him to a pole. She motioned to Matt. He turned on a set of heat lamps pointed at Brandon. She patted Brandon on the head. "Now you get to stay there for as many hours as the captain deems enough."

"But it's hot."

"I know. That's the same thing the pirates said when they were clapped in chains and held on the deck in the blazing sun."

"Where's the captain?"

Stephanie tried not to laugh. "I believe he's busy right now." She turned to the other children. "Okay, who's next?"

Jen and Andy looked at each other and then shoved their

hands into their pockets. The parents burst into laughter.

Stephanie put her arm around Jennifer. "Since there's no volunteer, I choose you for the next punishment."

"What is it?"

"It's called a pillory."

"A what?"

Stephanie motioned to the side again and Matt rolled out the pillory. Stephanie led Jen to it and, with Matt's help, locked her inside. "This is another of the punishments doled out by the law when they caught a pirate. Not as permanent as a hanging, but I think as you'll find out, not exactly comfortable and is a bit embarrassing."

"How long will I be stuck here?"

Stephanie patted Jen's head, leaned down and smiled, then walked away. "Your turn, Andy."

He was already shaking his head and backing away. "Nuh-huh! I don't want to be a pirate no more."

"Too late." She put her arm around his shoulders and led him to the mast.

"What're you gonna do to me?"

"This is the punishment phase of being a pirate, Andy. What do you think we should do?"

"Walking the plank would be good."

Everyone laughed.

"That's too easy. We're trying something new tonight."

"Like what?"

She placed his back against the pole. "We're tying you to the mast."

"Oh. That's not so bad."

She pointed up. "Way up at the top."

"Huh?" He looked up and shook his head. "It's dark up there, and I don't like heights."

"Don't worry, son." The voice came from above. Matt hit the lights and Andy's dad, Luke, could be seen tied to the top of the main mast. "I'll take your punishment for you."

Andy grinned and waved. "Thanks, Dad."

Jayne joined them on the ship. "Does this remind you of anything?"

The kids remained silent. Jayne sat on the treasure chest. "What holiday are we celebrating in a couple days?"

"Christmas!" All three kids chimed the word together.

"That's right. And why did Jesus come to earth?"

Still stuck in the pillory, Jen ran in place. "To save us."

"Right again. He took our punishment for us." She pointed up. "Just as Andy's dad is doing for him."

"Daddy?" Brandon's voice sounded pitiful. "You gonna come take my place?"

The barn filled with laughter. Steve waved to his son.

"You bet, buddy."

Stephanie motioned for him to stay seated. "I guess it's time to set everyone free. We just wanted to get the point across that the pirate's life wasn't glamorous like the movies would have you believe."

While she released Jennifer, Matt unchained Brandon, then disappeared over the side of the ship for the next part of the fun. Stephanie pointed to the chest and crates.

"Have a seat for a minute." She sat across from them but could still see those watching below. Jayne joined her. "We'd like to mention a few more things about what pirates were really like before we turn you loose to play like the movie pirates do."

The children grinned and cheered. "Do we get to walk the plank again?"

Jayne nodded. "Yes, along with some new things you haven't done yet. But first we want to tell you a little more about what real pirate life was like. For instance, did you know that most pirates died young? Very seldom did they live into their thirties. If battles didn't take their life, then sickness and diseases ended them early."

"That's right. And here's another bit of information I bet you didn't know." Stephanie leaned forward. "They didn't bury their treasure."

The kids looked at each other then at her again. "You mean we don't get to go looking for treasure?"

Stephanie laughed. "Like I said, you'll get to do the Hollywood version of piracy and you'll get to find a great treasure if you can follow the map, but I wanted you to know that pirates spent what they stole too fast to be able to bury it. Besides that, they didn't trust each other or their captain enough to turn over their loot and hope to get it back. They kept stealing because they ran out of money almost as fast as they stole it."

Brandon scooted forward on his crate. "What about the parrots and monkeys?"

"Some of them did have parrots and monkeys. They caught and kept them as proof they'd been to faraway tropical lands."

"Yeah, but do you have some here we get to play with?"

Jayne laughed. "Only stuffed ones."

Brandon shrugged. "So when do we get to hunt for buried treasure?"

"Not just yet. We have something else for you tonight. We also wanted you to know that rarely did the pirates swing from their ship to the one they were trying to rob."

"What? We don't get to swing?" Jen looked at Brandon. "We wanted to swing."

"Like this, me mateys?"

The lights went up and Matt could be seen at the top of the mast in the crow's nest. Luke was no longer tied but standing next to Matt, who opened the small door and leaned out.

"Avast, ye landlubbers. Prepare to be boarded." Just as Matt leapt, the barn door below the ship opened. Light glowed from the opening and Greg stood watching Matt with a smile on his face. Suspicion thumped inside Stephanie. She craned her neck to see Matt just as the sling around him came loose.

Chapter 7

Matt gripped the rope as the sling below him fell. He slid down the swing and landed on the padded platform as planned. He took a breath and gathered his wits before facing the kids.

"Well, shiver me timbers. What a ride."

They all laughed and ran down the steps to cluster around him.

"I want a turn."

Stephanie ran to him, her eyes wide. She mouthed the words, "You okay?"

He nodded. "Give me a minute, me buckos, and I'll have ye swinging in a jiffy."

Jayne joined them, a frown on her face. "Let's give the captain some time to get the swing ready, kids. We'll walk the plank until then. Climb back up on the ship and I'll get the cage."

Once the kids had left, Jayne turned back and spoke quietly. "What happened? You okay?"

"I'm fine. The buckle on the sling came loose. I'll have it fixed in a minute." He waved Jayne on. "Trust me. It'll be fine."

She raced off to tend the kids, but Stephanie remained with him. "Talk to me, Matt. What happened?"

"Just like I told Jayne, the buckle came loose. I don't

know how. I checked out the rigging this afternoon." He took a closer look. "It's not broken, just unlatched." But he no longer had Stephanie's attention. She was staring at the side door. "What's wrong, Steph?"

She opened her mouth, then closed it and shook her head. "I don't know." She touched the sling. "Can you fix it so the kids won't get hurt?"

He frowned. She wasn't telling him something. "Sure. All I have to do is buckle it back up, but this time I'll tape it closed so it can't work loose. The kids can just step into it."

She nodded. "Good. Let's make sure they have fun."

Stephanie headed for the side door. As much as Matt wanted to follow, he agreed that this vacation was for the kids and they needed to get what they came for. He had the sling ready in minutes and motioned to Luke to get ready. By then, Stephanie had returned, her expression concerned. He'd talk to her when he had the chance, but for now he sent Jennifer up the mast, hoisted by yet another pulley.

While Matt stayed at the bottom, Luke hooked Jen to the sling and waved at Matt. He grabbed the safety rope to keep control of Jen's descent, and the girl was on her way down, screaming the entire way, landing without a glitch.

The rest of the night was spent repeating the procedure many times with each child until everyone was ready to drop. After thanking them for the great time, the Tollivers headed for the house, more than ready for bed. Luke also left with Andy. Matt wanted to get there himself but he wanted to talk to Stephanie first.

She was nowhere to be found. Jayne stood at the light panel. He joined her at the door and gave her a quick hug.

"You were great tonight. Having Luke take the punishment for Andy was a stroke of genius."

Jayne started turning out the lights. "Wish I could take the credit but that was all Stephanie's idea. She's been trying hard to tie this pirate theme into Christmas. And trust me, it's not an easy task."

They parted ways outside the barn, but Matt knew it would take some time to fall asleep as he tried to figure out his former fiancée. He no longer doubted she was different from the girl two years ago, but just what kind of person had she become? Jayne's revelation that tonight's idea to have Luke take Andy's place made Matt's chest feel warm. He couldn't help but smile. He liked the change, but was it temporary or permanent? She'd burned him once. He refused to let it happen again. Time would tell, but they only had a couple of days left together. Maybe it was time for another long and serious talk.

Matt woke the next morning and headed straight to see Jayne with questions about the day's treasure hunt. He started his question the second he opened the door.

"Hey Jayne, got some questions about the hunt. First, what time—"

His question skidded to a stop at the sight of the luggage sitting in the middle of the kitchen floor. He looked up. Jayne sat at the table and Stephanie stood across from her, handing her several sheets of paper. He recognized them as the treasure hunt map and directions. He frowned and tried to put voice to his next question as his heart threatened to break again.

"What's going on, Steph? Running again? Leaving

someone in the lurch is becoming a habit, except this time it's a couple kids."

He could see tears running down Stephanie's cheeks. She wiped them away, grabbed her suitcase, and walked out the door. He moved to the window as she got into a cab and rode away from him for a second time. He clenched his jaw, determined not to let it hurt.

"You owe that girl an apology, Matt."

"Why? She's the one who left. Again."

"But not because she wanted to."

He turned from the window. "Then why is she gone?"

"To keep anything else from happening, especially to those kids. She's leaving to keep them safe."

"I don't understand. Nothing's happened to the kids."

Jayne motioned to one of the chairs and waited for him to sit. Part of him wasn't sure he wanted to hear what she had to say. The other part made him drop onto the chair.

"Okay, you've got my attention. Why is she afraid for the kids?"

"Because of what happened with that sling last night."

"But it was just—"

He was going to say it was an accident. Then he remembered the look on Steph's face and the way she went out the side door. She was quiet and withdrawn the rest of the night. He shook his head.

"All right. Why don't you tell me what it was?"

"She said she couldn't be sure but she thinks Greg had something to do with the buckle on that sling. She saw him in the doorway just as you were about to jump."

Matt's mind spun as everything came together. Greg had

the opportunity yesterday afternoon and getting Stephanie to himself was the motive. Anger ignited. The man was crazy and needed to be stopped.

"Did she talk to Steve and Emily about this? Tell them that Greg could have killed his own niece and nephew?"

"She gave me this note to give them but only after she had a chance to leave. She loves those kids but she just wants to make sure they get the Christmas they wanted."

"It's Greg who needs to leave, not Steph."

"I agree, but she figured this was the easiest way to please everyone." Jayne reached across the table and touched his hand. "I never met Stephanie two years ago, Matt, but the girl I've met this week doesn't sound anything like the one you described. This Stephanie has a heart for the Lord and for those kids." She gripped his hand until he looked at her. "And I believe she has a heart for you, too. She just can't seem to get over the past and tell you. Or maybe it's you who can't get over the past so she *can* tell you."

He couldn't deny what she'd said. He'd pushed Stephanie away just yesterday when she'd tried to spend time with him. Fair or not, he at least owed her some time to talk.

"I can't let her go yet, Jayne. At least not until we have a chance to talk."

"Then you'd better hurry to the bus station or you'll be making a trip to her parents' house in Pennsylvania."

Matt stood and headed for the door. "Hold off on that note to Steve and Emily at least until I get back. Maybe we can work something out."

❄

Stephanie glanced at her watch then swung her leg harder. Of all days for the bus to be late. After what Matt said, she couldn't get away fast enough. If she had any question as to whether or not they could work things out and get back together, this morning answered that for her. He'd just been nice these past days because he had to.

"I don't want you to go."

Matt's voice was right behind her. As sweet as it sounded, what he said was even sweeter. Tears sprang to her eyes as she turned to face him. He came around the bench and took her hands in his.

"I'm sorry, Steph. I had no right to say those things to you."

"Yes, you did."

She wanted to say more but he put his thumb over her lips as he cupped her cheek with his hand. "No. You've not done or said a thing while you've been here to earn something so mean. I never gave you a chance to explain but Jayne told me everything. I want you to come back with me."

Those words meant everything to her, but she shook her head. "I can't. Nothing's changed. I can't let those kids get hurt."

"They won't. I'll make sure of it."

"You can't know what Greg has planned, and as long as I'm there, he'll keep trying to get me to himself, even if it means getting you out of the picture. And next time, the kids might be the ones who pay the price."

Several people rushed to fill the empty benches while some ran to catch their bus. A few bumped them as they hurried by. He motioned to the bench behind her.

"Let's sit and talk."

"My bus will be here soon."

"Let's talk till it gets here."

She glanced at the door then at her watch. "All right. I guess I have a few minutes." And spending the few minutes with him would be much better than waiting alone.

"Tell me about Greg and his interest in you."

He certainly didn't waste any time getting to the point. "I'm not sure when it started. I've been working for the Tollivers for almost nine months now and have known Greg most of those. He stopped by their house for a visit about a month after I started working there, and he comes by at least weekly since then."

"When did he first start letting you know he liked you more than as a friend?"

She pulled up one corner of her mouth and shook her head. "He started flirting from that very first meeting, but I made up an excuse and left. After that, Steve and Emily insisted I stay, saying that I was part of the family and didn't need to leave."

Matt frowned. "You think Steve and Emily have something to do with Greg wanting to get to know you better? Like maybe finding ways to get you two together? Even inviting him on this vacation?"

She made a face. "Not sure about the other times he came around but Greg claimed he more or less invited himself on this trip, that Steve had nothing to do with it."

Matt nodded. "And when it comes to you telling him you're not interested?"

She looked him in the eyes so there'd be no mistake. "I've told him from the get-go that I'm not interested in him other than as a friend. He told me he doesn't want a friendship."

"And that doesn't scare you?"

"It didn't until last night. I just thought he was one of those egotistical guys who couldn't believe he wasn't the object of every woman's affections. But when I saw him in the doorway looking up at you, I thought it was possible he might do anything to get his way and not think about the consequences."

The number to her bus was called over the intercom. She stood with suitcase in hand.

"That's me. Time to go."

Matt grabbed the handle of her case as he stood. "Don't. Stay here. We'll work out this Greg thing."

And what about this thing between her and Matt? Just what was his real purpose in getting her to stay? With his free hand, he grasped her wrist then slid up to her elbow.

"We're not done talking yet, Steph. There's so much more I want to know about you." He licked his lips then looked in her eyes. "And so much more you need to know." He took a step closer and rested his forehead on hers. "Please stay."

Heart thundering up into her throat, she could only nod. He kissed the spot where he'd placed his forehead.

"Thank you." He took the suitcase from her and offered his elbow. "Aye, me beauty. Ye've made this old sea dog's heart very happy." He led her toward the exit. "Heave to me bucko. With fair winds, we'll be back in time for grub. Then it's the treasure we be finding."

She couldn't stop laughing as she squeezed his arm and leaned close. "Keep your voice down. You have everyone staring."

He grinned and winked. "Tis yer beauty, lass. Now, on to me galleon. Time to cast off."

She shook her head. There was no stopping him when he was on a roll. And if the past was still a good indicator, the fun had only begun.

Chapter 8

Stephanie helped Matt put together the finishing touches on the treasure hunt, keeping an eye out for Greg the entire time. She wouldn't get to talk to Steve about her suspicions until he returned from town. Nothing they did today should hurt the children in any way, but after last night, she wouldn't doubt if Greg wouldn't try to sabotage the fun in order to make Matt look bad.

Matt checked the angle of the light, then peered up at her, squinting against the sun. "Would you let me say something to the kids before you get them started on the hunt?"

"Sure. I think that would be great. They'll get a pep talk from their captain before they get to work."

He stood and smiled. "Work, huh? I think that's one job they'll enjoy. You have the gifts all ready to hide?"

"Yep. Once we get the kids started the wrong direction, you get to bury the gifts in the straw."

"Aw, now that's just mean, sending them the wrong way."

"Not mean, just wise. It'll take more time this way."

"And wear them out so they'll sleep."

She grinned. "Now you're learning."

Three hours later, everyone but Steve, Emily, and Greg stood on the porch closest to the lake. Steve had called to let Jayne know he and Emily would be staying in town for a quiet evening. So where was Greg?

241

Stephanie turned to look across the lake. The lowering sun glistened off the ice, creating a treasure all its own. Again, Stephanie wished for a camera. This place held a beauty like none she'd ever seen and it needed to be captured.

"Stephanie?"

Jayne pulled her attention back to the kids. "Right. Sorry." She smiled at them. "Before we begin, your captain would like to say a few words."

Matt stepped next to her in full pirate garb. "I won't be using my pirate talk this time. The story I'm about to tell is too special and important to be made into a game."

He picked up his Bible then perched on the porch railing. He flipped open to the passage he'd marked with a slip of paper.

"Now after Jesus was born in Bethlehem of Judea in the days of Herod the king, magi from the east arrived in Jerusalem, saying, 'Where is He who has been born King of the Jews? For we saw His star in the east, and have come to worship Him.'"

Matt closed his Bible. "The three Magi, the three kings that are always mentioned with the birth of Christ, they had their own map to follow but theirs was in the sky. They followed a star for a long time until they found their treasure. And who was their treasure?"

Jen raised her hand. "Baby Jesus."

"That's right. Those kings followed that map marking the location of baby Jesus. You three are like the three Magi. You're about to get started on your own treasure hunt with a different kind of map. As you go about following the directions to find your treasure, remember to think about the real treasure of Christmas. Jesus is our gift from God. He left His Father's side to come down here and take our punishment on Himself, just like you learned about last night. Think about Him as you seek your prize this Christmas Eve."

Stephanie smiled at him as she moved to his side. She turned her back on the kids so they couldn't read her lips. "That was a pretty big hint, but I love the parallel you drew for them."

"Thank you."

She faced the kids. "Who's ready for a treasure hunt?"

All three jumped to their feet and raised their hands.

"Good. You're going to work together to find the treasure, just like the Magi did." She held out the first slip of paper then pulled it back before they could take it. "Oh wait. I forgot something. You have to search for the treasure while wearing your eye patches and wooden legs."

The kids looked at each other then at her again. Brandon scrunched up his face. "But we have our own legs to run on. Why do we need wooden ones?"

Stephanie smiled. She had no doubt Brandon would be the one to question this part of the hunt. "You're pirates, so you have to dress and act the part." She motioned to Jayne, who pulled the patches and legs out of a box. "We're going to help you get these on. Then I'll give you the first set of directions."

The kids slid the patches over their eyes while she and Jayne strapped the wooden pegs to the kids' legs. Brandon grinned when he saw how they had to "wear" the pegs.

"I thought we'd have to use these fake legs instead of our real ones."

Stephanie grasped the rim of his tricorn and gave it a tug. "I know that's what you thought, and I can fix these up so you can do just that if you'd like."

He shook his head. "Nope. I like it like this better."

"I thought you would." She pulled the paper out of her pocket. "Written on this is your first set of directions that will lead you to the next location where you'll find your next set of directions. Keep following each of them until you reach the treasure."

Jen grabbed the paper. "The first step in this search of yours will take you down many more. Go down the stairs to the water's edge. More directions can be found on the shore."

Squealing, the children raced off the porch. Jayne leaned over the railing and cupped her mouth.

"Be careful. Those steps might be slippery."

Stephanie picked up the paper Jen had dropped. Then she returned to Matt's side to watch the kids find the next part of the hunt. "You sure the directions can still be seen scratched in the ice after all this time? They'll be mighty upset to get down there and not find anything."

He motioned with his head. "Watch."

She leaned closer so as not to be heard by others. "Have you seen Greg anywhere?"

"Nope. And I've been looking. You think he went out to eat with Steve and Emily?"

"Doubtful. They wanted a romantic evening alone before listening to all the noise of the kids opening their presents in the morning."

"So it's just yours and Jayne's gifts they'll get tonight?"

"If they can find them."

He laughed. "Oh come on. Knowing you, you made sure the directions were clear enough for a baby to follow."

She bumped him. "I'm not that easy. They have to work for the goods."

He pointed. "They're off to the third set of directions."

They all moved to the end of the porch to keep the kids in sight. Jayne gave Stephanie a hug.

"You did a great job on this hunt. This is the most excited I've seen them yet."

"Thank you, but they've loved every bit of this vacation, starting with the great rooms you decorated. I still don't know how you do it."

"I love it."

"It shows." She glanced at Matt. He was no longer watching the kids. "What's wrong?"

He shook his head. "A feeling. Did Greg see your list for the treasure map? Does he know all the locations?"

"Not that I know of, unless he went in my room without my knowledge."

Matt glanced at the kids one more time. "I'm going to go to the final stage. I just want to make sure nothing goes wrong. You did too great a job coming up with this idea."

"You need help?"

She could see his mind working. Finally he shook his head. "Best keep an eye on the kids. We'll join up again at the end."

"All right. See ya later."

Maybe that's when they'd get their chance for the serious

talk Matt had mentioned. Whenever it happened, she looked forward to some alone time with him.

"There they go." Luke had his arm around Jayne as she pointed at the kids. "Where to next?"

Jayne peeked at Stephanie. "The 'W' tree. You think they figured out that last verse in order to find that tree?"

"I hope so. I tried to make it as clear as possible. Plus Andy knows about the tree and I mentioned how the tree looked like a letter the other day. Hopefully, they'll remember."

Jayne grinned. "Matt's right. You made it easy on purpose."

She shrugged. "I can't help it. I want them to succeed."

As they watched, the kids did find the tree as well as the next three locations after that. Jayne smiled at Stephanie again as the children ran toward the barn.

"This one borders on mean, Steph. You know full well they're going to think their gifts are in that chest on the ship."

She laughed. "I know. But like the Magi stopping in Jerusalem and learning they still had farther to go, the kids will find the note inside the chest and learn they're not finished yet."

Jayne grinned. "Like I said. Mean."

Luke, Jayne, and Stephanie descended the steps of the porch and headed toward the place where the end of the hunt would take place. The kids only had one more stop after the chest before they reached their destination, and they all wanted to be there to see what happened. When someone yelled, they stopped and looked toward the barn.

Then they heard Jennifer's voice loud and clear. "No!"

The shout sent them running toward the barn as fast as they could.

Chapter 9

Luke was the first through the barn door with Jayne and Stephanie right behind. Stephanie moved around them for a better view. The three children stood on the ship with the lid to the chest open. They all looked down at them.

Jen stomped to the ship's rail. "Where's the next set of directions? The chest is empty."

Stephanie and Jayne blew out a breath and exchanged a look; then they hurried up the steps to see for themselves. Stephanie peeked inside. She'd put the instructions inside the chest herself. So where were they?

She shrugged at the kids. "I guess some other pirates got here before you. Lucky for you, I've got a copy of the directions." She dug into her pocket and tore out the missing verse from her sheet. "Here you go. Better hurry so the other pirates won't find the treasure before you."

Jen was the first to reach for the verse. "You're almost there. The treasure's near. But things aren't always as they appear. The three kings trailed a star to this place, in order to see their Savior's face."

Brandon stuck out his bottom lip. "We can't get to Bethlehem."

Andy hopped from one foot to the other. "No, but the manger scene's out in front of our house."

Once again, the kids were off as fast as they could run. The three adults tried to keep up. They came around the corner of the house to find the kids kneeling around the manger.

Stephanie groaned. "Man, I need a camera. That would make a great picture."

She spotted Matt standing at the panel waiting for the perfect moment to throw the switch. She gave him a smile and nod and received a thumbs-up.

The kids were moving, obviously looking for the final note. They glanced back at her. Stephanie's heart dropped. Were the directions missing again? She was about to join them when Andy gave a shout. He waved the paper in the air then handed it to Jennifer.

"The star was key back in Christ's day, and now you'll see it light your way."

Stephanie motioned to Matt. He lifted the switch and the bright beam of light rose into the sky from behind the head of the baby Jesus.

"Whoa!"

"Look at that!"

Brandon rose to his feet. "Oh man! It goes all the way up so you can't even see the end."

Their reaction was what Stephanie had hoped for. She had to admit, the sight was impressive, especially now that dusk was minutes away. Jayne moved to her side and gave her a hug.

"Very nice."

"Thanks."

Brandon dropped back to his knees. "What else does that paper say?"

As Jen started reading again, Stephanie motioned to Matt again, then waited for the reflector to move into place.

"Just track the beam and you will see a bounty of treasures for all you three."

Brandon scrunched his face. "Track the beam?"

They all looked up again and repeated their first reactions. Jayne and Stephanie laughed. All three kids stood as their eyes followed the beam of light from the baby's head, to the reflector several feet above them, and on to the large pile of straw mounded under a copse of trees.

"There's no treasure." Brandon scowled their direction. "I don't see no treasure."

Jayne took a step toward them with her hands out. "It's buried, hon. You have to dig for it."

Seconds after Jayne's words sank in, the kids raced to the straw and flung it everywhere. They squealed as packages were revealed. They didn't stop until the straw lay flat.

"Can we open them now?"

Jen's plaintive voice begged for a yes. Stephanie smiled and shook her head.

"Let's get them inside before the snow gets the paper all wet." She looked around. "And before it gets completely dark. I think opening them in front of a warm fire sounds best, don't you?"

The kids moaned but scooped up as many gifts as their small arms could carry. The adults gathered the rest and followed the kids inside. Matt fell in step beside Stephanie.

"That seemed to go well."

"It did. I think they had fun."

He smiled and winked. "What happened in the barn? I

wanted to run after you to make sure nothing had happened, but when I saw Luke with you, I stayed put to make sure nothing happened to the ending of the treasure hunt."

"The directions I'd put inside the chest were gone. The kids were upset."

"No doubt. What happened to it?"

"I have no idea. I put the paper in the chest myself."

They walked several seconds in silence. Then Matt stopped her by grasping her arm.

"Greg?"

She shrugged. "I don't know who else would have the chance or even want to try to ruin the game. I think maybe he wanted you to look bad again, like the first time."

Matt blew out a breath as he shook his head. "I don't figure this. How old is this guy?"

"Old enough to know better, which is the scary part of all this."

"Have you said anything to Steve and Emily? You think they know anything about Greg's odd behavior?"

"I don't know. They haven't spent a lot of time around him, but you can be sure we'll be having a talk when they get home."

He nodded. "Sounds like a good idea." He motioned to the kids. "You enjoy their fun. I'm going to see if I can find Greg. Maybe he can explain himself before this goes any further."

"Be careful."

"I will. Have fun. And let me know about your talk with the Tollivers."

Stephanie's eyes might have been on the kids as they

opened their presents, but her mind was on Matt and what he'd find.

❄

Matt headed straight for the parking lot. Greg's car was gone. He hadn't wasted any time running from trouble, even on Christmas Eve. Question was, would he be back? Matt returned inside and entered Greg's room. Shirts and pants hung in the closet. More clothes still sat inside the dresser. Either he was in too big a hurry to pack, or he planned on coming back.

Matt planned to watch him closely from now on. In the meantime, there was something he needed to do and was running out of time to get it done. The idea came to him the other day. Now he was convinced it needed to be done.

He went in search of Jayne and found her in the kitchen. "I've got an errand to run. I'll be back as soon as I can."

"And Greg?"

"Gone, but his clothes are still here. Tell Luke to keep an eye on everyone. Try to keep everyone together inside."

"All right. Thanks, Matt."

He wasted little time driving to his house and grabbing the needed items. Jayne would have anything else he might need. He didn't want to be away from the inn any longer than necessary.

Greg still hadn't returned when Matt arrived. Matt rushed to his room to get a new game put together. He didn't have much time, but if need be, he'd work all night.

With only a few hours of sleep, Matt rose the next morning and entered the kitchen with map in hand. "Merry Christmas."

Jayne eyed him for several moments. "Merry Christmas to you. You look tired. You play watchdog all night?"

Matt poured himself a cup of coffee. "Part of it. The rest was spent working."

She frowned. "On what? Your job for this reservation is almost over."

"I know. But what I was working on is personal, and I need your help on part of it."

"Oh? What do you need, Matt? You know I'll do almost anything for you."

He smiled. "Thanks, cousin." He slid the map across the counter. "First, I need you to put this in Steph's room for me. Then if the Tollivers need help with the kids, I need you to do that for Steph so she can go on her own treasure hunt."

Jayne's smile was slow in coming, then she beamed. "You gonna let me in on the game?"

He wiggled his brows. "You'll find out soon enough."

"Aw, now that's just wrong. You know I can't control my curiosity."

He waved over his shoulder as he left the kitchen, laughing as Jayne continued berating him and his inconsiderate attitude. The screeching and squealing coming from the Library Suite told him the Tolliver children were opening the gifts from their parents. Chances were, Stephanie wasn't in there with them, so where was she? Sleeping in?

Matt wandered to the parking lot. Greg was back. Was he in his room? Someone sneezed then blew their nose. Matt followed the sound to the porch facing the lake. Stephanie sat in one of the Adirondack chairs bundled in a blanket with a steaming coffee cup on the table next to her.

She tucked her handkerchief into the pocket of her coat and then cupped the coffee mug in her hands. He must have just missed her when he left the kitchen.

Nerves made his heart thump. He licked his lips and headed her way. She looked at him before he reached the steps.

"Hard to sneak up on someone when your boots squeak against the snow, isn't it?" She grinned at him and motioned to the chair next to her with her head. "Merry Christmas, Matt. Want to join me?"

"Merry Christmas." He climbed the steps and dropped onto the proffered chair. "Don't you think sipping coffee in front of a fireplace would be more appealing on a crisp morning like this?"

She took another sip from the mug. "Mmm. Maybe, but the view in there isn't nearly as good as here."

"But only as long as the hot coffee lasts?"

She laughed. "Exactly."

As she stared at the frozen lake, he stared at her. She was beautiful. And by all evidence, the beauty went all the way to her heart.

"What changed you, Steph?"

She turned to look at him, her eyes shimmering in the morning light. "What makes you think I've changed?"

"I don't think it. I know it. I've seen it. I've experienced it."

Stephanie turned back to the lake and he followed her gaze.

"I also experienced the other Stephanie, the one who always looked out for herself and put her best interests first."

"Goodness. She sounds awful. How did you put up with her?"

He laughed. "Oh, she wasn't *that* bad. She also had some good qualities. Likeable personality. Fun. You're still likeable and fun, but you're not the same girl I knew. Everyone else comes first now." He took a breath and looked at her. "So, what brought about the change?"

She took another sip of coffee, then set the mug aside. "Years ago, I remember someone telling me that we should take care of ourselves first, then others. At the time, I thought that sounded like wise living. Self-preservation." She blew out a breath and the steam rose above her head before disappearing. "Works great for animals, not so much for people."

"That's the way most of the world lives."

"Yeah. Shame, isn't it?"

"What changed your mind?"

"The Vicker family."

"Your ice cream employers?"

She smiled and he could almost feel the warmth and love she had for them emanate through the gap between them.

"They never preached at me. They just loved me and showed me what real life and living was like. They were the perfect example of real godly love and mercy." She took a deep breath. "I believed in God and that Jesus was His Son, but I only allowed that belief to go skin deep. Until I met the Vickers, that belief never reached my heart."

She turned to look at him. "This is the first Christmas that I've truly felt the real meaning. I mean, think of it, Matt. Think about how much love it took for Christ to leave His

Father's side to come to this world." She waved her hand through the air. "A world filled with pain, suffering, and so much selfishness. And He came as a baby so He could be an example of how we're to live before He sacrificed His life for us."

He could hear her throat growing thick. Tears would soon follow. But these would be good tears. He fought some of his own, but because of his own happiness. All his questions about the new Stephanie were answered.

"I'd like to meet the Vickers."

Her throat worked as she nodded and wiped at her eyes. "I have a two-week vacation coming up. I plan to visit them then, right after I spend some time with my parents and maybe get them attending church again."

He smiled. "I'm in need of a vacation, too." He shivered. "But only after we get inside and warm up." He stood and held out his hand to her. "How can you sit out in this cold? I haven't even seen you shiver."

She laughed and put her hand in his as she rose to her feet. "I'm warm from the inside out."

"Which explains your cold fingers."

She grabbed her mug as she followed him inside. "Will I see you later?"

"Count on it. I have a little work to do first, but the rest of the day is free until tonight."

And he couldn't wait to see the look on her face at the result of his so-called work.

Chapter 10

Stephanie returned to her room for some warmer socks. What she'd said to Matt about being warm on the inside was true, but her extremities were frozen. Despite the freezing temperatures, she wouldn't trade the time on the porch with Matt for anything, even if it meant fighting frostbite.

She stopped at the mirror to check her hair. A light brown sheet of paper sat on the dresser next to a small box. Her smile grew as she realized she was being sent on her own treasure hunt. She opened the box and discovered a compass. After taking a minute to put on her warm socks, she grabbed the map and compass and headed for the starting point.

From the manger of the nativity scene, the map said she needed to take fifty-eight paces to the northeast. As she held the compass in front of her, she counted off each step. At fifty-eight, she read the map and turned south for another forty-nine steps, then turned north for sixty.

She stopped then to blow on her hands. She wasn't quite halfway through the map's instructions. If she didn't hurry, she'd have frostbite for sure. Certain the map came from either the kids or Matt, she hoped they realized just how cold it was out here while they sat in their heated rooms.

After another blow on her hands, she read the map and started off to the east for forty-five paces. She ended up at the edge of the woods, putting her in the shade and even colder than before. She glanced at the map. At least the next set of paces sent her back toward the inn. She pulled her collar up higher and started counting. Before she reached three, she was grabbed from behind.

❄

Matt waited in the barn until he could stand it no longer and went in search of Jayne. She sat reading in front of the fireplace in the Abbott's Chamber.

"Did Steph get the map I made?"

Jayne gasped and jumped to her feet. "Oh Matt. I'm so sorry. I forgot. It's still in the kitchen."

Disappointment filled him but he'd never let Jayne know. She usually had her hands full with the guests. He shook his head.

"You're too young to be so forgetful, cousin."

She patted his arm as she rushed past. "It's not going to work, Matt. You can't make me feel better about dropping the ball."

He trailed behind her. "It's all right, Jayne. We'll just get started a little later than planned."

"I hope she's not in her room. Otherwise I don't know how I'll get it in there without being seen."

"Jayne."

She waved her hand at him. "I'll make it right. Just get ready."

Matt smiled and shook his head. He'd never get her calmed down until Stephanie found the map to her treasure. He headed back out into the cold to wait once again. Right before he reached the barn, an odd noise came from the woods. Almost like a screech but like none he'd ever heard before.

"Steph?"

Greg!

Matt raced toward the trees.

❄

Stephanie only managed one strangled scream before a hand was clamped over her mouth. She recognized the aftershave. She was so stupid not to realize Greg would try something like this.

As he pulled her backward, she yanked at his hand and finally freed her mouth.

"Stop this, Greg."

"You never gave me a chance. Now I'll make sure you do."

She tried to tangle her legs in his to slow him down. "Do you really think this is going to make me like you more?"

"If you'd have given me even a night of your time, it wouldn't have come to this." He tightened his arm around her neck. "Stop fighting me."

"I don't want to go anywhere with you."

He growled in her ear. "Don't make me hurt you, Steph."

"Well, you're going to have to because I'm not going with you."

She lifted her arm then shoved her elbow into Greg's ribs as hard as she could. He coughed and backed off a step. Before she could struggle harder and get free, his arms were ripped from her. She ran a few steps away before turning around.

Matt had Greg pinned to the ground by sitting on him.

Greg swung at him while trying to buck him off. Matt planted his fist in Greg's stomach, ending the fight as fast as it started. He yanked the scarf from around Greg's neck then turned him over and pulled Greg's arms behind his back, tying his wrists with the scarf. He stood and helped Greg to his feet then shoved him in the direction of the inn.

"You should have settled for a simple no, Greg. This stunt may land you in jail."

Stephanie didn't say a word. She didn't know what to think. She couldn't get her mind to slow down enough for a coherent thought. Matt stopped her and turned her to face him.

"Are you all right? He didn't hurt you, did he?"

She shook her head. "I'm fine. Just a little shook up."

He examined her eyes then nodded. "Okay. Let's get back."

Matt kept pushing Greg ahead of them, not allowing him any opportunity to attempt an escape. When they entered the house, Jayne ushered the kids into the kitchen. "Let's find a snack, shall we?"

Luke approached them. "What happened?"

"Greg tried to kidnap Steph. Find Steve and bring him into the office. We'll also need to call the police."

Luke nodded and pulled his phone from his pocket as he climbed the stairs to Steve's room. He entered the office minutes later with Steve and Emily on his heels.

"The police are on their way. I'll leave you to talk alone."

Steve headed right to Greg and leaned over him. "Have you been taking your medicine, Greg?"

Stephanie frowned and looked at Matt. "What medicine?"

Steve joined Emily on the loveseat. "Greg is borderline bipolar. He's not himself when he goes off his medicine."

Matt frowned. "And you didn't think it necessary to tell Stephanie? Didn't you notice his infatuation with her?"

Steve and Emily exchanged a look, then Steve shrugged. "We knew he liked her, but she never showed any interest. We figured that's as far as it went." Steve looked at Stephanie. "Did he hurt you?"

"No, but he did try to kidnap me just minutes ago. I also think he almost hurt Matt by tampering with the buckles on that swing. It could have been Jennifer or Brandon that got hurt if Matt hadn't ridden that swing first."

Steve's mouth dropped open and he scooted to the edge of his seat. "Is that true, Greg? Did you tamper with that swing?"

Greg lifted a shoulder. "Only a little. I thought if I could get him away from Steph, she'd give me a little more of her time."

Steve's hands curled into fists. "And it never crossed your mind that was wrong? You could have hurt my kids." He shook his head and faced Stephanie. "I'm sorry. I didn't know."

Luke tapped on the door frame before he entered. "The police are here."

Twenty minutes later, both Matt and Stephanie had given the police their statement. They led Greg away in handcuffs. Steve followed them to town in his own car. Matt pulled her into his arms.

"You look like you want to cry."

"I do. I'm torn with how to feel." She lifted a shoulder

and let it fall. "I told Steve and Emily that I was giving them a month's notice. I won't desert the kids during the holidays, but I don't think I can continue working for them."

He hugged her tighter and she had to admit the contact helped her feel better.

"Why don't you go on up to your room and get some rest?"

She nodded. Some time alone might do her some good. She didn't get far before Matt called her back.

"Ah, you're probably going to find a map in your room. You can trust that one."

She searched his eyes then smiled. "I thought the last one might be from you."

He winked. "That's what I get for trying to be original."

She smiled and couldn't resist kissing his cheek. "Thanks for rescuing me, Matt."

He bowed at the waist. "Aye, me lassie. Tis my pleasure. It's fun we be having from here on out."

"Arr. And yo ho ho. All is shipshape now, Captain. Or something like that."

He laughed and gave her a gentle push. "Go rest."

But once she saw his treasure map, she knew she couldn't sleep until she found the treasure waiting for her. As she headed back outdoors for another hunt, she reread the map written in Matt's scrawl.

"If a special treasure is what you seek, then this I say with tongue-in-cheek. Set sail to the place of pirate's appeal, and plant yer feet at the captain's wheel."

She grinned as she strolled across the yard toward the barn. It didn't matter what she found at the end of this map.

As far as she was concerned, her renewed friendship with Matt was the greatest treasure she'd received on this trip.

The barn door squeaked as she pulled it open. After what she'd just been through, the noise sent a shiver down her spine. The dark and dusty interior didn't help the creepy feeling. She stepped inside and climbed the stairs to the deck of the ship. After a quick look around to make sure she was alone, she crossed the deck and scaled the steps to the wheel.

She read the paper nailed to the wheel. "Give me a spin."

She smiled and turned the wheel. Something creaked above her. When she was sure nothing would fall on her, she kept turning, lowering a small chest. Once it settled on the floor, Stephanie left the wheel and knelt in front of the chest. She caressed it several moments while wondering about its contents. Unable to stand it any longer, she lifted the cover.

Nestled on top of hundreds of fake gold coins sat a very expensive camera. She lifted it from the bed of coins and held it close. It was the very camera she'd wanted two years ago. The same type of camera she planned to buy once she'd saved enough. She turned it around as she would to take a picture. Taped to the back was another slip of paper.

"Dig for more treasure."

Dig? Where? In the coins?

She ran her fingers through the plastic coins and found nothing. She tried again and again, going deeper each time. Finally, her fingertips landed on something smooth. She grasped what felt like a book and pulled it from the chest.

In her hands lay a photo album. She opened the cover. Matt's face looked back at her. It was her favorite of all she'd ever taken of him. His eyes and smile showed his love. Tears sprang to her eyes. She lifted the paper flap taped below his chin. The tears slid down her cheeks.

"I've never stopped loving you."

She turned as Matt's voice recited what she'd just read. He nodded to the album.

"Turn the page."

She tore her eyes from his face and did as told. The second page revealed another picture of Matt, but this one had a paper fist taped to it. She lifted the paper. She gasped and turned back to Matt. He closed the distance between them and helped her to her feet. He took the album from her and removed the engagement ring he'd taped to the page.

He held it out to her. "You accepted this from me once before. Will you accept it again?"

Unable to speak, she nodded. He smiled and slid the ring onto her finger. He motioned to the camera. "I'd planned on giving you that on our honeymoon two years ago."

"You kept it all this time?"

He shrugged. "I guess something inside me told me to keep it."

"I'm glad."

He took the camera from her hands and set it back in the treasure chest. Then he pulled her into his arms. "I love you, Steph."

"And I love you."

He leaned in for a kiss and held it for several seconds before pulling away.

She took a breath and smiled. "Blimey."

He laughed. "Aye. Yo ho, yo ho, an adventurer's life for thee."

She grinned at Matt's attempt to imitate the pirate's song. As she snuggled into the warmth of his embrace, she treasured all that had happened and pondered them in her heart, knowing life with Matt would most certainly be an adventure.

 Janelle Mowery has been writing for many years and signed her first publishing contract in 2006. She enjoys writing both contemporary and historical fiction as well as for children's ministries. She lives in Texas with her husband and two sons.

FIRST CHRISTMAS

By Darlene Franklin

Dedication

To my mother who taught me the joy of Christmas.
To Talia and all the other cats who have agreed to
share their lives with me throughout the years.
And most of all, to the Lord, who gave me
both Christmas and cats.

"For I know the plans I have for you,"
declares the Lord, "plans to prosper you and not to
harm you, plans to give you hope and a future."
JEREMIAH 29:11 NIV

Chapter 1

Waverly Coe peeked past the receptionist's desk at the people and patients in the waiting room. Doc Alec devoted Tuesday afternoons to small animals. His staff had scheduled shots for Mrs. Jamison's new Lab puppy and an operation to prevent young Robbie's Velvet from increasing the surplus population of cats in Bennington County. The doorbell rang and Waverly caught sight of a familiar angular face pushing a baby stroller. Was it that time of day already?

When the stroller came to a stop, Waverly heard smacking and whimpering sounds, accompanied by the yips of Mrs. P.'s dachshund. If Waverly didn't take immediate action, her baby Cinnamon would erupt in full-fledged cries.

Waverly went out to the waiting room. "Hi, Mrs. P. How's she been today?"

"She's been a doll, as always." Mrs. Paulson, Waverly's landlady, took care of the baby during the day.

Waverly bent over the stroller and looked at the auburn-haired infant, blue eyes scrunched together, chewing on the fist in her perfect bow-like mouth. What a marvel that God had allowed this miracle to come from her sin. "Hi, there, Miss Sunshine."

At the sound of her mother's voice, Cinnamon slowly swiveled her head until she found Waverly's face. She kicked, all arms and legs. Quickly Waverly unbuckled her and grabbed the diaper bag.

Mrs. Jamison lumbered to her feet and made a beeline for the baby. Goldie, her Lab puppy, also wanted to make the baby's acquaintance. "Isn't she precious? How old is she?"

"Two months yesterday. Excuse me, but I need to feed her before she tells the whole world she's hungry." The infant's whimper turned into a low cry as Waverly scurried into one of the exam rooms and shut the door.

Waverly settled Cinnamon into the crook of her arm and soon the baby was nursing happily, the cries settled into small burbles of contentment. Waverly brushed her fingers through her daughter's soft auburn hair, twirling it into a curl on top. A year ago she would have laughed at the picture of herself nursing a baby in one of Doc Alec's examination rooms. She would have insisted she'd be well into her junior year at the University of Vermont, looking forward to vet school after graduation.

Waverly had thought about staying in Burlington and returning to school in the spring. She'd hoped she and Cash would make things work, that they'd marry. But Cash had left her as soon as he found out about the baby, and Waverly decided to come home to Castlebury, at least for a while.

The decision hadn't come easily. Her father had retired from his vet practice—now Doc Alec's—and her parents had moved to Florida. Most of her high school friends had either gone on to college or were married themselves. She didn't fit in anywhere.

Except here. She shifted Cinnamon to the other side and closed her eyes. "Thank You, God, for Alec." In her private thoughts, she allowed herself to think of him as

"Alec," not as "Dr. Ross" or even the informal "Doc Alec." As a teen working at the clinic during school breaks, she had spent long hours mooning over the good-looking vet student interning with her father. Even then she dreamed of working with him someday. He had acted every bit the knight by offering her a job when it seemed most of Castlebury wanted to close their eyes to her situation.

While Cinnamon fed, Waverly's gaze wandered around the room, dedicated to Alec's feline patients. His gift to the owners of his patients—a calendar featuring local prized pets—hung on one wall. Mrs. P. had been delighted that her Misty had made the cut for next year's edition. A variety of toys designed to catch the eye of a cat lay jumbled in a basket in the corner. Every day Waverly disinfected them, but she didn't mind. Every possible need or desire of a cat made the room, if not a cat's favorite place, at least a little more tolerable.

Alec allowed Waverly to nurse Cinnamon as often as needed during office hours, and this was her favorite spot. She couldn't ask for a better boss.

Waverly held Cinnamon against her shoulder to burp her. She hummed a few bars of "Carol of the Bells." The song had stuck in her head after she'd heard it on the radio that morning. This would be Cinnamon's first Christmas. Waverly's heart fluttered at the thought. How significant Advent loomed now that she had a child of her own to teach about the baby born so long ago, God with us.

Someone knocked on the door. "It's me. Jenny." The receptionist interrupted. "I'm sorry to bother you but Doc asked for your help with young Robbie's cat. So as soon as you're finished. . ."

"I'm coming." She had dawdled longer than necessary. Cinnamon's eyes had closed and her chest rose and fell in a regular rhythm, sound asleep. Waverly lost track of time when she held her daughter. She kissed the top of her head and opened the door.

Alec stood at the next door, his hands cradling a snarling black adolescent cat as gently as she held Cinnamon. He smiled when he saw the two of them, a dark auburn curl falling over his forehead. "She gets sweeter every day." The cat Velvet hissed, and Alec laughed. "But you'd better get her out of here."

Mrs. P. had taken a seat in the waiting room, but she held a sheet of lime-green paper in her hand. When she saw Waverly, she grinned broadly. "All better now, is she?" She waved the page. "I was just reading how the Barncastle Inn is looking for local animals to be in this year's Christmas program. Why, they need a little bit of everything. Do you think they could use my Misty?" She clucked at the dachshund at her feet, who wagged her short tail and barked as she ran in circles.

"Waverly? Are you about ready?" Alec's voice called to her from the back of the office.

"We'll talk about it later, all right?" Waverly buckled Cinnamon into her stroller and kissed her one last time before heading to the operating room.

❄

Alec sucked the finger that Velvet had scratched to inform the stranger with the needle that she didn't appreciate the indignity fostered upon her body. Nothing was cuter in Alec's mind than a cat hunching its back and hissing at an opponent ten times its size. But if he didn't start the operation soon, they might have to wait another week. Seven more days when Velvet would seek a mate by any means available. Besides the problems with population control, the poor thing, at six months, was too young to bear a litter of kittens.

Through the door he glanced at Waverly kissing the top of her baby's head. She thought he was doing her a favor, giving her a job until she returned to school. The truth was, he didn't know what he would do when she left. The practice had kept him and Dr. Coe busy before his partner had retired, and Alec worked twice as hard to keep up with the demand now. Waverly grew up with animals, and she had completed training as a veterinary assistant along the way toward earning her degree in animal science. She'd make a fine vet some day, and he intended to make sure she had every opportunity.

She slipped into a fresh jacket and stopped by the sink to lather up her hands. "I got everything together for the operation earlier."

The radio played soft Christmas tunes while they worked. Waverly kept gentle hands on the cat, keeping her still as Alec gave her a sedative. She crooned over the cat much the same way she crooned to Cinnamon, and even the fiercest of animals responded to her. Alec made a minute incision in Velvet's shaved belly. "Have you decided about whether or not you're going back to school for the spring semester?"

Waverly's face scrunched. "I hate to put Cinnamon in day care so soon, but I know it'll be better for both of us in the long run after I finish my education. But then again, if I work until next fall, I'll be saving money for when I do go back." She peered over her mask, deep green eyes boring into his. "If I decide to stay home for a while longer, will I still have a job?"

"As long as you need one." Alec didn't speak for a while. *How do I ask this woman out?* It should be easy. No one would interrupt them here. Why was he such a coward? "Waverly. . ."

"I wonder if she feels cold, with all her fur shaved away." Waverly shivered. "At school, I saw a few cats that looked like feline hobos until their fur grew out after an operation."

"I guess I never thought about it."

She smiled at him while she continued stroking Velvet's head. "The less it irritates her, the less she'll lick it and maybe cause infection." She looked up at him. "I'm sorry, I interrupted you."

He gazed into her green eyes, all that was visible of her face over the mask she wore, watching them flicker and flow like grass in summertime. A man could lose himself in those eyes. "Would you do me the honor of going to dinner with me tomorrow night, after the rehearsal at the Barncastle?"

Her hand stopped moving down Velvet's back. "You mean, like on a date?"

"Yes, that's what I mean."

Her hand moved over Velvet's back again. "I. . .Yes. I will." He could see her smile in her eyes.

"Good." He turned his attention back to the cat. "Now let's finish up here."

A few minutes later, Waverly scooped Velvet up in her

arms. "I'll get her settled while she recovers." She paused by the door, and he opened it. "I should warn you. Mrs. P. thinks Misty would be 'perfect' for this year's Christmas programs up at the Barncastle."

He groaned. "Thanks for the warning." He removed his scrubs, washed, and went down the hall. From behind Jenny's desk, he heard telltale whimpers. "Don't tell me. Another litter of puppies needing homes?" He glanced down at the half a dozen squirming black-and-tan bodies. "Mrs. Overton's Schatzi again?"

Jenny nodded.

"Did you remind her we'll take care of that for her? For free?"

"She promised she'll be back. After the holidays."

Alec grunted. He picked one of the babies up and stared into his eyes. "You are adorable, aren't you?" He nestled the fellow next to his sister and went into the waiting room.

Young Robbie jumped to her feet. "Is Velvet all right?"

"She's fine. She just needs to rest here for the night and then she'll be ready to go home tomorrow." Alec saw Waverly at the door leading to the back. At her nod, he said, "Would you like to see her?"

"Can I?"

Alec nodded, and Robbie dashed after Waverly. He turned to follow.

"Dr. Ross?"

Mrs. P.

Alec made himself smile before he turned around. He let his gaze fall on the sleeping baby first. Aside from her red hair—more like Alec's own head than Waverly's strawberry blond locks—she was a miniature of her mother. He would like to hold her, if Mrs. P. wouldn't fuss at him for disturbing her sleep.

Only after he had sated himself with looking at the baby did he look at the dachshund leaping in the air at the sound of Mrs. P.'s voice. "I see that the Barncastle is looking for local animals to take part in their Christmas extravaganzas this year. And that you will be coordinating the efforts." She picked up Misty. "Misty is a natural at acting, aren't you, snookums?" She rubbed noses with the dog, who gave her face a long-tongued kiss.

Alec looked at the dog, wrapped in a bright red holiday sweater and internally shook his head. Mrs. P. inserted Misty into as many productions as she could in Castlebury and beyond, often with hilarious results. Only last spring the dog had romped through the set of *The Sound of Music* and pulled down the curtains. "You do realize they're re-creating the first Christmas this year, don't you?"

Mrs. C's smile widened even farther if possible. "Oh *yes*, of course." A wrinkle of doubt appeared in her brow. "Are you saying there weren't dogs around in Bethlehem? Why, I happen to know there have been dogs on the earth ever since Adam first named man's best friend." She winked. "And I can't imagine a heaven without dogs either. Though some people disagree with me."

Alec stuck his hands in the pockets of his lab coat while he searched for words. He could describe an animal's condition—although Waverly teased him that he used the biggest words he knew—but he felt more comfortable using his hands than words.

A whiff of a light gingery scent alerted him that Waverly had come into the room.

"Dr. Ross was just telling me that God didn't create dogs." Mrs. P.'s nose jutted in the air. "If you don't want my Misty in your production, just say so."

"I didn't say. . ." He turned in mute appeal to Waverly. No one had the guts to tell Mrs. P. no. At least not when it came to her doggie. And since Mrs. P. was little Cinnamon's caregiver and one of Waverly's strongest supporters, she wouldn't say boo against. . .

"It's just that this production will be outside, you see. And you know how sensitive Misty is to the cold." Waverly sank to one knee and went nose to nose with the dog. "And we wouldn't want to get sick, now would we?" Her voice took on a perfect imitation of Mrs. P.'s tone. She glanced up. "Especially since she couldn't wear her sweater. I'm pretty sure they didn't do that in the first century."

"I never thought of that." Mrs. P.'s eyes widened. "Maybe next year." Misty barked in response.

The baby stirred and cooed in her seat. Waverly kissed her forehead. "My Cinnamon's first Christmas will be one to remember here in our village, for sure."

Chapter 2

God didn't create dogs? Mrs. P. actually thought Doc said that?" Jayne Gilbert, owner of the Barncastle Inn with her husband Luke, laughed when Waverly told her the story about the confrontation at the vet's office when they got together in the evening. "If you talked Mrs. P. out of having Misty in the play, you must be a miracle worker."

"I only reminded her how miserable her poor baby would be in the cold." Waverly paused. "I'm a little scared about bringing Cinnamon out in this weather."

"Nonsense. This first weekend, the play is during the daytime. Plenty of sunshine."

"I only remember the one night we choose to do something outside during December, like caroling, always turns out to be the coldest night of the Christmas season." Waverly turned the row of the blanket she was crocheting for Jayne's baby, due in mid January. She joked it was too bad their little tax deduction wouldn't arrive until the New Year.

"You should call the baby Matthew."

Jayne arched an eyebrow at her.

"You know, because he was a tax collector?" Waverly shook her head. "Never mind. How are reservations coming for this year?"

Jayne's eyes lit up. "We're full up, and we've had people

asking if we're doing the same thing again next year. Be careful, Andy."

Jayne's stepson was rocking vigorously while holding Cinnamon. She lowered her voice. "He's so excited about having a brother, but I'm afraid he might be too rough." Speaking again in a normal voice, she said, "It's a lot easier preparing, since we chose the setting." She wagged her finger at Waverly. "I still wish you would agree to be Mary the first weekend. You'd be a natural."

Waverly blushed. "Absolutely not. Audra is perfect for the role."

The high schooler was young, well spoken, passionate—innocent. In that direction lay pain and doubt. Waverly knew God had forgiven her, but she still had to live with the consequences of her choices—no husband for her, no father for Cinnamon, future plans more difficult to realize. "I'll be just fine making sure the animals stay where they're supposed to."

"A partially sedated cat. A dog on a cleverly hidden leash. A cow munching on hay in a stall. Chicken clucking underfoot." Jayne smiled. "It would be easier not to bother with the pets, but. . ." Her face softened. "I believe someone as bighearted and as well-to-do as Elizabeth would let animals have a special place in her heart."

"That's why you're so good at this." Waverly grinned. "You fill in the rest of the story, like Paul Harvey always used to say."

"Then why do I feel like everything's spinning out of my control?" Jayne placed her hand to the small of her back. "I hope things will seem less hectic after little Matthew"—she flashed a smile at Waverly—"gets here." She gestured for Andy to bring Cinnamon to her. She held her close, burying her nose in the baby's hair and breathing deeply. "Nothing like the smell of a newborn."

"I bet Mary did that with Jesus," Waverly said.

Jayne opened her eyes and looked at her. "See, that's why *you* should play Mary. You would add those little touches."

Waverly groaned. "Not that again." Cinnamon rooted around on Jayne's shoulder, a sign for Waverly to start nursing her.

"So how has it been, going back to work?" This was Waverly's second week back after Cinnamon's birth.

"So-so." Waverly tilted her hand this way and that. "I can't complain. I love the animals, you know that, and Alec is so understanding."

"I see." Jayne grinned.

Waverly tugged the receiving blanket around Cinnamon's shoulders. "See what?"

"You said *Alec* is so understanding."

Waverly felt heat rising into her cheeks. "I meant Doc."

Jayne waved her finger in Waverly's face. "You won't get by with it that easily. You *said* Alec. I've never heard you call him by his first name before."

❄

"So I asked her out." Alec paused alongside Luke at the temporary stalls that Matthew Raynor, the carpenter, had built to accommodate the animals for Zechariah and Elizabeth's household for the Annunciation play.

"It's about time." Luke grinned at the young vet. They had become good friends in the three years since Luke had arrived at the Barncastle and convinced Jayne to marry him.

Alec didn't say anything. A puzzled look on his face, Luke asked, "Did she say no?"

Alec shook his head. "She accepted. But I keep wondering if it's too soon."

"Let's see." Luke bent over and checked the latch meant to keep sheep penned in. "When I met you, she was still in high school, and you thought it was too soon. And I agree with you there. This isn't Bible times, or even Amish country, where you can sweep a seventeen-year-old girl off her feet." He pulled a screwdriver out of his tool belt and tightened the hinge.

"Not to mention the fact her parents would have killed me." Alec kicked the side slats to test their strength.

"Then it was too soon after she graduated and went off to college, because you wanted her to have time to experience life on her own before being tied down."

"Hey, I was in school, too." But not dating, at least not seriously. Alec used his busy schedule as an excuse but the truth was his heart burned for a woman—hardly more than a girl, really—who was too young for him.

"Then it was too soon—or should I say too late?—when she started dating that kid at college and came home last Christmas all dreamy eyed. She was convinced she would be wearing an engagement ring this year."

Alec popped his right hand into the top slat so hard that his knuckles throbbed. He massaged the hurting member with his left hand.

Luke grinned at him, and then his expression sobered. "And then we learned she was pregnant and her boyfriend turned out to be a user and a loser. You're not holding that against her, are you?"

Alec shook his head so hard that his bangs fell into his eyes, obscuring his vision. "Of course not. But what"—his breath caught in his throat—"what if she can't forget him?" He sagged against the rails. "How do I know when she's ready to move on?"

"She said yes." Luke headed for the hay bales "I think that's your answer."

※

Once she arrived at the Inn, Waverly hesitated at the door to the building that would serve as the staging area for the annunciation. She had dallied too long, deciding what to wear. A nice skirt tempted her, but she dropped that idea when she considered her options. The problem was she still couldn't wear most of her old clothes. She needed a whole new wardrobe, but had no money to buy one. She settled for her favorite sweater, a deep green knit, and a pair of comfortable jeans with lambskin lined boots. Fortunately, she had an abundance of outfits for Cinnamon, at least until she outgrew the three-month size.

Alec probably didn't expect Waverly to bring the baby on their—she could hardly bring herself to say "date"—but she wasn't going to leave her precious baby at home, not after working all day. Besides, Cinnamon would get hungry before long. Her tiny stomach wanted filling every couple of hours.

Alec gestured for Waverly to join him on the hay bale closest to the action. Even dressed in everyday clothes of a beige sweater and off-white jeans, Audra looked otherworldly, the perfect person to portray Mary. The angel Gabriel appeared and Audra shrank back in fear. He reassured her. "Do not be afraid, Mary; you have found favor with God."

Waverly closed her eyes. Oh, how she wanted that for herself.

But then Audra's crystal clear voice spoke the words that reminded Waverly of how far she had fallen. "How will this be, since I am a virgin?"

Waves of regret flowed over Waverly, and she rocked Cinnamon in silent agony. Alec looked sidewise at her, as if the same questions arose in his mind, and the urge to cry almost overwhelmed her.

Cinnamon stirred, wanting to eat, providing Waverly an escape. "Excuse me." She gathered her things and found Jayne in the dressing room. "Do you mind if I nurse Cinnamon?"

"Go ahead."

Waverly clasped her child close to her breast. Did knowing she had done nothing wrong make Mary feel any better during the long months—years, probably—of censure over getting pregnant outside of wedlock? *Oh God, I know You have forgiven me. Help me to forgive myself.* Waverly pled for peace, not wanting her distress to disturb her little girl. *She's innocent of my sins, Father.* Every time she looked at the baby, she marveled that God would create something so beautiful out of something so wrong.

God brought peace, and by the time Cinnamon had finished, the cast was changing the set for the next scene, Mary's visit to her cousin Elizabeth. Waverly returned out front and laid Cinnamon in her seat. Waverly was tasked with keeping an eye out for Morris the cat, in case he misbehaved.

Watching the familiar Bible story come to life transfixed Waverly. Elizabeth rushed out the door. Her dog raced by her side and greeted Mary, wagging her tail, begging for attention. Mary paused, shocked to see the evidence of the growing life in her cousin's womb. Elizabeth exclaimed, "Who am I, that the mother of my Lord should visit me." Morris, the ginger tom, rubbed around Mary's legs in welcome, and she hesitated before saying her lines.

"My soul glorifies the Lord." Waverly spoke the next words out loud like a prompter, and light laughter broke out.

"I'm sorry. I'll try again." Audra edged away from Morris, but the cat persisted in rubbing his tail along her exposed ankles. She sneezed.

Waverly frowned. Did she need to get Morris away? Waverly glanced at Alec for direction, but he made no sign.

Audra started again. "My soul glorifies the Lord and my spirit rejoices in God my Savior." She rubbed her nose while Waverly silently added "from now on." Years ago she had memorized Mary's *Magnificat* as one of her favorite parts of the Christmas story. Morris's tail twitched in time with the words, striking Mary's robe with each beat, as if he was worshipping God along with Mary.

". . .Has done great things for me. . ." *Sneeze.*

". . .Generation to generation. . ." Instead of the look of adoration appropriate to the words, Audra's face looked bright red. Morris added a soft meow.

". . .Has lifted up the humble. . ." When Audra lifted her

arms to the heavens, her sleeve fell to her elbow. Huge red bumps appeared on her forearms.

"Stop!" Waverly called out at the same time as Alec. She dashed forward and grabbed Morris.

". . .Remembering to be merciful. . ." Audra forced the words out through puffed lips.

Alec helped Audra sit. "Do you have an epi with you?" Audra pointed to her purse and Alec had found it and plunged it into her skin before Waverly could move.

Waverly decided the most important thing she could do was to get the offending cat as far away from Audra as possible. "I need the keys."

Alec tossed them in her direction, and she managed to catch them while holding on to Morris. The tom blinked round yellow eyes in her direction and meowed, squirming. "Oh no you don't."

Jayne's mother opened the door for them, and Waverly went to the van to grab the cat carrier. The Barncastles had returned for an extended visit until after the birth of Jayne's baby.

When Morris saw what Waverly intended, he extended his claws and jumped out of her arms. If Mrs. Barncastle hadn't already closed the door to the theater, he might have headed back inside, where it was warm. Soft moonlight bathed the yard, but even in bright daylight a cat could find a dozen places to hide, some of them so small not even a mouse could fit in.

All they asked Waverly to do was take care of one measly cat, and she had already lost him. She grabbed a towel, determined not to get scratched this time. "Morris. Here, kitty, kitty." She clucked between her teeth.

Meow. Gravel skittered across the drive, near the tree guarding the entrance.

The door opened, and a square of bright light sparked highlights in Alec's red hair. "Let me help. Chase him toward me." He armed himself with a towel and stood near the van.

Waverly caught sight of a shadow dashing between trees and she ran toward it. Morris ran in the opposite direction, toward the main house. "We could just wait him out. Morris likes his creature comforts. He'll get tired of being cold and hungry." She stopped scanning for the cat. "How is Audra?"

"She should be okay. They're meeting the doctor at the hospital. She never told anyone about her allergies." He shook his head at the foolishness of it. "She never should have agreed to be around hay and animals."

Waverly's heart clenched, and she sent up a prayer for the young girl. If Alec hadn't been there. . .

"Here they come." Audra's mother bundled her into the car and they shot through the parking lot, spewing gravel in their wake.

"Join us for some hot cocoa?" Jayne stood in the doorway, rubbing her hands together, her face lined with worry. "We need to make some plans." Without waiting for an answer, she headed for the inn.

Waverly heard Cinnamon's soft cry and took a step forward. "What about Morris?"

"No worries." Alec ripped open a packet of feline delights and dropped them in his food bowl—which he left inside the cat carrier.

Conversation flowed around the kitchen table, between the various actors, the Gilberts, and other staff at the inn. Waverly focused on Cinnamon, who was passed from one willing lap to another. Cinnamon didn't fuss, but too much attention left her exhausted.

A cell phone rang, and Jayne flipped hers open. The table fell silent. "Uh-huh. Good. I'm glad to hear it. I understand." She closed it and looked at the gathered group. "Audra is fine. She's going to get a breathing treatment and then she'll probably go home."

Waverly released the breath she didn't know she had been holding. Somehow she felt responsible for what happened, for allowing the cat to rub all that dander onto the girl's sensitive skin.

"But we—the Barncastle—still have a problem. She can't come back. And our first guests are arriving this weekend."

Silence fell around the table. Then Lois, the pastor's wife chosen for the part of Elizabeth, asked, "Who will play the part of Mary on such short notice?"

Waverly felt Jayne's eyes upon her, willing her to volunteer, but she kept her mouth closed. Forgiven she might be, but she was still no fit role model to portray the mother of the Lord.

"I know someone who already knows every line."

Everyone's head turned in Alec's direction.

"I saw her saying them tonight, right along with Audra. She needs very little rehearsal, very little at all." He looked straight at Waverly. "What do you say?"

"That's the best idea I've heard tonight." Jayne grinned.

"But the costume"—Waverly grasped at straws—"won't fit."

"We could hide a camel inside that costume." Jayne brushed her worries aside. "We need you, Waverly. Please say you'll help."

Alec looked at her, his brown eyes sure and steady, and nodded. She drew in a deep breath. "I guess I don't have a choice."

Chapter 3

He has helped his servant Israel, remembering to be merciful to Abraham and his descendants forever, just as he promised our ancestors."

A holy hush fell over the crowd as Waverly finished reciting Mary's song. The spotlight on her face caught the look of wonder, of adoration, of trust and wholehearted commitment that Alec knew sprang as much from Waverly's heart as from any acting skill she possessed. He stood to his feet and brought his hands together, and soon everyone in the audience—standing room only, between inn guests as well as community members—joined him. Applause echoed as the actors returned to action, heading inside the house to prepare for the birth of John the Baptist three months later.

Next to him, Mrs. P. covered Cinnamon's ears and glared at him. "You'll wake her up with all that racket, and then where will Waverly be?" Alec just smiled. He felt too happy to take offense.

The night's performance ended with Zechariah's song after the birth of his son, John. Luke came to the front. "Please return tomorrow night, to learn what was happening back in Nazareth with Mary's lonely fiancé."

Alec remained seated and listened as bits of conversation drifted in his direction.

". . .Felt every word."

". . .Like it really was Mary."

Waverly would be pleased by the response to her performance.

Cold air whooshed in as people exited the building. Mrs. P. wrapped Cinnamon's blanket more tightly around her. "How did your date with Waverly go last night?"

Date? Alec wanted to slap his head. "Uh. . ."

"You didn't go?" Mrs. P. shook her head. "That poor girl paced the house for hours trying to decide what to wear, and you stood her up?" Her voice rose in pitch and volume like it had when she'd accused him of saying God didn't create dogs.

"Things got crazy."

"I know. Audra got sick and was whisked to the doctor. But then you drove Waverly home and you forgot about the date?" She wagged her finger under his nose. "I thought you were a better man than that, Dr. Alec Ross."

Heat flamed in his face, probably turning it a shade to match his hair. Across the floor, he saw Waverly talking with Jayne. A shy smile lightened her ordinarily serious face.

He might have messed up the date, but he didn't have to let tonight get away from him. "If you'll excuse me, I have an apology to make."

Mrs. P. nodded approvingly. He heard her say, "Tell her I'll take care of Cinnamon," as he trotted across the floor.

Waverly removed her head shawl, allowing the cool air from the side door to flow across her overheated skin. Aside from that, she was in no hurry to change out of the soft white robe she wore. As long as she had it on, she could imagine she was Mary, chosen by God to bear His Son. She could believe herself highly favored by God. As soon as she changed into her street clothes, into the sweatshirt that still stretched too tight across her pregnancy-expanded body with the small stain from Cinnamon's throw up on one shoulder, reality would crash in.

Well-wishers crowded around her. Mr. Eggers, her high school speech teacher, as tall and lanky as ever, wrung her hands between his own like an enthusiastic Bob Cratchit. "You were amazing, Waverly. I knew you were something special when you were in my class, but after this, you could find a career in Hollywood if you decide animal science isn't for you."

Waverly laughed self-consciously. *Right.* "I learned all about projecting my voice from you."

Next the guests from the Inn—Mr. and Mrs. Sanderson? Anderson? Sanders, that was it—came forward. "We've heard such wonderful things about the Barncastle. But you surpassed all our expectations."

Behind Mr. Sanders she spotted a cap of bright red hair. Alec. She fought to keep a smile on her face. Most of the guests left, and Jayne, Luke, and Andy walked in the direction of the main house, leaving her alone with Alec. He stared without speaking, his mouth opening and shutting without any sound coming through. He cleared his throat. "You were terrific tonight."

She smiled and half-turned her face away, knowing heat had gone to her cheeks. Over his shoulder she saw Mrs. P. waving at them.

"If you'll excuse me, I need to change and get on home."

She took a step in the direction of the dressing room.

"Please, give me a moment."

She paused.

"I'm a jerk for forgetting about dinner last night." With each word, the color in his cheeks increased. "If you can find it in your heart to forgive me, I'd like to make it up to you tonight."

Waverly blinked. She was sure he had changed his mind, and now he was asking her out again? *Fool me once, shame on you, fool me twice, shame on me.* "I need to go home with Cinnamon." She moved another step back.

"Mrs. P. said she'll take care of Cinnamon for a while longer. Please, Waverly. It's important to me."

Not again. I won't be fooled by a man's sweet talk, not even one as good as Doc. Over Alec's shoulder, she caught sight of Mrs. P. heading for the exit. Her landlady winked at her and opened the door.

"Mrs. P." Waverly ran after her, but the white robe tripped her feet and slowed her down. The older lady waved good-bye and whisked the stroller through the door before it closed behind her with a whoosh. *I'm going to give her a piece of my mind when I get home.*

"It looks like I need a ride home." Waverly's voice sounded as thin as poster board even to her own ears.

"Happy to oblige. And Joe's Java is right on the way home." Alec grinned. "Eggnog latte sounds pretty good about now. With a snickerdoodle cookie?"

He remembered her favorite cookie. A small piece of Waverly's heart warmed at the thoughtfulness. "Very well."

✳

Alec had rarely seen Waverly so radiant, as if she carried part of Mary inside her. He pulled out a chair for her in front of the stone fireplace that drew people to Joe's Java on cold winter days.

They each had a large cup of eggnog latte in front of them. Waverly sprinkled a dash of cinnamon into the foam on top. He wondered if her fondness for the spice had influenced her choice of her baby's name. The shop sold cookies at half price at this time of night, so he'd bought four. Waverly broke off a piece of hers and dunked it in the latte before eating it. "Delicious. Even better than chocolate chip." She devoured the cookie. "I'm ravenous. I didn't know acting could work up such an appetite."

"Do you want to get a sandwich?" Alec rose halfway out of his chair.

Waverly narrowed her eyes, considering. "Sure. One of their turkey-and-cranberry specials."

"Be right back." He added a bag of chips and a small fruit cup. From what he knew of Waverly, he doubted she'd eaten much all day. At least that was how she handled the stress of finals back in high school.

Her eyes widened a bit at the several items he set in front of her but she didn't object. She bit into the sandwich and closed her eyes in appreciation. "They had nothing like this at school."

"I know what you mean. There's nothing like coming home." He paused and took a sip of his latte. "But even coming home wasn't the same for me after you left for school

295

yourself. I always felt like something was missing."

Color flared in her cheeks, and when she didn't speak, he wondered if he had said too much. She raised her eyes to his. "I enjoyed seeing you when I came home during breaks, too. I know Dad was glad to have you join the practice."

"I'm only holding down the fort until the next Dr. Coe is ready to practice medicine." Dreams—that's what he saw in Waverly's face tonight. A dreamy look that lately had disappeared, replaced by resignation. If only he could help rekindle those aspirations. "You were terrific tonight, you know."

"I knew the lines, like you said." She felt uncomfortable with his praise. She always did.

"There's more to a play than saying the lines. You had a—presence—on the stage. It was like hearing Mary herself."

"I'm no Mary." Some of the dreamy look fled Waverly's face, and Alec wanted to restore it.

"God only created one Mary. And He only created one Waverly. That's all He wants."

"Yeah, but I've already messed up whatever perfect plan He had for me. I know God has forgiven me, but I can't get back what might have been."

If Alec knew a way to ease Waverly's shame over having a baby out of wedlock, he'd do it. He'd pound it out and iron it smooth or give her a magic potion. Instead, he offered his only gift—his words, his heart. "But don't you see, God redeems even the times we stray. Like tonight. I don't think you would have been nearly so good playing the part of Mary if you weren't a mother yourself."

She looked at him as if he were crazy. She pulled the top

of the potato chip bag apart and crunched on a chip. "Audra would have been better."

The conversation had come full circle, and Alec let the subject drop. Waverly finished her food and checked her watch. "It's getting late. Cinnamon will be getting hungry soon." Her laughter hovered just this side of brittle, and she appeared to hear it. "But this has been nice. Thanks for taking me out."

"Do you have time for a walk around the town square?"

She hesitated and then nodded.

They strolled down the street, their breath forming smoke rings in the cold air. The temperature hovered right around freezing. The sky was crystal clear, the stars creating a laser beam picture in the heavens. "On a night like this, I can imagine what the star of Bethlehem looked like."

Waverly gazed upward with him. "Me, too." The trees on the town common all had white lights, enhancing the effect of the stars overhead.

"And I imagine Mary and Joseph stared at the sky on their trip to Bethlehem. When they lay down at night, you know. And thought how big God was, and how small they were, and wondered why God had chosen them."

"Maybe Mary even felt as unworthy as I do, although I'm only pretending to be her. She seems to accept it, without question. 'May Your word to me be fulfilled.'" Waverly sighed. "Her faith astounds me and inspires me at the same time." She looked down the street, in the direction of the apartments where she lived. "Faith. That's Cinnamon's middle name, you know."

"That's beautiful," Alec said.

They sat on a bench under the trees and tipped their heads back to look at the panoply of the heavens overhead. It felt like the most natural thing in the world for Alec to rest Waverly's head on his shoulder and put his arm around her, drawing her close. Her lips hovered oh-so-close, but he wouldn't sample them. Not so soon. He hoped that faith, and patience, would win the day in the end.

After a while, they made their way back to Alec's truck and he drove her the short distance to the apartment she rented over Mrs. P.'s garage.

"I had a wonderful time tonight, Alec." Waverly rested her hand on the door handle.

"Maybe we can do it again sometime."

She smiled in response. "See you at the office in the morning." Then she unlocked the door and disappeared into the house.

❄

On most Saturday afternoons, Alec enjoyed a bit of a breather, unless one of his patients had an emergency. But he arrived at the clinic only five minutes early—already late, according to his usual practice—and a steady stream of patients arrived until 11:59, guaranteeing he wouldn't leave until well after noon.

"This is the last one." Waverly brought in a rabbit. "I think the problem is she's pregnant and her owner doesn't know she's about to become a grandmother." Laughter lit her eyes. "Do you mind if I lock up and leave? I was hoping to get some Christmas shopping done before the program tonight."

"Go ahead." Alec had hoped for a few minutes of quiet

chat with Waverly, but the morning onslaught had made that impossible. Transforming the stage from Elizabeth's home to Joseph's carpenter shop would occupy his afternoon. But he could look forward to seeing Waverly again that night.

After working on the set, Alec whipped home long enough for a bowl of hearty beef stew before returning for the evening's performance. Today's order of animals included a couple of chickens and a dog that traipsed everywhere under Joseph's feet. The play didn't really call for two animal handlers, but Alec and Waverly's supposed expertise allowed them to watch for free. Waverly arrived about fifteen minutes ahead of time and they looked across the audience.

"There's a lot of people here." Waverly squinted against the bright lights overhead.

"About the same as last night."

"The President of the United States could have been here last night, and I wouldn't have noticed, that's how nervous I was. I see a lot of town people."

"While the guests at the inn have the best seats." He pointed to the comfy chairs spread along the front.

"What's on the table?" She squinted.

"Fruit. Nuts. Trying to keep to the first-century theme." They pulled their heads back into the dressing room and shut the door.

"Hmm. That explains the sorbet Jayne served last week. They say Emperor Nero enjoyed a dish of something like ice cream in his day. Elizabeth and Zechariah *might* have been rich enough to indulge in it."

The houselights blinked twice, and after a few minutes,

they dimmed and the waiting crowd hushed. The curtain rose, and from their spot in the wings, Alec and Waverly could see Joseph at work in his shop.

The actor captured Joseph's dilemma with all its nuances. Alec saw his compassion, felt his perplexity and betrayal. His fiancée, pregnant and unmarried—a sin punishable by death.

His dilemma echoed with Alec, except all Joseph's uncertainty vanished with the angel's message. *Take Mary as your wife. The baby is God's Son.*

How could Joseph accept such an impossible task? Raise God's Son? The Messiah? No wonder the angel said, "Don't be afraid."

Waverly watched, the shadows from the stage lighting playing with her features. "Immanuel. God with us." She repeated the prophet's promise to herself.

Could Alec be as brave, as selfless, as Joseph? Raise a child not of his body as his own?

Don't be afraid. God's still, small voice repeated the angel's words.

Chapter 4

An entire flock of sheep? Won't two or three do?" Waverly switched her glare from Jayne to Alec. "And *we* have to make sure nothing happens to them?"

Jayne only arched her eyebrows. "You must know Luke's words. They were keeping watch over their *flocks* by night."

"I didn't know the interpretation was going to be so literal. Besides, a flock is anything more than two animals. Where are you going to put them all on the set?"

Alec turned to Jayne and shrugged. "*You* explain."

"We're doing this part of the play *al fresco*. Outside."

"What? In Vermont? In December?"

"But the weather has been mild these past few days, and the forecast says it shouldn't turn cold until Sunday at the earliest. And the moon will be almost full. Perfect conditions."

But how would they do the angel choir? *Not my problem.* "Even worse. How can we keep the sheep from wandering?"

"Waverly." When Alec said her name like that, like warm maple syrup, she melted like butter. "I, um, volunteered us to be the lead shepherds."

Waverly sank onto her chair. "And who is assisting us?" She didn't think she wanted to hear the answer.

"Our guests. Who else?" Jayne grinned.

"I guess Mrs. P. can keep Cinnamon for the night. Unless she thinks Misty would make a good sheepdog."

"No way. My folks raise sheep, so our collie will be coming with the flock. And I might even convince my parents to serve as shepherds. They've done it in enough church plays. How bad can it be? We get to sit around a fire and listen to angels sing." Alec grinned, and Waverly decided it might be fun after all.

How bad can it be. Alec's words taunted Waverly when they arrived at the Rosses' farm the next day. This was worse than a cowboy trying to move his doggies along. At least then the horse provided the herder some protection from the crush of the animals.

"Just let them know you mean business." Alec aimed another animal through the chute onto the waiting truck bed.

Waverly didn't have a problem cornering an individual animal, but she'd never tried to manage an entire group at once. That lamb looked harmless enough. She went after him with bangers, urging him toward the chute. The baby complied until he heard his mother's bleating. He ran straight toward her, knocking Waverly to the ground.

When Waverly tried to stand, the ewe bumped into her, paying her back for disturbing her baby. "Ow!" Waverly rubbed her elbow.

"Come on, Lucy." Alec steered the ewe away and she trotted behind him like one of Hamelin's rats, her lamb in her wake. He returned and extended a hand to help Waverly to her feet. "You gotta get the mothers first; then the lambs will follow." He took a step back and looked at her, dirt and other unmentionable substances spattered from her boots to her hips and dripping from her hair. "It gets easier, with practice."

"Fat lot of help I'm going to be, if one of these guys decides to make a break for it tomorrow."

"Laddie will keep them in line. Won't you, boy?"

At the sound of his name, a handsome collie ran to Alec and barked.

"Laddie?"

"As close as we could get to Lassie for a boy dog."

"Weren't most of the Lassie actors male?"

"We can't all be Waverly and Cinnamon." He winked.

Mr. Ross, Alec's father, chased the last of the sheep onto the truck and shut the tailgate behind them. "That's that." He caught sight of Waverly. "Come on back to the house for a spot of cleaning up."

"I didn't bring anything. . ."

"Not to worry. Doreen will fix you up."

So Waverly was going to visit in the home of Alec's parents looking her spectacular worst. She stared down at her boots and lifted her foot as high as she could until it finally made a plopping sound and released from the— well, "mud" would be a euphemism for the muck of sheep droppings mixed with snow and mud. She shivered, and the prospect of drying out by a warm fire appealed to her.

Alec's mother, Doreen, met them by the back door. "So good to see you again, dear." She acted as if people arrived at her door covered in mud all the time, but then again, perhaps they did. She hung Waverly's coat on a peg and took her boots before leading her upstairs to the shower.

Doreen had turned on the space heater in the bathroom earlier so the room was steamy warm when Waverly climbed into the shower. The warm water cascaded over her body, releasing some of the kinks she'd developed when she'd fallen down. Someone knocked at the door. "It's just me, dear. I've laid out a robe you can use while we wash your clothes."

"Thanks," Waverly called over the splash of water. She stayed in the shower until the hot water turned cool. The robe Doreen had laid out for her was made for Christmas, a plush green velour with red poinsettias up and down both sides of the center zipper. She combed her hair into a ponytail and joined the others in the living room.

The Rosses' home hadn't changed much since the last time she had been there, the summer before she left for college. A picture of Alec at his graduation from vet school took pride of place among the family pictures, next to a portrait of him with Laddie. He looked impossibly handsome and serious. All the things that had drawn her to him back when she was a gawky kid in junior high, and he came into her father's office the first time to work his summers between semesters at college.

Oh, Dad. Waverly still missed him and his wisdom. But he and her mom had sold the business to Alec, with a clause allowing her to join the practice in the future if she so chose. Her mother's worsening arthritis had mandated an early retirement to a warmer climate. Waverly had thought about heading to Florida when she discovered she was pregnant, but when Alec offered her a job for the summer, and then extended it into the fall, she found she wanted to come back home to Castlebury.

Waverly took the chair closest to the fireplace and slipped her feet out of the fluffy slippers and wiggled her toes on the warm hearth. Alec appeared through the doorway to the kitchen, two steaming mugs in his hands. "I fixed us some hot cocoa."

She peered into the cup, and spotted a handful of miniature marshmallows floating on the surface, with cinnamon sprinkled on top. "My favorite." She lifted it to her mouth and took a sip. "I thought you'd be gone with the sheep. Sorry about the delay."

"The sheep aren't going anywhere without me." Alec grinned but then his expression sobered. "I'm the one who should be apologizing. I should have asked you before I agreed to us taking part in the play this weekend. You don't have to if you don't want to."

"You're the boss."

"I mean it." Alec sat down across the fireplace from her.

Waverly sipped her hot chocolate, her tongue finding one of the miniature marshmallows. "I'll do it. It can't be any worse than today."

"That's the spirit."

First I'm roped into playing Mary. Now the shepherds. What next?

❄

What Waverly didn't realize, Alec thought, was that he could almost thank the sheep for giving him an excuse to spend extra time with her. Fresh from the shower, her hair shimmering a pale strawberry gold, the green of the robe bringing out the color of her eyes. *She should have a robe like*

305

that. But although his mother would be happy to give it away, it wouldn't be appropriate for him to give nightwear to a female employee.

"Here you are, dear." His mother appeared through the door with Waverly's clothes, warm from the dryer. "All ready for you. Are you all dried out?"

"She'd like a second cup of cocoa." Alec stood to his feet. He liked seeing her there, in his parents' house, and wanted to delay their departure.

"Don't worry, I'll get it." His mother left and returned a few minutes later with a tray holding three cups of cocoa and a plate of frosted sugar cookies.

"Sorry it's not snickerdoodles," Alec said.

Waverly bit into one of the cookies. "Frosted sugar cookies run a close second. I always had fun decorating cookies at Christmastime when I was a kid. I thought about doing it this year, but Cinnamon's a bit too young to take part." She giggled.

"How is that darling baby doing? She's what, two months old?" Alec's mother settled on the couch. "Is she turning over yet?"

"Oh, yes. Just yesterday. And she's got her first tooth. I felt it last night."

"Oh my. Alec didn't get his first tooth until he was almost five months old. A late bloomer."

Alec grinned, baring his teeth. "Not to worry. I have a full set now."

The two women swapped baby stories. Alec learned a bit more about his infancy than he cared to, but he enjoyed watching them interact. *Mom would like to have another woman in the family*, he realized

"Do you have any plans for Christmas, Waverly?" His mother held her cocoa mug by the handle, her right pinkie extended.

"Mrs. P. and I are going to keep each other company." She shrugged.

Alec knew what his mother would say before she opened her mouth. She needed no encouragement.

"Join us here, then. It must be hard on Mrs. P., this first Christmas without her husband."

"I couldn't impose." Waverly shrank back into the seat.

"Nonsense. You'd be doing us the honor, allowing us to celebrate Cinnamon's first Christmas with you."

Waverly looked at Alec as if seeking his permission, and he nodded.

"I'll ask Mrs. P., but if you're sure—"

"I'm sure."

Take Mary as your wife. The angel's words to Joseph ran through Alec's mind.

If only Waverly was willing.

❄

"Waverly, let me introduce you to our guests, Greg and Karla Andrews, and their children, Lexie and Marcus. They'll be your undershepherds for the evening."

Waverly studied the family. The Andrews had to come from money to afford a weekend at the Barncastle, but they looked pleasantly down-to-earth.

"When we heard what y'all were doing for Christmas this year, why, I told Greg we just had to come." Karla beamed.

"We wanted to see y'all Yankees handle sheep. I do a little ranchin' myself, down Texas way."

Waverly could guess how "little" their ranch might be—not—but she couldn't help liking the couple. "Then you should feel right at home tonight." And with experienced animal handlers, she would have less reason to worry about stray animals.

"Yup. Just a humble shepherd out mindin' the sheep under the starlit skies. 'Cept I figure Bethlehem was a might warmer than Vermont." Greg winked at her, and she grinned in return.

"I'll see you when it's time to start the show, then. I'd better go out and help Dr. Ross with the sheep."

"That doctor, he's a fine young man. If I was younger and not married to the love of my life, I might go after him myself." Karla flashed her diamond-studded wedding finger in front of Waverly. "Get out there and keep him company, before he gets too lonesome."

Waverly laughed. "I will." She pulled a lightweight sweater over her shirt and jeans, then added the shepherd's robe and headdress over it all. The long robe hid her wool stocking–covered feet and lambskin boots, which those first-century shepherds didn't wear. The weather might be mild for December in Vermont, but it still turned downright cold after the sun went down.

Alec was already among the animals, Laddie at his heels, his father walking beside him with a shepherd's crook on his arm. Hmm, when did people start developing different breeds of dogs, collies in particular? Waverly decided it didn't matter. The shepherds on the ancient Judean hillside probably had a dog to help with the sheep.

The sheep ignored her as she picked her way over the rocks in the field. As she drew near, she heard Alec saying, "testing, testing" into a miniscule earpiece.

"I hear you loud and clear." She waved to him from the edge of the field. At least this week she had no speaking part. She passed the rows of seats and bun warmers prepared for the audience at tonight's show. Jayne also arranged for families to spread blankets and watch that way, if anyone wanted to chance the cold earth. Children did better where they could move around a little. Before the show, Doreen would run a petting stall, where curious children could stop by and touch a lamb firsthand.

She reached the spot where Alec and his father waited. "All ready for your big debut?"

Alec had been chosen to say the "Let's go into Bethlehem" line. Jayne had asked Greg first, but he had demurred, saying no one would mistake his Texas drawl for a temple shepherd. Not that they sounded like a New Englander either, but. . .

Alec's look spoke volumes. He dreaded that single moment more than the rest of the season, all three weeks put together. And to think he had insisted Waverly take a major role in last weekend's production.

Chattering voices announced the arrival of Karla and Greg, nondescript in their matching shepherd's costumes.

Showtime.

❄

"For unto you is born this day in the city of David a Savior, which is Christ, the Lord."

Waverly heard the angel say the words, and all her worries

about possible mechanical difficulties and misbehaving sheep disappeared. She felt like one of the shepherds hearing the words for the first time, or as close as anyone could over two millennia later.

"Glory to God in the highest! Peace on earth."

Waverly wanted to jump up and down and sing the "Hallelujah Chorus." *This* was what Christmas was all about, the birth of the Savior. She wanted to make sure she taught Cinnamon the truth, starting this year.

Chapter 5

Sheep date number two, Alec thought on Saturday night, as once again he and the other shepherds donned their costumes. He only had eyes for one special shepherd, whose baby had been chosen to play the infant Jesus in the manger.

Back on Thursday night, the Barncastle had presented the scenes of Mary and Joseph's arrival in Bethlehem, their fruitless search for room at the inn, and the arrival of the baby. Aside from showing the actress how to ride on a donkey—no more comfortable for her than it must have been for Mary, after all, just as bumpy and uneven—and supplying animals for the barn, he'd had a quiet night. Last night he'd survived his first words on stage. Tonight they'd all be cooing at the baby, but no mics for the shepherds. He could relax.

Instead of Friday's flock, the shepherds brought one apiece with them, gifts for the baby Jesus. A lock of Waverly's hair escaped from her headdress, and he adjusted it for her. "Not sure if any of the shepherds had long strawberry blond hair."

"I'm glad this is the last time I have to wear this costume." She shrugged uncomfortably. "It will be hot inside the stable. I'm glad it's heated, for Cinnamon's sake, but I'll be sweating up a storm." She stopped. "What a silly thing to worry about, when you think about how hard it must have been for Mary and Joseph."

"It's okay." He longed to reach out again, this time to caress her face, but didn't dare. "It's almost time for our grand entrance."

"'Come, they told me. Parum pum pum pum.'" She sang the familiar tune. "I heard that drummer boy song on the radio this afternoon and can't get it out of my head."

"Want me to fetch a drum for you? That can be arranged."

She fake-jabbed him in the ribs. "Like that's in the Bible. But I love the sentiment."

"We all do. That's why the song gets played every Christmas. But us, we'll just have to settle for a gift of sheep."

Karla and Greg joined them in the dressing room. "If y'all don't mind, I'm not going to try to kneel at the manger. I don't get up and down so good anymore." Karla waved a fan in front of her face. "Is it hot in here, or am I having a hot flash?"

They all laughed, and the auditorium lights dimmed. After a bit of a scuffle, they led a handful of bleating animals through the side door. The actress now playing Mary held Cinnamon in her arms, while Joseph hovered protectively behind her. Waverly's baby had never looked so serene or sweet, and Alec wanted to take Joseph's place as their protector. One of the sheep trotted toward the side rail, her lamb trailing behind, and Alec guided them back to the manger. Everyone held the baby and exclaimed with plenty of praise-Gods, amens, and hallelujahs. The birth of a baby always heralded joy, but this baby, this night—the celebration would last for eternity.

When the time came for the shepherds to leave, Alec felt like it was the most natural thing in the world to run down the aisles shouting, "An angel told us! The Messiah is born! Come to Bethlehem and see!"

Out of the corner of his eye he saw Waverly, his father, and the Andrewses doing the same thing in other aisles.

They congregated behind the audience in time to hear Mary's final words. "Everything that has happened on this night of nights is a treasure. I will never forget."

Nor will I. Alec clapped along with the audience, celebrating the God of the miracle of Christmas.

The door closed behind them on the final performance of the weekend, and Christmas was only three days away.

❄

Cinnamon lay in her baby seat, her bright eyes following the sound of her mother's voice. Waverly had spent the night in the kitchen, fixing a simple supper of chili and cornbread followed by a baking extravaganza.

The whole time, Waverly sang along with the radio. The station played Christmas music with no commercial interruptions for thirty-six hours, from Christmas Eve throughout Christmas Day. Cinnamon had fussed once for a dirty diaper and again because she was hungry, but she seemed as content as her mother to welcome in the birthday of the Savior with music and food.

After baking cookies and rolling date nut balls, Waverly tackled the most important project of the night: Jesus' birthday cake.

"Maybe I should have used the Christmas tree pan. It

would have been easier."

Cinnamon gurgled.

"What? You disagree? You're probably right. Christmas trees didn't come along until years after Jesus was born."

The cake, a treasure chest recipe chock-full of fruits and spices worthy of the Magi, had cooked perfectly in the rectangular pan. The cream cheese frosting, compliments of a handy can, spread easily across the top. She had used a special tip to scallop the edges with red frosting. She wanted to add a blue star, one with six points and a long tail, but the hands that handled a scalpel with confidence trembled when she practiced the star.

Someone knocked at the door—Mrs. P. "I saw you were still up. And how is the little munchkin?" She leaned over Cinnamon, who wiggled and smiled at her. She handed Waverly a wrapped dish. "These are for you."

"Thanks." Waverly laid down the tube of frosting and took the plate. Even without removing the wrappings, Waverly could smell the tantalizing aroma of cinnamon and ginger. "You must take some of mine with you as well. Do you have any hints on how to get a star on the cake?"

"Do you have a stencil?" Mrs. P. peered around the table searching for one.

"No."

"Well, that's the solution. Lay a waxed paper stencil over the cake. It will catch any spills and leave you with a perfect star." She dug through the cabinets and pulled out a roll of waxed paper.

Fifteen minutes later, Waverly had finished. She sank into her rocking chair with one of Mrs. P.'s gingerbread men while she nursed Cinnamon and visited with her landlady. The phone rang—her parents, calling to wish her a Merry Christmas Eve—and Mrs. P. excused herself.

"One last thing," Waverly told Cinnamon after she got off the phone. "We have to hang your stocking so Santa will have a place to put your Christmas presents." She picked up the darling pink-and-white quilted stocking she had found, embroidered with "Baby's 1st Christmas."

Cinnamon slumped against her shoulder, fast asleep. Waverly kissed her softly, laid her in her crib, and pulled her blanket over her. Once again the enormity of the task in front of her—making sure her daughter met the Christ of Christmas, every December and all the days in between—loomed in front of her. How much better it would be if Cinnamon had two parents, sharing the job, as God intended.

Waverly shook herself. No use wishing for what wasn't going to happen. "God, with You on my team, I can't fail." She turned on the nightlight and left the room, adding a stuffed mouse into the pink stocking before turning in for the night.

Her mind strayed to last year. Her mom and dad had stayed in Castlebury for Christmas, but had already packed to move. They seemed pleased that Waverly had "found someone," as her mother so quaintly put it, glad Waverly wouldn't be all alone this year.

No one suspected her special someone would desert her. No, Waverly wasn't alone this Christmas, but a child wasn't the companion anyone had expected. Would she ever have someone again? How old would Cinnamon be? How many

Christmases and birthdays would pass before—if—that happened? Alec's face swam in front of hers, and she blinked back the tears that threatened. He treated her kindly, as one might a younger sister. Nothing more.

❄

Alec might not be a child any longer, but he still woke up at farmers'—and vets'—hours on Christmas morning. Well before daybreak, as excited as a six-year-old about the day ahead. He took his time dressing, wanting to look his very best for their guests. His favorite Vermont sweatshirt, green mountains in the background with gangly moose and stately deer munching on grass peeking through a covering of snow, looked well with his ruddy coloring. He lingered in the bathroom, making sure every hair was neatly groomed.

"You almost done in there?" His father's voice boomed through the door. "You're taking as long as a girl."

"Just a minute." Alec tilted his head each way and laid down his razor. He couldn't change his basic looks. He was who he was, for better or for worse. He splashed on aftershave, one he liked that reminded him of pine woods in spring, and opened the door.

"About time." His father squeezed past him into the bathroom, and Alec went downstairs to the kitchen where he could smell cinnamon rolls baking in the oven. His mother hummed Christmas carols to herself while she washed dishes in the sink.

Alec turned on the oven light.

"They won't be ready for another ten minutes, so no use peeking." His mom handed him a dish towel. A slow smile spread across her face. "Don't you look fine." She leaned forward and hugged him. "Smell fine, too."

He dried a measuring cup and put it back on the shelf with the flour without commenting.

"Couldn't have anything to do with our guests today, could it?" Her eyes twinkled as she handed him a coffee mug.

His neck tickled under his collar, but he shrugged it off. "Can't a guy get dressed up for a holiday?"

She raised her eyebrows. "Most men I know use it as an excuse to dress down. It's like pulling hen's teeth to get them to look presentable." She looked at him again. "Did your father notice?"

Alec shook his head.

She winked. "Don't worry. Your secret is safe with me." She ran rinse water over a handful of silverware before standing it upright in the cup at the corner of the dish rack. "But don't keep it a secret from that sweet young thing for too long."

Heat rushed into Alec's face until he was certain his face must be as red as his hair, and he turned his back on his mother, drying each piece of silverware until it shone. Maybe it would help if he opened the front door and stood in the cold air for a few seconds. At last he regained some degree of composure. "Mom, I'm not sure if she's ready." *If I'm ready.*

His mother snorted. "Ready or not, she's a mother, and she could use a good man to help her raise that precious baby. If Americans practiced arranged marriages, the two of you would have been promised years ago. So what's holding you back?"

Tires crunched on the drive. The car door opened and Mrs. P.'s Misty bounded out. He turned to his mother, a silent plea in his eyes.

"Don't worry. I won't say anything—except to God." His mother dried her hands and headed for the front door.

Waverly leaned into the backseat, where she must be unlatching Cinnamon's car seat. Babies traveled with a lot of baggage, he'd noticed. Diapers, wipes, clean clothes, bottles, changing pads. . .a whole assortment of things longer than his mother's shopping list. He tugged on a jacket and walked out the door. "Merry Christmas!"

"Merry Christmas to you, too." Waverly didn't look at him as she pulled the strap of the diaper bag farther up her shoulder.

"Anything I can carry?"

"There's food in the trunk." Mrs. P. popped it open.

Several stacked plastic containers, as well as pie plates and cake pans, lined the floor of the van. Alec's mother joined them. "You didn't need to bring anything."

"We wanted to. I don't get many excuses to bake anymore."

Alec started to pile some of the containers on top of the cake. "Careful, there!" Mrs. P. took the cake from him, and he could see the decoration.

"Nice work, Mrs. P."

"To tell the truth, Waverly did that."

Waverly beamed. The diaper bag hung from one shoulder and a baby seat dangled from her other arm, a blanket hiding Cinnamon from view. "Brr. Let's get inside."

Alec's mother bustled to the stove and extracted the pan of cinnamon rolls from the oven, as well as her favorite breakfast casserole made with croissants, eggs, bacon, and cheese. "Just in time for breakfast." She winked at Waverly. "That baby's still young enough to allow you to enjoy a good breakfast before she opens her presents."

"My parents spoiled me. When I was little, we'd all get up at midnight on Christmas Eve and open presents. Well, the kids got up. Mom and Dad had never gone to bed." She laughed. "But I intend to do things the old-fashioned way. No presents until Christmas morning, and that's that." She unzipped the bunting and picked up Cinnamon.

"Oh, how cute!" Alec's mother reached for the baby, who was dressed in a green-and-red plaid dress with gold worked through the material. "They make the most adorable things for babies anymore." For his part, he couldn't take his eyes off of Waverly, who wore a sage-green sweater adorned with a simple jingle bell necklace made to look like a snowman that rang whenever she moved.

After breakfast, Waverly sat on the floor next to the Christmas tree. Alec handed her the Santa hat. "You're elected to hand out the presents."

She raised an eyebrow at him. "Okay."

Before they opened the presents, Dad read from the second chapter of Luke. "The story we've seen acted out before our very eyes all month."

"Do you mind if we do one more thing before we open presents?" Waverly hopped to her feet and came back with her Christmas cake, complete with a burning candle. "Jesus' birthday cake. I know Cinnamon is too young to understand, but I want to start off right."

"Happy birthday, dear Jesus. Happy birthday to You!" The group held out the last note and then clapped. Cinnamon

319

whimpered at the noise. "Did we scare you, little one?" Waverly rocked her in her arms and kissed her forehead. "Merry Christmas, Jesus Christ is born," she whispered in her ear.

Alec looked at Waverly, his heart aching with the holiness of the moment. He could think of nothing more sacred than sharing the good news of Jesus with his children, and no one better to do it with than Waverly. He longed to spend this Christmas and every future Christmas with her and Cinnamon.

He had to find a way to talk with her. Soon.

Chapter 6

I don't mind keeping Cinnamon today." Mrs. P. repeated her offer.

Waverly didn't know what she would do if Mrs. P. didn't stop hovering over Cinnamon like a worried nurse. To hear her tell it, one would think no child had ever spent a moment outside in the winter.

"It's the day after Christmas, Mrs. P. I *want* to spend the day with my daughter, and besides, when else will she have a chance to meet camels up close and personal?" She zipped the pink baby bunting closed and looked at Cinnamon's scrunched-up face, smiling up at her in recognition. "We'll have fun today, won't we?"

"Of course you do, child." Mrs. P. picked up Misty, who wriggled out of her arms. "Don't worry about me. I have Misty to keep me company."

Oh dear, now Waverly had hurt Mrs. P.'s feelings. She sat down to listen to her landlady.

"I just thought you might like some time alone with Doc, is all. Does he even have a place for her car seat in that rattle trap truck of his?"

"Yes, he does. The backseat is cramped, but there's plenty of room to buckle her in."

"And I'm worried about the little one. She seemed a mite peckish last night."

"That was just the excitement of her first Christmas." Mrs. P. harrumphed.

The doorbell rang. Alec had arrived. "We'll see you when we get back." Now she'd have to spend the evening doing penance for hurting her dear friend's feelings.

If only this afternoon could mean more than an afternoon's drive through the still-brown, though cold, winter landscape. Waverly allowed herself a moment to dream, to wonder "what if" she wasn't a single mother with little chance of romance in the near future. Cozying up next to Alec, even in a truck with two smelly camels in tow, would be downright nice. Spending Christmas with his family had been so much fun, so natural, that she could imagine a whole string of Christmases just like it.

Waverly shook her head to clear it. Her top priority remained Cinnamon. That meant keeping her baby with her when she wasn't working, and that included today. She pulled on her lambskin boots, a warm sweatshirt and ski jacket, and gloves. She draped a blanket over the top of the carrier and opened the door.

"Happy Boxing Day." The flaps on Alec's cap had flipped up, leaving his exposed ears beet red.

The cold air tore into Waverly's throat when she opened her mouth. "Cold enough to freeze your blood." She shivered.

"Then it's a good thing we're warm-blooded." He offered her his arm, and she noticed a couple of slick spots where the driveway had frozen over.

"I need to get the car seat from my car."

"You and Cinnamon get in the truck, where it's warm.

I'll get it." He held the baby seat while Waverly hopped into the truck, then handed Cinnamon to her.

The truck's heater blasted, nice even after so few minutes outside. How well did camels tolerate cold, she wondered. They were creatures of the desert, after all. But these particular camels lived year-round in Vermont, so they must have adapted.

Alec snapped the car seat in place like an old pro. "I'll take her now." He looked down at the baby. "Good morning, Cinnamon. Are you looking forward to seeing the camels today?"

Cinnamon smiled widely. Waverly noticed she responded to the deep tones of a man's voice. Not just any man—this man. Alec was a good man, and good with Cinnamon. *Don't go down that road,* Waverly warned herself, again, but her heart didn't want to listen. She had learned the hard way not to put her heart's desires ahead of common sense and God's will.

"Here you go." Alec settled Cinnamon in the seat and secured the fastenings. Waverly twisted around to check that everything was snug tight. She gave Alec a thumbs-up and he trotted to the driver's side.

He got in, blew on his fingers, and grinned. "We all set to go?"

"As ready as we're going to be."

Alec plucked the hat off his head and set it on the console between them. How a man could look as good as Alec did, bundled up in a heavy ski parka with streaks of paint on it, mystified Waverly. *Stop looking.* She turned her attention to the skies overhead. "Think it might snow anytime soon?"

Although the opportunity for a white Christmas had already passed.

"Snow! Snow! Snow!" Waverly sang the first three notes of the song from the Bing Crosby/Danny Kaye musical *White Christmas*.

"It will come soon enough." Alec kept his hands lightly on the steering wheel but peered out the window. "Those clouds look promising."

Cinnamon whimpered.

"Another country heard from."

Waverly checked her watch—too soon for her next feeding. Cinnamon fussed for another minute, Waverly tense while she waited to hear if she would settle into sleep.

"I thought babies loved riding in cars." Alec shot a grin in Waverly's direction. "Do you want to check on her?"

"I'm sure she's fine." Waverly told herself to relax. "I may need to take a break before we get there, though." The closest exotic animal farm willing to rent them camels for the weekend was located in New York, a solid two to three hours' drive each way.

"I was planning on it. A meal, too, if I can twist your arm. There's the state line, up ahead." He nodded at the sign reading WELCOME TO THE EMPIRE STATE. "We're almost halfway there."

Cinnamon took exception to leaving her native state behind and bawled. Waverly asked, "Is there a welcome center or anything up ahead?"

Alec looked at her. "It's not the interstate. No, I don't think so. Ah, but I see a coffee shop." Without asking, he pulled into the parking lot.

As soon as the truck stopped, Waverly climbed down. Biting cold air slapped her face. She debated. Take Cinnamon inside or bring her to the front of the truck, where she could have privacy if the baby wanted to nurse for a moment or two? She wished she had packed a bottle like Mrs. P. had suggested, but she had expected Cinnamon to sleep until they reached their destination.

Waverly opened the back door and eau de dirty diaper assaulted her nostrils. "I need to get her inside." She didn't want to get Alec's truck dirty in the process of changing.

"Sure thing." While she unhitched the baby and wrapped the blanket around her, Alec came around the truck. "I'll get the doors for you."

Waverly bent her head into the wind and carried Cinnamon, now letting go with a gale-level squall. At the last minute the wind whipped the blanket away. "Go on in. I'll get the blanket." Alec dashed outside.

Waverly was glad to see the restroom came equipped with a changing table. She wrestled with the diaper bag and spread the changing cloth—still warm from the truck— across the cool surface. She laid Cinnamon down and unzipped the bunting.

"No wonder you were complaining." Waverly cleaned and changed her baby. "Did all the Christmas food Mommy ate yesterday upset your tummy?"

Cinnamon's cries settled to whimpers, but she ran her hand across her gums. "Went right through you, did it, and now you're hungry again." The bathroom was devoid of any chairs or other comforts. Waverly snapped Cinnamon's bodysuit back in place and found the hostess.

"Do you have a chair I could borrow? I need to feed my baby."

"Of course. Isn't she sweet?"

While the hostess bustled around for supplies, Waverly explained the situation to Alec. "Why don't you order something for me, and I'll eat in the truck." She looked out the window. "We really don't want to get caught in the snow."

❅

Alec found a spot far removed from cold windows, near the warm kitchen, and drank two cups of coffee.

The hostess—who also appeared to be the only waitress—plunked down across from him while she poured a third cup of coffee. "Ready to order?"

He glanced at the bathroom door and then at the snow driving against the window. "I guess I better."

"I know, it's hard when they're little like that." The waitress—her name tag read Rosie—tapped her order pad. "Don't know that Donnie and I got to eat a single meal together as long as the kids were little."

"Oh, we're not a couple." *Now, why did I feel compelled to say that?*

"Could have fooled me. You look right natural together."

Alec scowled. What had happened to his plans to share his heart with Waverly today? He hadn't expected Cinnamon to take over the entire trip. "I guess we'll have two cheeseburgers with fries to go. And if I bring in a thermos, can you fill 'er up? With a large cup to go?"

"Sure."

He pushed his arms into the sleeves of his coat and

walked out into blowing snow in air that had dropped ten degrees. Grabbing the thermos, he went back inside.

Waverly stood at the cash register, chatting with Rosie.

"You all set?" Alec looked down at Cinnamon, eyes closed, her forehead wrinkling in sleep, the same look he had seen on Waverly's face when she concentrated on something. The baby looked a lot like her mama. "I bet you feel better now."

"She should. I wonder if the pickled beets I ate yesterday gave her a tummy ache."

"Here you go." The heavenly aroma of burgers and freshly toasted buns wafted from a bag in Rosie's hand. Alec opened the thermos, and she filled it up. "That should do it for you." She beamed at the two of them. "Hope to see you again sometime."

Waverly paused at the door, staring at the flying snow. "Oh my. How are we going to make it?"

"We don't have much choice." Alec held the door open for her and then ran ahead of her to the truck. She hustled and bundled Cinnamon straight into her seat.

"We promised Jayne and Luke. Can't have Magi weekend without camels."

The truck had grown cold and Alec kept his ridiculous hat on his head until the heater kicked in. Waverly buckled her seat belt. "Every nativity set I've ever seen has camels, but does the Bible even mention them in the Christmas story? Why do we assume the wise men rode camels?"

Alec shrugged and removed his hat. "I don't know. But my Bible's in the glove compartment there. You could read the second chapter of Matthew and check, I suppose."

Waverly pulled out the Bible and plucked off her gloves so she could turn the pages. "It says 'magi from the east came to Jerusalem.' And later, after they left Herod, 'they went on their way.' 'On coming to the house.' 'They returned to their country by another route.' Nope, not one word about their mode of travel."

Alec's side window was frosting over. The windshield wipers fought the snowfall. Behind them, the animal trailer swished a bit.

"It's getting bad out there." Waverly wiped at her window with her mitten.

Alec checked his odometer. With the stop at the state line, they had covered only a little more than half the distance. Pulling out his cell phone, he dialed the animal farm.

"Alec, where are you?" Ken, the owner of the farm, asked.

"Just over the state line, and we've got a real storm brewing. I'm heading back to Castlebury. Don't want to risk damage to your camels."

"I'm relieved to hear it. Not fit weather for man nor beast out there. Skedaddle on home and let me know if you decide to come down tomorrow."

"Ten four." Alec shut the phone.

"You mean it? We're headed back to Castlebury?"

"I think it's the best course." He maneuvered the truck so that he could turn around.

"I'm sorry if we slowed you down."

He looked at her, smiling. "You're the best part." He rubbed his gloves against the windshield, clearing off a patch free of ice, and pulled back into traffic.

He concentrated on driving—and only driving—for the

next fifteen minutes. Waverly ate her food in silence. "I think that's the sign for the state line."

He grunted. Still fifty miles to go.

"You haven't eaten."

"Gotta keep my hands on the wheel."

"Here, let me help." The paper bag rustled, and the aroma of grilled meat tickled his nose. "I tore off a piece. Just bite into it."

He took the small piece and stuffed it in. It went down as quickly as a ravenous wolf's first bite. "More. Please."

Laughing, she fed him in small bites, a single french fry at a time. His lips brushed her fingers once or twice and they burned, although the food had grown cold. She giggled, and he laughed with her.

"No more. The windshield wipers aren't working well enough."

"Okay." She leaned back, and a bite of cold air sliced across his face. He wiped his glove across the windshield to clear a small patch. "Defroster's not working fast enough." He frowned. "It's fogging up inside the cab. I'm gonna have to open the windows a crack." He slipped it open a quarter of an inch, and the temperature in the cab dropped about ten degrees.

"But Cinnamon." The baby cried and Waverly twisted in her seat. "I don't want her to get sick." A certain amount of panic rose in her voice.

Alec stared out the narrow strip of the windshield that was clear. The wheels slipped.

"What was that?"

"The road's getting icy. They weren't predicting this

much snow." Alec eased up on the gas pedal. "About Cinnamon, I don't know."

Waverly unbuckled her belt and knelt on the seat, reaching for Cinnamon. "I can't reach her." Frustration edged her voice and she ran her arm down behind Alec's seat, reaching for something on the floor. She found the diaper bag and sat frontward again. "Maybe I can add more layers to help keep her warm. But what? I have a change of clothes, but that won't do any good since I can't reach her."

"And I don't dare stop, afraid I might not get going again."

Waverly pulled out a changing cloth. "Better than nothing, I suppose." She slipped off her coat before kneeling over the headrest again. Alec heard her settling the extra layers over Cinnamon, and the baby's cries grew muffled.

"Are you warm enough?" Alec looked at Waverly with concern.

She put on the scarf and hat she had removed in the cab and folded her arms around her waist. "I'll be okay. I have more resistance to winter than my baby."

A mother's love. . .the closest thing that could compare to God the Father's love, the kind that sacrificed without any expectation of getting anything in return. Waverly was a good, godly woman.

And once again he had to postpone that serious conversation he kept rehearsing in his mind. Getting them home safely through cold and snow was his top priority.

❄

They couldn't get back to Castlebury soon enough to satisfy Waverly. She wasn't dangerously cold, a lesson she had learned in her first time on the ski slopes as a kid, but she was chilled through and through. Cinnamon's constant crying caused Waverly's milk to flow. She hoped Alec wasn't paying attention to the dark spots appearing here and there on her sweater. She didn't think he had. His attention had riveted on the road and the weather radio. The predicted snow flurries had changed to near blizzard conditions, with snowfall of up to a foot in some areas. People thinking of traveling for New Year's Eve were encouraged to exercise caution. At last the sign for Castlebury appeared, and Waverly relaxed a bit. Alec's fingers relaxed their grip on the steering wheel as well. "Oh, look, Joe's Java is open." She spotted the cheery neon sign. She glanced at Alec. "But can we stop?"

Alec grunted. "A hot drink sounds good about now, but let's park by my office and transfer us all to one of our cars and come back. I don't want to move the trailer after I've stopped."

"Of course." Heat jumped to Waverly's cheeks, warming them from their cold state. "You don't need to come with us."

"Oh but I want to." Alec flashed a grin at her. "I need you with me when I explain to Jayne why we don't have three camels as ordered."

Waverly glanced at her sweater. The spots had become fairly noticeable. She'd put her coat on when they went inside and she'd keep it on, even if she warmed up so much she felt like a furnace.

They left the truck at the vet's office. In spite of the weather, the parking lot was full. "I guess everybody else had the same idea." He opened the door.

Waverly didn't know if she could manage a cup of cocoa with her shivering fingers, but Alec solved the problem by carrying their order on a bright red tray, in keeping with the "ho ho ho" cups holding their drinks. "She even warmed the muffins for us. We had a choice of apple cinnamon or apple cinnamon."

Waverly laughed. "Sounds good." She peeked at Cinnamon's face but left her in the bunting until they both warmed up a bit. "Bet they won't be half as good as you." She rubbed noses with her baby, and she gurgled, her cry calming down in the warm room.

"Is she hungry?"

"She probably could snack, but I'll wait awhile. Mama needs to warm up first." She tucked Cinnamon into the crook of her arm and gave her a pacifier. The baby sucked peacefully and curled up against her mother.

Waverly bit into the muffin and washed it down with a mouthful of whipped cream that she spooned from the top of the hot chocolate. "Are you coming to Jayne's baby shower tomorrow?"

"That's tomorrow?" Alec's nose wrinkled the way it did when he was puzzled, a trait she found endearing.

"I thought I told you. We're planning the baby shower after we have the wise men rehearsal tomorrow. Speaking of Jayne. . ."

"Yeah, I know." Alec scooped a crumb of cinnamon streusel into his mouth before he opened his cell phone. "Hi there. . . No, we didn't get through. . . You know, Waverly checked that while we were on the road. The Bible doesn't even mention camels, I think it's just tradition. . . Extra horses? Sure."

"So if they can't arrive by camel, we're going to put them on horseback?"

"You know they weren't going to ride the two-humped critters. We were going to show them arriving with the camels and gifts in tow."

"I know." Waverly looked out the window at the snow that continued falling. "Have her guests arrived?"

"Apparently the snow started down south before it got here. They left early to miss it. So the show will go on." He glanced at his watch. "I hate to rush things, but I need to pick up something for tomorrow. Are you ready?"

"Sure." Waverly reversed the dressing for outside weather in record time. Minutes later, Alec dropped her off at her apartment. He lifted the blanket long enough to peek at Cinnamon, and a soft expression crossed his face, like the smiles she had seen on Luke's face when he felt Jayne's baby moving about inside. Waverly pushed down the longing that came with the gesture.

❄

I almost blew that one, Lord. Alec breathed a sigh of relief that the local businesses had kept their doors open—local drivers put on their winter gear and tire chains if necessary and went where they needed to. Unless they were transporting expensive cargo like borrowed camels. He stopped by a couple of stores before he had everything he needed.

Tomorrow, Lord, for sure.

Chapter 7

I confess I'm just as glad you found me a horse. I was a mite worried about camels," Omar Shippen, a local playing one of the Magi, said. Inn guests would portray the other two wise men.

"Yeah, Prince here will be just fine. Worthy of carrying gifts to the Lord of Lords." Alec offered the Morgan an apple and rubbed his nose. He wouldn't admit he felt the same way. Vets knew a little about many different animals; he'd dealt with everything from a porcupine in heat to somebody's pet python. He'd felt confident he could handle the camels—with a little know-how from the owner of the exotic animal farm. But then he thought of Waverly slipping and sliding around the sheep and shook his head. Maybe not.

"Especially since we've got quite a load for them to carry today." Omar nodded toward the parcels, bundled in burlap sacks died purple and red. "More than Santa Claus carries on Christmas Eve."

"How else are we going to get wrapped presents into the Barncastle without Jayne knowing?" Alec winked. "I doubt that the original gifts of gold, frankincense, and myrrh took up so much space."

Omar waved his hand in the air. "Travel supplies. They'd been on the road for two years, isn't that the estimate?"

"According to King Herod." When Omar turned away, Alec slipped his gifts into one of the bags.

The snow had stopped falling during the night, after dumping eight of the predicted twelve inches. White Christmas had arrived a week late, but didn't some Christians celebrate Epiphany on January sixth? "So we have a white Christmas, after all."

"What's that you said?" Omar asked.

"That we're having a white Christmas after all. For the wise men's Christmas."

"Hah." Omar snorted. "That's one thing I doubt the Magi had to contend with. Not much snow in the Middle East."

"True enough. Say, can you help me get the horses in the trailer? Usually Waverly helps me, but I'll be picking her up on the way."

"Sure." Before long, they had loaded the horses into the trailer and the bags into the dry safety of Omar's van. Alec called ahead to alert Waverly to his arrival. "And my dashboard says the current outside temperature is thirty-two degrees, and the sky is clear. There should be no worries about little Cinnamon today."

"I guess I was a worrywart. She was fine."

"You're a mom. That's your job. But how about you? You looked a little frosty around the edges before we got hot cocoa into you."

"I'm fine. But just in case, can I have a sick day?" Waverly faked a cough. "See you in a few."

Mrs. P. popped out the door when Alec pulled into the yard. "I'm so happy Jayne invited me to be one of the wise men's servants. I would hate to miss the excitement today." She lowered her voice. "And here comes Waverly."

Waverly wore what Alec thought of as her workaday outfit, much like she wore yesterday. He frowned when he considered her limited wardrobe. One more of her many needs that she handled without complaint. Cinnamon, on the other hand, was bundled in a different bunting this morning, this one a pale lavender with pink daisies embroidered on it.

"How are my two favorite redheads this morning?" Prince snorted, and Alec realized what he had said.

Aside from a funny look, Waverly didn't comment. "We're fine. Prince seems ready to play his part."

"He was born ready. And let me take that." He accepted the bag with wrapped bundles from Waverly's hands and put them on the backseat. "I suggested people bring their gifts to the office. We've hidden the gifts in the burlap sacks the horses are carrying. Omar has the sacks in his van. We'll add yours when we get there."

Waverly giggled. "What a wonderful idea! Jayne will never guess. Would you grab the baking pan from my kitchen? I made those chocolate chip brownies Jayne is so fond of."

Alec whipped into the apartment and took a deep sniff of the wonderful aromas, part spice, part baby powder, everything Waverly, then opened his eyes and spotted the brownies in a blue foil pan. Numerous photographs dotted the room: a few of favorite patients at the clinic, one of her parents at their home in Florida. Pride of place went to a formal portrait of a smiling Cinnamon, propped up against a lambskin blanket. Tucked into the corner he found a snapshot of Waverly holding the baby, joy beaming from her face. His heart heaved. The clock on the microwave blinked, reminding him to get on the road.

He found Waverly staring out the open window. "The snow gave us a miserable time of it yesterday, but I don't mind so much when it looks so beautiful today. Kind of nice for New Year's, don't you think? Fresh snow, fresh year, fresh start."

Color sparkled in her cheeks, as if she had been reborn with the year. He put the brownies next to the presents and climbed into the truck beside her. "To new beginnings, then. Thinking of the New Year—have you made up your mind about going back to school this term?" He held his breath. His own dreams for the coming twelve months might depend on her answer.

"I have a few more days to register for the spring semester, but I think I'll wait until next fall." She rolled up her window. "I want to enjoy Cinnamon while she's still so little, before I jump back into classes and studies. Not to mention vet school and clinical training. . ."

"You know you'll always have a place here." *In more ways than you know.*

She flashed him a brief, tentative smile. "I'm counting on it."

Alec tapped his fingers on the steering wheel, raw nerves making him fidgety. He swallowed and started the engine.

❄

Waverly hadn't known what to expect of Jayne's father in the role of King Herod. She doubted the genial older gentleman could play the hard-hearted king, but when he told the Magi, "Search carefully for the child. As soon as you find him, report to me, so that I too may go and worship him," she shivered. He drew a knife across his palm when he instructed his soldiers to kill all baby boys under the age of two. Waverly clutched Cinnamon close to her chest, and tears tickled her eyelids for all those parents and the boys so needlessly sacrificed to the king's ambition.

God loved those parents and those babies, she reminded herself, and prayed she would never endure a similar trial. How her worries about Cinnamon getting too cold during the ride yesterday paled when compared to a bloodthirsty king.

Next up, the wise men approached the house where Mary and Joseph had set up housekeeping. "My turn?" little Justin Taylor asked, and the spectators giggled. Justin was a precocious toddler with a good vocabulary but no one could predict how the two-year-old would react.

As soon as the Magi presented the gifts—even without the wrapping paper any American child associated with gift-giving—Justin squealed "Mine?" Mary opened the bottle of frankincense for him to smell, and he screwed up his nose. "Ugh." Waverly bit her lip to keep from laughing. Jesus might have reacted the same way when he was a little boy. But he took a gold coin and bit into it, and again, laughter rippled across the crowd.

Mary packed the spices away in a basket with a thoughtful look on her face. "Such strange gifts for a child. Frankincense—used in offerings. Myrrh—a spice used to wrap a dead body." A shudder crossed her face and a spotlight created the shadow of a cross behind the spot where Justin sat pounding on a nail. Then the angel spoke to Joseph in a dream and he hurried with his family to Egypt. Waverly brushed away tears from her eyes.

Alec took the horses to the barn and came back in with the brownies Waverly had baked. She joined Mrs. P. in setting up a folding table for the wrap party—their pretext for the shower—while the actors changed clothing. "Do you have the cake?"

Mrs. P. winked. "I have it hidden away. We'll bring it out later."

Jayne joined them at the table, rubbing her lower back. "I am so ready for this guy to make his entrance. There's been a time or two when we thought we might get our little tax deduction early." She looked down at her protruding belly. "I'm glad you decided to wait. We didn't need a birth in the midst of the Christmas Any Time plays."

"What all did you put in those sacks, Alec?" Omar rumbled as he exited the changing room. "They felt like you loaded them with rocks."

"I can't imagine. Just a few odds and ends." Waverly wondered if everyone else heard the false note in Alec's answer. "Let's check it out." He went into the props room and emerged with the two bags. "Phew, these are heavy. Let's check them out."

He pulled out a rectangular box wrapped in baby blue paper. "Look what I found." He grinned.

"Mine!" Justin grabbed for it.

"I don't know. Look here. There's a gift tag that says 'Jayne.'"

Jayne straightened. "What's going on?"

"Surprise!" The gathering shouted.

"Have a seat." Luke pulled out a chair at the end of the table.

"You guys."

Alec dug his hand into the bag again. "Look what else I found!" Grinning, he removed a pink-wrapped box. "This one says it's for. . .Waverly and Cinnamon."

Waverly's mouth dropped open. "What's going on? This is Jayne's shower."

"No, poppet." Mrs. P. patted her shoulder. "We decided to make it for both of you." Misty ran around her feet, barking. "Come on in, folks."

Waverly stared openmouthedly as the back doors opened and a number of townsfolk came in. Alec's parents, the owner of Joe's Java, the pastor and his wife. . .they formed two concentric circles around the table.

"Mine?" Justin reached for the pink-wrapped box.

"This one is for you." Alec found a box wrapped in bright red-and-green paper. "We decided our favorite child actor should get some gifts as well. And here is one for Andy."

"What do you say?" Jayne prompted as Andy tore into the present.

"Thanks. Look, Mom, it's a super secret spy kit." He hoisted the box over his head for everyone to see.

"Why don't our guests of honor sit together." Waverly took the seat next to Jayne.

"And here is the cake." Mrs. P. opened a bakery box and pulled out a sheet cake decorated with pink and blue bottles and diapers and everything baby. It read, *Congratulations, Jayne and Waverly.*

Mrs. P. busied herself cutting cake and pouring punch while Waverly and Jayne opened gifts. "This next one is from Doreen." Waverly rattled the box but it didn't make a sound. She pushed against the wrapped gift and it sunk beneath her fingers. Probably another cute baby outfit.

Instead she found a plush sweater in pale lavender, with a matching infant bodysuit tucked in below. "New mothers need pampering too," Doreen said. Waverly hugged her.

Alec sat at the opposite end of the table, but Waverly felt his eyes on her as she opened every gift. With so many gifts from so many people, she could hardly keep track. But none of them bore Alec's name, not even when every gift had been distributed. Did he mean the present from his parents to be from him as well? The thought sent a chill to her soul. *Stop it. He's been kinder to you than you deserve.* She bit into the rich cake but the sugar did little to cheer her up.

After she finished the cake, Waverly stood to help clean the table. She hoped all the gifts would fit in the backseat of Alec's truck. At the moment she wished she didn't have to ride back with Alec. Why had he given a gift to Jayne, but not to her?

"A penny for your thoughts?" The man appeared in front of her as though conjured by her thoughts, his eyes locked on hers as if nothing else existed in the world for him.

"Wondering how I'm going to get all this"—she waved a hand at the array of boxes piled on the floor—"home."

"We'll make two trips if we have to. Come with me for a sec." He didn't wait for her to agree, but instead took her hand in his and tugged her in the direction of the now-emptied burlap sacks. Hoisting the sack over his back, he led her into the dressing room and closed the door behind them.

"There are two gifts left, but I wanted a moment of privacy."

His smile was so tender, her heart melted with the beauty of it. So he hadn't forgotten her, after all. But why all the secrecy? She giggled. "You didn't have to do that." *Yes you did.*

"Oh but I wanted to." He opened the top of the sack and revealed a hefty box wrapped in a cute paper with ribbons and bows. "Here's one." Next he dug his hand deep into the sack and pulled out a small, gold-wrapped gift. "I wanted gold foil. Keep with the Magi theme." He took a deep breath. "Which one do you want to open first?"

Waverly's eyes fastened on the gold box in Alec's hand. It couldn't be what it looked like. "I'll start with the big one." Her voice trembled and she sat on the couch where actors rested between scenes. Alec sat next to her, and heat wrapped her body where their arms touched. She took her time untying the bow and running her fingernail along the edge of the wrapping paper, as if she wanted to preserve the paper for all posterity.

"A car seat? But I have one." Why all the secrecy for a car seat? Her heart slowed down. That gold box—It couldn't be. . .

"I hate seeing you move it all the time. And I hope for you and Cinnamon to take many trips in my truck."

"That's. . .thoughtful." She stared at the gold box.

Alec moved, and air rushed in to take his place by her

side. He knelt in front of her.

This can't be happening. Waverly wanted to hide her face behind her hands.

He wrapped her fingers around the gold box. "Open it."

This time she tore into the paper, uncovering a square jewelry box. She hesitated, running her finger over the solid dark blue velvet lid engraved with the name of the local jewelry store.

He smiled at her and opened the lid, revealing a diamond ring. "Will you marry me, Waverly Coe? Will you trust me with your love and give me the opportunity to be a husband to you and a father to your daughter?"

The ring sparkled through the tears in Waverly's eyes. "If I have learned anything this first Christmas with Cinnamon, it's that with God, I can trust Him with everything—He gives me more than I could ever dream." She leaned forward and met Alec halfway, their lips touching in a soft kiss.

"Even you. With all of my heart, yes."

 Award-winning author and speaker Darlene Franklin recently returned to cowboy country—Oklahoma. The move was prompted by her desire to be close to her son's family; her daughter Jolene has preceded her into glory.

Darlene loves music, needlework, reading, and reality TV. Talia, a Lynx point Siamese cat, proudly claims Darlene as her person.

For information on book giveaways and Darlene's upcoming titles, visit www.darlenefranklinwrites.blogspot.com.

A Letter to Our Readers

Dear Readers:

In order that we might better contribute to your reading enjoyment, we would appreciate your taking a few minutes to respond to the following questions. When completed, please return to the following: Fiction Editor, Barbour Publishing, Inc., P.O. Box 719, Uhrichsville, OH 44683.

1. Did you enjoy reading *Christmas at Barncastle Inn*?
   ❑ Very much—I would like to see more books like this.
   ❑ Moderately—I would have enjoyed it more if _____
   _____
   _____

2. What influenced your decision to purchase this book?
   (Check those that apply.)
   ❑ Cover   ❑ Back cover copy   ❑ Title   ❑ Price
   ❑ Friends   ❑ Publicity   ❑ Other

3. Which story was your favorite?
   ❑ *Love Comes to the Castle*   ❑ *Where Your Heart Is*
   ❑ *Christmas Duets*   ❑ *First Christmas*

4. Please check your age range:
   ❑ Under 18   ❑ 18–24   ❑ 25–34
   ❑ 35–45   ❑ 46–55   ❑ Over 55

5. How many hours per week do you read? _____

Name _____

Occupation _____

Address _____

City_____ State _____ Zip_____

E-mail_____

CHRISTMAS
BELLES OF GEORGIA

by Jeanie Smith Cash, Rose Allen McCauley,
Jeri Odell and Debra Ullrick

Love finds four separated sisters when
and where they least expect it, in these
tender tales of Christmas romance set in a
quaint Georgia town.

Christmas, paperback, 352 pages, 5.1875" x 8"

Please send me _____ copies of *Christmas Belles of Georgia*.
I am enclosing $7.99 for each.
(Please add $4.00 to cover postage and handling per order. OH add 7% tax.
If outside the U.S. please call 740-922-7280 for shipping charges.)

Name _____

Address _____

City, State, Zip_____

To place a credit card order, call 1-740-922-7280.
Send to: Heartsong Presents Readers' Service, PO Box 721, Uhrichsville, OH 44683